D1368800

SPUR TO THE SMOKE

**Center Point
Large Print**

**This Large Print Book carries the
Seal of Approval of N.A.V.H.**

SPUR TO THE SMOKE

Steve Frazee

CENTER POINT PUBLISHING
THORNDIKE, MAINE

This Center Point Large Print edition
is published in the year 2008 by arrangement with
Golden West Literary Agency.

The text of this Large Print edition is unabridged. In other
aspects, this book may vary from the original edition.
Printed in the United States of America.
Set in 16-point Times New Roman type.

ISBN: 978-1-60285-273-0

Library of Congress Cataloging-in-Publication Data

Frazee, Steve, 1909-1992.
    Spur to the smoke / Steve Frazee.--Center Point large print ed.
      p. cm.
    ISBN: 978-1-60285-273-0 (lib. bdg. : alk. paper)
      1. Large type books. I. Title.

PS3556.R358S58 2008
813'.54--dc22

2008016246

CHAPTER ONE

THEY SWAM the Sapinero River six miles below the town of Kebler. The pounding current shouldered their horses downstream to a poor landing in dense willows, but Roderick Vail did not try to go around the obstacle or pick his way. He crashed his tall buckskin straight through, cursing when the animal floundered in a tangle of bone-gray debris left from floodtime, and then the horse had to lunge and dig to climb the steep north bank.

Roderick's son, Lee, came on more carefully, but when his horse kicked the willows behind there was no choice about the hundred yards ahead. The bay was heaving when it surged up to where Roderick waited.

"That thing has got no guts," Roderick said. He was a high-shouldered man, broad across the back, lean throughout. Wet to the waist from the crossing, he took his pistol belt from around his neck and strapped it on. He checked his pistol with cold blue eyes, with tapering, powerful fingers. His hair was tawny, going down in curling stairsteps at the back. "No guts at all," he said, looking at his son's horse. The comment seemed to spread to cover other things.

Lee raised one leg at a time to let the water run from his boots. "There's a ford a half mile upstream."

"I rode this river when you were a snot-nosed brat." Roderick gave his son a look charged with a thin stream of doubt, and then he rode on.

These moments of weighing had come more frequently of late. Lee had seen Roderick look at Mrs. Vail like that, mulling something in his mind, then turning away with the doubt unsatisfied. In Lee's case the scrutiny had been sharper-edged, but each time Roderick had withheld his comment, as if he were struggling to be sure, or fair.

At such times Roderick was never pleasant company and often not for days afterward. So now Lee took his time and let his father ride ahead through the stiff sage, across the flinty ruts of old erosion marks where hoofs raised scant dust.

After a while Roderick twisted around. "Don't hang back there like a damned squaw. I want to talk to you."

They walked their horses side by side. Lee Vail was four inches shorter than his father, who stood six feet two. The son was heavier, lacking the whipthong litheness of Roderick. His face was cast in even planes while Roderick's features thrust out aggressively. The son's coloring was dark, his hair a few shades less than black, and in those respects he was like his mother, Maureen Vail. All he had from his father was blue eyes, but much darker than Roderick's.

On the scattered ranches of the Sapinero country it was said that Lee would never be the man his father was; and this Lee knew and was content, for he knew also that Roderick had paid a price for everything he was and everything he owned.

"Worthless country over here." Roderick looked at

the empty land, at the humped ridges pouring down from the Fossil Mountains to the north. East, toward Kebler and beyond, lay the home places of those who had been too late to settle on the south side of the Sapinero. "And worthless people too," Roderick gave his son a cutting glance. "Are you still running out with Iris Meeker, Lee?"

Lee took anger from the question and then he let the anger die. Consideration before answering one of his father's questions always irritated Roderick, although Lee had no desire to dig cross-grained into his father now. "Yes, I am," Lee said, and then he watched the surge of fury on his father's hawkish face.

"What kind of marriage would that be?" Roderick demanded.

"We haven't talked of marriage."

"What else would she have in mind!"

"I'm well past twenty-one, so let it be."

Roderick's eyes narrowed. His lips went tight; and then, surprisingly, he smiled. "A trip to the brush now and then—that's fine. You'd be a stale, miserable man otherwise. That isn't what I wanted to talk about anyway." The sweep of Roderick's hand took in a quarter of the compass east and north. "Worthless land, Lee, and worthless people. It's a combination that threatens a man."

The gesture was too dramatic, the words high-flown. Lee would have laughed at another man who did the same, but Roderick's violent background and his present grim intentness gave a dangerous edge to both the movement and the words. Lee was uneasy. He always was when caught in the swirl of one of his father's driving moods.

"The people are all right," Lee said. "Just because they didn't get here as early as you did is no reason to call them worthless."

"They're all right—if you keep them in their places."

Lee stared uneasily at his father. "The Crawfords, the Meekers, Joe Emmet, the Roods—all the rest of them on the north side of the river. . . . What's got into you all of a sudden?"

"It's not sudden." Roderick looked south across the river toward his Broken Diamond. Calvin Houghton's Two Teepees was the only other ranch on that side. "Houghton is figuring on starting something, and then the others will take it up. You kill trouble before it gets a hold, Lee." He was so sure, so savage, that Lee was startled.

Looking at the ruthless jut of his father's features, Lee swallowed against a pressure in his throat. Before he met Lee's mother Roderick had been a marshal in a trail town. Only bits of that history had seeped from him while Lee was growing up. Ten men killed . . . Never give a sonofabitch who's after you an even chance. "Start what?" Lee asked. "Why would Houghton—"

"He's started already. In Union Park."

The park was Diamond's stronghold, a great basin that foamed with aspen thickets. Without apparent depletion of the graze, Roderick ran three thousand cattle there year after year. Yesterday when Sam Harvey, the Diamond foreman, rode down for supplies he had mentioned seeing a few head of Teepees cattle the week before on Ballou Creek.

"You don't mean those strays?" Lee asked. "We both know there's always been a few head of Houghton stuff in the park. When it comes time for fall—"

"Call them strays," Roderick said. "It sounded to me like there was more than usual. Let them keep coming year after year and then some of the dryland loafers on this side will get ideas. No, Lee, I've had all I'll take."

Even in view of his father's quick shifting moods, this was a remarkable leap away from reason, Lee thought. Yesterday when Harvey dropped the news about the cattle as a casual fact, Roderick had been undisturbed; Now he was on the warpath. The time lag between thought and action did not make sense, for in most things Roderick acted on impulse. Lee said, "It can't be those usual strays. What else—"

"That's plenty. I say it's damned good and plenty!"

"You could have seen Houghton last night at home." That was the proper way. Houghton was hot-tempered and blunt but he was a good neighbor. He deserved privacy in a matter of this kind.

"Houghton will be at church today," Roderick said. "Him and most of the would-be ranchers on this side. We'll make it clear to all of them in one whack."

"That's a poor way to do things."

9

"It bothers you, Lee?"

"Yes."

"Why?" The question was a deep probe.

"It's not a public matter," Lee said. "Your way of handling it doesn't make sense to me."

"Afraid?"

"That's got nothing to do with it. If you insult Cal Houghton and everybody else, you're deliberately inviting their hatred. Not that the northside ever loved us anyway, but why go out of your way for trouble?"

"Trouble!" Roderick cut the air with his hand. "They'll do nothing. There isn't a thimbleful of guts in the whole bunch. We'll tell 'em how the boar ate the cabbage and that'll be the size of it."

"I don't like it, Roderick."

"Ann Houghton, huh?"

"No. It's just that you're making a mountain of a molehill."

"You always were a bear for arguing!"

Lee met his father's angry look. After a time Roderick turned away, pointing this time across the Sapinero to where the Razor Mountains lay misty in the afternoon sun. "There were only a few of us here when they started sniping at me in Union Park. Just a steer now and then, but it could have built up to something big. The park was full of prospectors and drifters in those days.

"I got old Cannon Ridgway and his crew from the Teepees. We did what was necessary, and since then there's never been any trouble in the park, until now.

If a man can't see a lesson in that he's a fool." Roderick looked at his son with a waiting expression that demanded confirmation of the principle he had drawn.

Lee knew. History here was brief. Acts of violence were the great rocks that ripped high in the meager stream of living, and so time was marked from the day Roderick and Cannon Ridgway, now dead, had led a crew into Union Park and hanged four men for stealing cattle. Whispers ran yet around the deed: Two of the men were innocent; the other two might have taken an occasional beef for food.

"I stopped trouble before it had a chance to grow." Roderick still waited for Lee to speak, and when Lee said nothing the father turned away with anger thin across his bony face.

Trouble, Lee thought, was a chain that repaired its own broken links. Friends of some of the hanged men came to the Diamond by night three years after the hanging. Lee remembered how the crash of pistols and the slamming of a rifle tore him from sleep.

He ran into the yard that night and there he saw Roderick standing near the lantern pole. Pale starlight showed him with a pistol in his hand, stooped, unmoving, clad only in a long nightshirt. On the ground there lay two men. One of them was making bubbling noises as he waved his knees from side to side. The other was a motionless bundle of clothing, dark against the earth.

From the shadows at the end of the porch Maureen Vail cried, "Lee! Get away from there!" Her voice

11

started dully, then rose until it almost broke.

Roderick turned slowly, the pistol still at arm's length against his thigh. He said, "Go in the house, Lee. Go back to bed—"

Until he fell asleep much later Lee heard his parents talking. For the first time in his life he heard his mother crying, and it was a sound that terrorized him and filled him with a feeling of helplessness that seared his very being.

When he rose in the morning he did not try to make a dream of the night. He went directly to the lantern pole and looked at the ground. Someone had shoveled dirt around, but he saw the flies scrabbling thickly on the earth. Roderick was gone then. The four Diamond riders had been in the park all summer. Alone with his mother, Lee tried to find out what had happened. She told him that three men had come to hang his father and that one had got away. And then she drew within herself and did not hear his questions; and she would not let him leave the house again.

Sometime in the morning Roderick returned with old man Ridgway and one of Ridgway's riders. Lee saw them take two tarpaulin-covered bundles from the barn and later he saw them digging on a sage hill west of the house. About that time Mrs. Ridgway arrived in a buckboard. She stayed a week at Diamond.

Ridgway and his rider did not even stay for dinner. They left right after the burying. Lee heard his father say, "Do you suppose we ought to go after the third one?"

Old man Ridgway laughed shortly. "Two out of three planted is a fair showing, I'd say. If you want a perfect score, go ahead."

"I guess not," Roderick said. He walked away almost aimlessly.

Ridgway was mounting when the third man said, "He's hell on wheels, ain't he? How many does this make for him?" His voice was full of admiration and Lee was impressed, although he did not like the looks of the man.

Ridgway settled himself in the saddle, a red-faced, burly man with bitter little eyes. He gave the rider a sour look. "He's hell on wheels, all right." Ridgway went out of the yard on the run.

For several days Roderick was most patient with his wife, hovering about her, doing small things for her that Lee had never seen him do before; but there seemed to be a compact between Mrs. Ridgway and Maureen Vail against Roderick. By the time Mrs. Ridgway left the Diamond, Lee's mother had become a quiet woman, unresponsive to Roderick's efforts to make her talk and laugh. She stirred about the house at night, often coming into Lee's room to stand silent beside his bed. After the first few times, troubled, Lee pretended to be asleep when he knew she was there.

Mrs. Vail began to ride at night, leaving while Roderick's voice, plaintive, followed her and tried to argue her out of going. Lee remembered yet the sounds of her horse thudding away as if desperation drove her. He seldom heard her return, for she always came in quietly. And then there was a night when she did not return.

Lee was thirteen then. His father hauled him from bed in the chill predawn of a spring morning. The sun was rising when they found Maureen lying in the rocks on Stormy Ridge where her horse had spooked and thrown her. She was conscious. She had no broken bones, but her back was injured and she could not move. Her face was white. Her black hair gleamed against the nest of rocks where she lay. She stared at Roderick and said, "Leave me alone. I don't want to go back."

Roderick gave his son a swift look. High willfulness was in his cold blue eyes, and anger. "She's out of her head, Lee." He lifted his wife carefully. She looked at him as if she hated him all the while he was carrying her down the hill to a meadow they could reach with a wagon. Her horse was grazing there. It came trotting toward them, whickering, holding its head high and sidewise to keep from stepping on the dragging reins.

Even yet Lee remembered the white blaze on its forehead just touched by the rising sun. It was an ugly little horse, short-barreled, hard-gaited, strong. Maureen Vail loved it.

Roderick put his wife down. He shot the horse in the head even as his wife cried out against the act. Mrs. Vail's eyes blazed in her colorless face. She cursed Roderick and tried to sit up, but pain whipped her across the will and forced her back. This time it was surely hatred in her expression, Lee thought; but of course she was hurt and had been lying out all night.

One hind leg of the horse was raking through the dew on the grass. Roderick put his pistol away. "She's out of her head, Lee." He looked at the horse. "When something you trust lets you down, there's the answer. Remember it, son."

Years had washed the memory, fading Roderick's part to something that now seemed falsely dramatic; but the coloration of Maureen Vail's part was still strong. Lee never saw her in another outburst against Roderick; and so in time he thought he had succeeded in glossing her action over with: *She's out of her head, son.*

About the time Sam Harvey came to the Diamond there was a change in Mrs. Vail. She emerged from behind her shield and faced the world again, visiting around the country, driving to socials, asking people to call once more at Diamond. This lasted only a brief time and then she resumed her recluse life, but Lee sensed a new fever behind her outward bearing. He was older then and he thought he detected a desperation in his mother that threatened to break through; but gradually it subsided and the curtain closed around her again.

Harvey had nothing to do with it, Lee decided. Harvey's arrival was merely a mark of time. He was the only man who had ever worked more than one season for Roderick.

Riding now toward Kebler, Lee wondered why he

was remembering old events and trying to link them with the present.

Roderick said, "I settled things in the park before they got out of hand." He stared at Lee, telling him obliquely to speak up.

Settled trouble? A direct line of trouble stemmed from the hangings in the park. It was clear to Lee; he thought it should be plain also to Roderick.

"You heard me," Roderick said. He was a man demanding confirmation of his action, past and present.

Lee studied the tight-lipped face. Except for the lack of mustache, Roderick appeared little changed from the wedding picture of him, straight and tall beside Maureen's chair. Even then a pistol showed under his long coat. The reason for today was somewhere deep in his character, and Lee could not touch it. Maybe it was that a pistolman could never rest, that the recoil of his weapon carried deep into him and bruised him into new violence.

Whatever the reason, it must follow some uncertainty, Lee guessed, for the demanding in Roderick now was that of a man who wishes to be told he is right. To tell him he was wrong would infuriate him, and to tell him he was right would merely bolster a plan he would not change in any event.

"It was different when you came here," Lee said. "Maybe you had to act quick with a pistol or a rope, but—"

"People never change. They get manners. They

build a church and get a hypocrite to preach to them but they cheat and steal as much as ever. They'll run over you if you let them."

"Nobody is trying that."

"The hell you say. We're serving notice about the park. Go home if you can't stand the strain." It was the final statement.

Roderick quickened the pace of the tall buckskin.

CHAPTER TWO

THE TOWN was on a fiat above the canyon where Silver Creek cascaded toward the Sapinero. It was named for big Pete Kebler, who had built the first structure, a saloon and general store. Some people still recalled that Roderick had been enraged because the place had not been named Vail.

A working man for all his size and full of unusual ideas, Kebler had plowed two furrows a hundred feet apart and a quarter of a mile long to mark the street. Into these he had laid the trunks of budding cottonwoods so that now the street was a wide lane so thickly lined with trees that the few buildings at the lower end of town were almost masked in summer. A white-painted church stood alone at the head of the street, and that had been built largely because of Kebler's efforts.

As soon as Roderick and Lee rode off the hot mesa and into the street Lee felt the violation of their presence. It was the Sunday of the month when the circuit preacher came across the Fossils to hold services, a sermon in the morning and more preaching in the evening. Between times, members of the congregation visited and ate lunches in the cool grove behind the church.

Roderick went down the middle of the street. His high cheekbones and narrowed eyes made him look like an arrogant Indian chief on his way to council. Lee thought there was something obscene in his willingness to plunge a knife into the peace of the afternoon.

They passed Kebler's place. No one was in sight. The saloon would be locked, as it always was on Sunday.

Lee said, "I'll go ahead and tell Houghton you want to see him."

Roderick reined in quickly. "What are you afraid of?" The weighing look was in his eyes. He drew his pistol and checked it. "Look at your six-shooter."

"What for?"

"Check it, I said!"

"No."

"I've spent time and money teaching you how to handle a pistol. You mean you won't back me up?"

"It's not coming to that," Lee said. "Nobody wears a pistol to town any more. If they do it's always left in Kebler's, especially on Sunday." He saw the anger pulse in Roderick's face. "I can go tell Houghton you want to see him."

Roderick chipped his words through his front teeth.

"Sometimes I wonder what's inside you." His fury almost exploded, but after he had stared at the even set of his son's face for several moments, he rode on.

From Mell Crawford's harness store to the church there were no buildings. Water gurgled in and out of boxes set in the ditches for houses that had never been built. The murmur of voices came from the grove behind the church.

Lee saw Iris Meeker first. She was sitting on a log bench with Tony Alarid, beyond the long plank tables where the married women chatted. She was a strong woman, wide-hipped, full in the bosom. Even in the shade her hair was a bright golden shine. She gave Lee a slow smile and then she looked at Alarid, who was watching Roderick.

The men were scattered around the grove. Gramps Rood was asleep on a blanket under a tree, his hands folded on his stomach, his mouth a round hole in his bushy gray beard. The largest group was squatted in a circle where Joe Emmet was drawing on the ground with a stick and talking of an easy wagon route across the Fossils.

George Cantonwine came forward as Lee and Roderick dismounted. He was a tall man whose skin fitted like loose clothing. He misquoted the Bible freely in all his sermons but he spoke with such fervor of hellfire and damnation that his listeners did not care about the defect. Even in normal conversation he made his voice a promise of punishment. In Preacher Cantonwine there was no meekness. He rode a great stallion

19

with a misshapen jaw. He fixed Roderick and his son with a brooding look, noting the pistols they wore. The slashes in his loose cheeks pinched in as he said, "Welcome to the gathering, brothers." He paused. "Where's Mrs. Vail?"

He knew as well as anyone that Maureen Vail seldom left the Diamond.

Roderick was curt. "She's not feeling well."

Lee looked around the grove. Cal Houghton was nowhere in sight. His wife was sitting at one of the tables. There might be a chance that Houghton had not come to church, and in that Lee found some measure of hope.

Cantonwine said, "On the Lord's day it would seem that Mrs. Vail—"

"She doesn't feel a damned bit better then." Roderick did not even look at Cantonwine.

Lee saw the tightening, the exchanged glances, the protective bunching around the rupture he and Roderick had caused in the peaceful scene. Joe Emmet tossed his stick away and straightened up. The men near him rose. Tony Alarid stretched his legs. He hooked his thumbs into his belt and cocked his head, watching the Vails with a half smile on his dark, sharp features.

Alarid was Cal Houghton's foreman. He had hated Roderick since the day he rode into the country and asked for a job at Diamond. Roderick had listened to his drawl, looked at his rig, and then told him bluntly that no Texan would ever work at Diamond. Before he caught on at Teepees Alarid had worked for Landon Crawford. He fancied himself around Iris Meeker until the day he came upon her and Lee high on Gothic Creek. Alarid made a quick guess, which happened to be right; and then there were two Vails that he hated.

As tangible as weight his attitude carried across the space to Lee. Roderick was not unaware of the man either. Lee saw a moment's hesitation in his father's manner, a tiny run of balancing that a man who was afraid, or careful, might make before a critical move. It seemed that way to Lee, although he knew that neither fear nor carefulness was a quality of Roderick.

"Your weapons are unseemly," Cantonwine said. "I must insist—"

"Be quiet, Cantonwine," Roderick said, as if the man were a noisy child.

Anger spouted from the preacher's eyes, a wrath fit to call upon the heavens for destruction, but it curdled off into temporal fear. Lee looked away from Cantonwine, ashamed of the man's expression. Roderick's insult had raised resentment in everyone but Alarid, whose faint smile was as much contempt for the preacher as it was hatred of the Vails.

"Where's Houghton?" Roderick demanded.

Nettie Houghton rose quickly, a stocky woman, gray-haired, sharp of movement. "What do you mean coming here and asking for Cal, or any other man, in that tone? That pistol gives you no right to be here at all." She glanced at Lee and lumped him into her challenge. "If you have business with my husband, Roderick Vail, you can wait until after church. I should think you'd have the decency to consider that in the first place. Who do you think you are?"

Shamed by a woman, Cantonwine tried to regain position. He stepped toward Roderick. "If you choose to stay, I insist that you remove your pistol."

Roderick knocked the preacher aside carelessly, giving him no more than a casual glance. "Where's Houghton?"

"At the creek," Mrs. Houghton said. "You—"

Roderick said, "Go get him, Lee."

Alarid's voice was lazy. "Sure, Lee, trot down there and do that little thing." Iris jogged Alarid with her elbow. He raised one brow and smiled.

Cantonwine's face was pale and his lips were jerking.

"Get Houghton and bring him here, Lee," Roderick said.

Lee had not moved. He did not know whether he would or not. The problem solved itself. Houghton and Pete Kebler came through the trees, laughing, talking. Houghton was carrying one of his grandsons on his shoulders. Huge, smooth-faced, with shrewd horse-trading sense written all over his features, Kebler caught the full force of the scene before Houghton did. Kebler hoisted the boy clear of Houghton's shoulders, and the movements of the child's legs raised Houghton's thin red hair in untidy wisps.

"Been waiting for you, Cal," Roderick said.

Houghton's small eyes gleamed with a sharp, aroused intelligence as he stumped forward. He was a rounding sort of man who rolled in the saddle when he rode. His nose was small, tightly fitted to his facial bones, his mouth small and thin-lipped. He barely glanced at Lee as he walked up close to Roderick. "What's sticking in *your* craw, Vail?"

Like all the rest Houghton was unarmed, but Lee recognized the fact that his forthright manner would be unchanged whether he wore a pistol or not. Again Roderick hesitated, and Lee hoped that he was realizing how foolish he was being. Roderick glanced at his son and then he said, "There's too many of your cows in Union Park, Houghton."

For an instant Houghton's face was blank. He looked like a man who had set himself for a heavy blow and then had been lashed by a string. His eyes bunched at the corners. His voice was puzzled. "What's got into you?"

"I said too much of your stuff is wandering into the park, Houghton." Roderick looked at Lee again.

No longer off balance, Houghton let his temper flicker all over his face. His voice went up. "I'm glad you call it wandering, Vail."

"We'll let it go at that." Roderick swept his gaze on all the other men. "I'll take it unfriendly if I see any brand but Diamond even close to the park from now on."

Alarid shook his head gently, still smiling.

Bliss Rood said, "You're taking it unfriendly now, Vail. Since I been in this country I never knew of anything from this side to stray a mile across the river." He was a squat man, dark-browned, with a neck that rose from his body in a brief, powerful run. His ears were small and flat, his arms so short they stood out from his body as if he were carrying stones against his armpits. "You're inviting unfriendliness, I'd say.

Rood looked to no one for support, but little Ben Meeker, Iris' father, standing next to Rood, stared at the ground quickly as if the act would disassociate him from any share in Rood's blunt statement.

Roderick looked hard at Bliss until Houghton asked, "How many of my head up there?"

"Too many," Roderick said. "Let Alarid count them when Harvey shoves them out on Cannibal Mesa three days from now."

The sides of Houghton's neck were pulsing. "I've no use for a man who makes a show of everything he does. By Christ, Vail—"

"Save your wind." Roderick turned away. "Come on, Lee."

Tony Alarid was on his feet now. "Go on, Lee," he mimicked. "Trot along at the tail of the old he-lion, or would you like to take off the pistol and stick around."

The challenge was a lift to resentful men. They raised their heads and studied Lee. Cantonwine started to protest, and then a moist cruelness crossed his eyes and he stayed silent.

Pete Kebler said, "That won't help matters one bit,

Alarid." Almost together three men told Kebler to shut up.

Alarid's dark coat was neatly fitted and it masked the wiry, explosive strength of his trim body. He looked small as he brushed past Kebler and came toward Lee in an easy, controlled movement. "Take off the pistol. Stay a while, Lee. Maybe we can have a special service for you."

Landon Crawford, pressing forward with the tightening semicircle of men, stepped on Gramps Rood's leg. The old man woke up and yelled, "What the goddamn hell here!" He sat up and caught the drift of affairs and then he scrambled forward, still cursing excitedly.

A stubbornness he did not try to reason out held Lee where he was, silent. This was the shape of things that came from seeking trouble. He resented the fact more than he did the personal challenge, and he saw in Alarid the same quality that Houghton had accused Roderick of having: a wish to be big before people, to show off. Lee glanced at his father. The fierce expression of the bony face said, "Fight him!"

Iris Meeker shoved in beside her father. She watched Lee steadily.

"Well?" Alarid said.

Lee shook his head. He turned away and almost bumped into Ann Houghton, Cal's unmarried daughter. She was a tall woman with hair like dark copper. There was none of her father's ruddiness in her face, none of her mother's plumpness. Each feature was cleanly defined, a trim, straight nose, high cheekbones, controlled lips; and over all there was the calmly speculative expression of one who makes her own decisions.

She too watched Lee steadily, and he could not tell what was in her mind. He had thought he knew her, that someday he would marry her; but now she was like the others who stood apart and set themselves against the Vails. She mattered more than all the rest. Lee needed her understanding, some sign to tell him that she knew why he had no wish to plunge into a useless fight.

She watched him quietly, conveying nothing. Lee turned back to Alarid. Bliss Rood said, "Hell, you're wasting time, Alarid."

"Give him what he asked for, Lee," Roderick said.

The forces twisting Lee were not of his own making. Nothing in him stampeded away from what his own will told him, but his father's command lay on him with hard authority and the faces behind Alarid taunted him and Alarid was smiling. From the corner of his eye Lee saw Ann walking swiftly toward the tables where the women were. He avoided Iris Meeker's direct gaze. For an instant he wanted to cast reason away and step savagely into Alarid without considering the motive.

But he went toward his horse instead. Gramps Rood cursed disappointedly. The stinging slap of laughter followed. Cantonwine regained his voice and boomed, "Let us sing 'Shall We Gather at the River?' "

Lee rode down the street alone. The singing of the women came thinly, mingled with the heavy tones of man talk and laughter. Roderick's buckskin came up beside Lee with a surge. "You pup! They're laughing at us!"

"You made the quarrel with Alarid, not me," Lee said.

Roderick's fury was strained like a tight wire. "You backed down! You shamed me!"

Roderick had never backed down. Lee recalled how his father had probed at the courage of every man who ever worked at Diamond, except Sam Harvey, picking at men even after he knew they were afraid of him. He could understand his father's feeling but he had his own anger and humiliation too. "You made the enemy of Houghton and the rest for your own reasons. I had no reason to roll in the dirt with Alarid because of that."

"You made a fool of me!"

That too was so, for Lee knew his refusal to fight had turned the edge of the whole affair against them after Roderick had held the dominant position. They rode another hundred feet. Suddenly Roderick threw the buckskin against Lee's horse and crowded the bay around. "Go back there and fight him!"

"No."

Red and white blotches showed on Roderick's high-peaked face. "You're afraid of him."

"I don't think so."

"You're gutless, damn you. I've been wondering for a long time and now I know."

So that was what had been in Roderick's mind during those moments of moody appraisal. Lee said, "I won't fight him or anyone else just to please you."

Roderick's long arm flashed across the space between the horses and the flat of his hand rocked Lee's head sidewise. "So help me, I've raised a miserable coward!" The words came out with groaning fury.

The affair in the grove had poured its poison into Lee, the turning away when he knew the cost; but he knew what it had cost Roderick too, and so he strove to make a balance and hold his temper.

Roderick struck him again and all Lee's striving splintered. He leaned out in the saddle and smashed his father in the face. The blow reached only near the end of its power but it snapped Roderick's head back and knocked his hat off. The bay jostled when Lee tried to strike again. Lee's father caught his wrist. The two men tugged awkwardly across the space until Lee's horse sidled away and dragged him from the saddle.

Lee clung to his father, trying to pull him down. Braced against the unbalanced weight, the buckskin held like a rock until Roderick kicked out of the stirrups and let his weight plunge down on Lee. They crashed to the ground, and the horse stepped clear of them. In rough and tumble Lee found his strength greater than his father's. He hammered Roderick's face with the sides of his fist. He jolted Roderick with the heel of his hand against the jaw and jarred him away and tried to get on top of him. Roderick rolled like a cat and leaped up.

There was dust on his face, blood at the corner of his mouth. His tawny hair hung wildly. "Come on!" he cried.

Lee went in swinging. His blows found nothing. Roderick's fists streaked out, cracking into Lee's mouth, raking his cheekbones. His left eye went dim with water. He walked straight in, trying to beat his father's arms aside and reach him. A spearing blow made his knees unhinge. Weaving on his feet, Lee held stubbornly to getting in close, but Roderick's fists slammed him, stopped him.

With his clear eye centered on his father's belt buckle, Lee rushed. Roderick sidestepped. He turned Lee by the arm and shoved him violently and Lee plowed into the dust on hands and knees. He scrabbled around to face his father, rose, and tried to rush in again. Roderick knocked him flat with one clean blow.

There was only a tall blur before Lee when he got up. He lunged toward it, stumbling. His father drove him back with punishment that Lee no longer felt until the last blow hurled the son on his backsides in the ditch, with one arm flung across a water box. Lee heard Roderick breathing gustily. He saw him but vaguely and tried to rise to go at him again. Lee's efforts put him deeper into the ditch. Water rose across his thighs as he tried for leverage with muscles that were poisoned by fatigue and shock.

Lee could not rise. He knew it, and so he muttered, "Wait a minute."

Roderick walked away. He smoothed his long hair back with his hands. He wiped his bleeding mouth on his sleeve and stooped to retrieve his hat. He found his pistol lying in the street and spent several moments blowing dust from it. For a short time he stood beside his horse, looking toward his son. Then he swung up easily and rode out of town.

The singing in the grove was just ending when Lee crawled out of the ditch. He saw his horse in the shade on the other side of the street. It was a long trip. He scuffed over his hat and almost fell when he bent to pick it up. When he reached the bay he was sick and dizzy again stooping for the reins. He leaned against the horse until his head cleared.

It was then he saw Alarid and Iris standing near the church, watching him. Pride prevented Lee from risking failure in an attempt to mount.

Walking slowly but straight, Lee Vail led his horse down the street and out of Kebler.

CHAPTER THREE

AFTER THE evening sermon the women went toward home in spring wagons, with most of the men coming behind in a loose group. Preacher Cantonwine rode beside the Crawford wagon. He would spend the night with them and go across the mountains in the morning. He rode bent forward slightly like a man contemplating the evils of the world and how to combat them. Pale moonlight made deep troughs of the furrows in his cheeks. There was a hot rage in him.

Roderick Vail was a killer with a long record of violence. His wife was high and mighty and would not come to church. She had an Irish name. Cantonwine had never seen her, for the Diamond was the only ranch in the country where he had not been invited. He wondered darkly if there was an altar with heathen images in her home.

There must be punishment for Roderick Vail, swift and visible and under Cantonwine's control. This day the man had sorely affronted Cantonwine, striking him, making him small before the world. One flaw kept fracturing the cankerous thoughts: the preacher was mortally afraid of Roderick.

In spite of the crunching of his revengeful lust, Cantonwine was sensitive to every movement of the dangerous horse under him.

"The sermons were wonderful, Reverend Cantonwine," Mrs. Landon Crawford said, for the third time.

"The Lord directed my tongue." Cantonwine tried to balance a line of action against his fear of Roderick. The son was craven; perhaps it would be better to strike through him. But it would not be a sweet revenge that way.

Moonlight touched bits of metal among the riders behind the wagons. Their conversation came unevenly, covered when the wagons were grinding over rocks, clear when the wheels were creasing dust. Ben Meeker was talking now.

"Some big fellow always pushing a man around. It's the same wherever you go. I've made four starts and it was the same every time. Once in Texas—"

Joe Emmet listened to the whine with disgust. Old Ben had been here early enough to take up the best land north of the Sapinero, and with normal effort he could have held the best range on the Fossils, such as it was; but he had let things drift away from him. Right now the old fool ought to be worrying about his youngest daughter riding home with Tony Alarid. Emmet was worrying about it plenty.

". . . Then I moved up into Kansas," Ben said, "and that was even worse."

The wagons ground through McGraw Wash, and Ben reached his fourth start on the Sapinero. The others heard the sounds he made and that was all.

Bliss Rood cut in suddenly without offending Ben or anyone else. "He had no call to do that."

"It's just Roderick's way," Chauncey Meeker said. "He was aiming at Houghton but he had to make a holy show of things. It's just his way." The dim light fell on Chauncey's big white teeth as he spoke. He was Ben Meeker's oldest son, a hard-working man who had taken up his own place soon after the family came to the Sapinero country. His ranch was small and his range uncertain, but he managed both well and everything he did was planned with an eye to the future.

"He aimed at all of us." Rood spoke with stubborn anger. "I never heard of Roderick Vail until I came here. I like to judge a man first hand, not from what people say about him. There could be a lot of bluff in him. I'm wondering what would happen if someone did drop a few hundred cows into that park he thinks he owns."

They dipped into the wash and the hoofs of the horses clopped softly in the sand. Landon Crawford said, "You'll think about that dumping business twice, won't you, Bliss?"

There was a short laugh.

"Vail brought the idea up himself," Bliss said. "Nobody ever bothered him over there. He must be more afraid than he has a right to be to come busting in with a warning to all of us. There's a heap of bluff in Vail. I still wonder what he'd do if some of us pushed cows into Union Park."

"He'd do plenty," Chauncey said. "Him and Sam Harvey. I'd as lief take a chance on Vail, I think, as that Harvey."

"All right, they're both tough, let's say." Rood's slow speech was like that of a man musing aloud. "I ain't saying I'd care to tackle Vail alone even if I think he's part bluff, and I ain't sure Lee was as afraid of Tony Alarid as some of you seem to think, but I still ain't convinced of just what they could do if a bunch of us moved into Union Park."

"You started with yourself," Chauncey said dryly. "Now you've got us all in Vail's back pasture."

Once more there was a quick laugh but it ran along the edge of a sullen resentment over the affair in the grove and it did not hold long.

"Maybe it wouldn't work." Bliss Rood's even, stubborn tone was unchanged. "But when a man comes dusting in at me with his hair on end and slaps me across the chops for nothing, then, by God, I figure he has to be paid back."

It was almost tangible, the silent agreement with the principle Bliss had stated. There had been insults and a challenge, all unnecessary; and they had helped point up the fact that Roderick Vail was big and the northsiders small. The feeling was there in the silence, the moody pondering of men who have economic troubles enough without the arrogant jostling of someone who lacks understanding of their problems. But no one cared to agree aloud with Bliss, and in that was an admission that the matter was merely something that must be borne.

Joe Emmet, for one, found logic in Rood's words but he was not greatly interested. Emmet ran a few cattle but his main concern was his sawmill on Gothic Creek. He had problems enough there, what with a shortage of timber. Roderick Vail controlled the answer to that. But at the moment an even greater worry was Iris and Tony Alarid back there in the night. Emmet looked over his shoulder. When he turned back he knew that Chauncey was watching him.

"I just don't care about being insulted," Rood said. "I'll figure out something."

"You had your chance," Landon Crawford said. "Alarid tried—"

"Alarid!" Bliss spat the name. "He's a bigger show-off than Roderick. The main question was about Union Park, not who was the best man at knocking out teeth before the women."

This direct economy of thought laid another thinking silence on everyone but Ben Meeker, who said, "Someone like Vail is always around to ruin things for a man. I guess he wants everything on this side too. That's about the size of it, boys."

Even Rood did not care to comment on the lack of substance in the words. The wagons ahead bumped on through the sage and an odor of dust as bitter as smoke drifted back. Cantonwine's stallion spooked and went buck-jumping through the moonlight. The preacher sawed him around and brought him under hard control.

Crawford said, "Handles that brute easy enough, don't he?"

"Yeah," Rood grunted. "But he was just like the rest of us today, crawling when Roderick Vail snapped the whip." He would not let the subject change. Bliss Rood was a man of few ideas but tenacious when one did reach him. "You haven't said a word, Emmet. What do you think?"

"I'm hard to insult," Emmet said. "That seems to be the bone you're growling over."

"You want to shift your sawmill over into Vail's timber," Rood said. "Think he'll let you?"

"One way or another it'll be my business," Emmet answered.

Bliss Rood turned his blunt head and stared a long time through the shifting layers of moonlight at Joe Emmet. When they came to Gothic Creek, Emmet said good night curtly and rode away. Soon afterward the Crawfords turned toward the river on a rocky road. Cantonwine answered one of the women's questions. "Yes, Sister, he was bold and prideful with his weapon girded about him, but we must find forgiveness for Roderick Vail and all his kind." And then he added, "Of course, pride goeth before a fall."

There was a savageness in the last statement and it caught Rood's interest. Cantonwine was a queer one, what with his mealy mouth, but at times Bliss had sensed a boiling inside him. He was a coward, no doubt, but Bliss was smart enough to know that cowards are the world's most dangerous people.

When Chauncey Meeker came to his turnoff he rode ahead to the wagon and said something to his mother. Then he went down the backtrail on the trot, and everyone knew he was going back to check on his sister.

Rood said good night to no one when he turned away. He rode toward home scowling. Iris Meeker had chased around some with Emmet before Lee Vail got after her. No matter what Emmet said he couldn't feel very happy about the Vails. Then there was Cantonwine. A man might be able to do something with him, but he wasn't around very much. Rood's plans were muddled, but the base of them was strongly rooted in a sense of personal injury that would keep growing as he brooded about it.

Lee Vail was almost to the river before he noticed that his pistol was gone. He guessed it must be lying in the street yet. He crossed at Island Ford where the Sapinero was only knee deep on the bay. On the far side he undressed and bathed in the icy current. It was mainly his face, all cut and swollen, with one eye closed and his jaw moving as if the hinges were full of cinders.

He felt no pity for himself; he wondered how he had lived so long without knowing certain things about his father. He shook the dust from his clothes and dressed and then he sat beside the riffling water, flipping pebbles while his mind resisted the idea of going home. At last he got the bay from the willows and rode on.

The hills broke down to flatness where Diamond lay. For a mile the river ran slowly beside meadows that were subirrigated by warm springs which made a great white fog in winter. Buildings at Diamond were not large or many, for the economy of the ranch was simple, three or four riders in summer to patrol the natural confines of Union Park, and only a minimum of effort in the winter when part of the herds were brought out of the park. Natural losses were high but normal increase was also high.

It occurred to Lee that there were better cattlemen than Roderick, men who had to shave through on tight margin, men who had problems which Roderick attributed scornfully to shiftlessness. Lee examined the thought and found it a fact to accept, rather than an idea which, at first, had seemed to smack of disloyalty to his father.

He rode into the yard.

All around the house were white gravel walks and planter walls of red rock. Maureen Vail had built them with her own hands in the years following her slow recovery from her accident.

She was sitting on the porch with Sam Harvey. She had a fair look at her son's face as he dismounted reluctantly. She came toward him quickly, a tall, slender woman with jet-black hair. Her eyes were flaky gray and for a long time they had looked on life with a detachment that was more than reserve.

"What happened, Lee?" Mrs. Vail was concerned but not excited. She had seen her son with both legs broken. She had seen him with one arm fractured, and once with his scalp ripped open for six inches and five of his ribs cracked. Roderick had brought Lee up the hard way around horses and cattle.

"What happened, Lee?"

"A fight." Lee glanced at Harvey.

"Who with?" Mrs. Vail asked.

Roderick, then, was not yet home. "A man." Lee looked at the corral. "Where's Roderick?"

"He was with you."

"I guess he went to the park." Lee paused uncertainly. An intentness was growing in his mother's expression.

She said, "It must have been a tough man. Look at his face, Sam."

"I'm looking." Harvey was still on the porch, standing with one foot on a stone wall. He was of medium size, a man with close-knit, wavy hair that had once been red. Now it was grayed to roan. Compressed upon his face from some depth of quietness was an expression that just missed being blank, but his dark eyes, restless and penetrating, belied the composure of lips and facial muscles.

Mrs. Vail asked, "Joe Emmet?"

Emmet! She knew about Iris and how Emmet had been cut out. "No," Lee said. He wanted to look away, but Mrs. Vail's intentness held him. "Roderick."

The sudden change in his mother amazed him. The same fury she had flashed at Roderick when he shot her horse at chill sunrise long ago leaped into her expression. Her hands clenched into Lee's jumper. "You and Roderick? Why?"

"We disagreed. I didn't want to fight Tony Alarid." Lee gave a bare account of the afternoon. His mother's hands slipped down from his jumper, but her anger was unchanged. She turned away suddenly and started toward the house. Lee tried to find something in Harvey's face but the man's look was bleakly wary.

"I'll fix some coffee, Lee," Mrs. Vail said, "and then I want to patch your face up." She went up the porch steps almost on the run, pausing just an instant to look at Harvey, and then she swung into the house.

Unformed thoughts swirled through Lee's mind as

he took care of his horse. He kept glancing toward the house. Harvey was sitting down again. It was the depth of Mrs. Vail's rage that troubled Lee; it was no transient surge of emotion but something that ran far back to the day Roderick had carried her down from Stormy Ridge.

She's out of her head, Lee.

But that was not true of a few minutes ago. Ever since her accident Maureen Vail had not been well, or at least Roderick and Lee had told themselves so until the thought became an assumption needing no examination. Yet when they were in the park Mrs. Vail had built stone walls and wheeled dirt like a man and refused afterward to answer their outraged protests. Frequently she changed the design of the walls or moved them and they had come to laugh about that as being a woman's way of doing things; but now Lee remembered the times he had seen walls knocked out as if his mother had gone at her work with hell driving her.

The knowledge smashed into him: there was nothing physically wrong with his mother and probably had not been for years. If she had lived behind a barrier of fragility, it was of his and Roderick's making, for never by complaint or pretense had Mrs. Vail promoted the idea that she was not well.

Harvey walked down the yard slowly and ducked through the corral poles. "He called Houghton about the strays in the park?"

Lee glanced sharply at the foreman. "How'd you know?"

"I saw it coming when I made the slip about Teepees cattle."

"Then you know Roderick better than I do."

"Yes," Harvey said. There was meaning all around the edges of the word, like a flickering light that defies identification.

It was either sudden doubt or quick realization that stripped Lee's mind of another easy line of thinking. For six years Harvey had been at Diamond, from spring roundup to late fall, spending most of his time in the park. Although Lee had never heard him and Roderick talk fully of their past, he had heard enough to know that they had been friends before he was born. Harvey had been easy to accept. He came in the spring and left in the fall. Roderick always said that when Harvey was around the park Diamond's interests were so secure that Lee and Roderick could spend their time playing poker in Kebler if they wanted to.

But now it struck Lee that he did not know Sam Harvey at all, although his trust in the man was still the same.

"He went to Kebler, to the church. He spoke his piece before everyone," Harvey said. In his choice of words, rather than the tone, ran condemnation that raised at once a stiffness in Lee.

"Yes," Lee said. No matter what he thought and what Harvey thought, Roderick was not a matter to maul over with adverse criticism. "Who told you?"

"I said I saw it coming." Harvey studied Lee, quietly. "In case you feel you didn't do very well, I'll tell

41

you that Roderick has always been about the handiest man with his fists I ever knew."

"That part doesn't bother me one bit."

"I know."

Lee slapped his horse away. "You know what?"

"That a licking doesn't bother you."

"I can't say that I care about it."

Harvey nodded. His eyes lighted almost to a smile but they grew dark in an instant and he said carefully, "No man likes a beating, Lee, but it happens to all of us in one way or another." He paused, watching Lee gravely. Harvey seemed to be balancing thoughts, trying to estimate in advance the impact of something he was going to say, but whatever it was did not emerge.

"What brought you here today?" Lee asked. It was a casual question but as it hung unanswered, with Harvey studying Lee, implications grew and colored the inquiry.

"I came to get orders to move Houghton's cattle out of the park."

"You were sure there would be such orders?"

Harvey nodded. His assurance nettled Lee because it was based on an understanding of Roderick's character that Lee did not have; it gave him a feeling that he had grown up at Diamond without knowing more than surface facts about his parents.

Harvey said, "Alarid wanted a pistol fight?"

"He wasn't armed."

"Did he call you both?"

"Just me."

Harvey glanced at Lee's empty holster. His reaction slid away behind some withheld thought. "I'll go on back to the park. Roderick must be there."

Lee nodded. "I imagine he went straight there from Kebler to tell you to move the strays."

"Partly that." Harvey did not turn away soon enough to hide the savage glitter that ran across his dark eyes. "The rest was because he didn't want to be the first here to tell about the fight."

Lee watched Harvey ride across the yard. Maureen Vail came out on the porch. As Harvey passed her he raised one hand slowly and let it fall, and the gesture was a gentle salute carrying a full measure of communication. Mrs. Vail's eyes followed him until he put his long-legged claybank into a trot. It all passed in seconds. A treacherous thought ripped through Lee. He wondered how many times in six years he might have seen a small, sharp moment like this one without observing anything.

Mrs. Vail said quietly, "The coffee is ready." She said it again before the words struck through to Lee.

Sleepless in the night, Lee heard his father sliding corral poles. Later, the long strides in the yard. These were familiar sounds that had always brought him an unrealized sense of well-being, a comfortable feeling that needed no analyzing; but now his sleepless unease was like the night when gunfire had sent him rocking up in terror.

He knew his mother was sitting in the living room beside a dead fire. He heard Roderick trying to cross the porch softly. The door opened, and before it closed Roderick said, "Maureen, what are you doing up at this hour?" His voice was plaintive. "Good Lord, woman, you're not going to start that all over again, are you?"

The anger Lee had seen in his mother's face now came in her voice. "What are *you* starting, Roderick?"

"Lee told you about the business today?"

"Only a little. I guessed the rest."

"Nothing will happen," Roderick said. "There won't be any trouble. Houghton will growl and grunt and that will be the size of it."

"When you and Cannon Ridgway started to Union Park I recall you said there wouldn't be any trouble."

"That was different!" Roderick's voice was persuasive now. "There'll be no trouble this time. The old days are gone."

"Are they?"

Lee rose and slipped into his clothes.

Roderick did not answer his wife's question. "Lee here now?"

"Yes."

"I called him a coward, Maureen. I was wrong, but my temper was up and I couldn't help myself."

"Temper against yourself or him?" Mrs. Vail asked coldly.

Lee walked into the living room. His mother looked small and quiet sitting in a chair beside a lamp that was turned low, but Lee felt the pressure of her will as she stared at Roderick. Shadows took the sharp lines from Roderick's bony face, but his driving vitality was still evident in the way he stood, in the way he swung to face his son. "You sulking, Lee?"

Lee shook his head.

Roderick grinned. He held up his left arm. "You whacked that so hard a time or two that I could scarcely use it the rest of the day. But you were swinging wild." He crossed the room and grasped Lee by the shoulder. "It's not going to happen between us again. Hear that, Maureen?"

Mrs. Vail watched the two men bleakly.

"Anything around this dump to eat?" Roderick asked. "Two fighting men like us—Never mind, we'll rustle something up."

Lee crossed the room with Roderick, and his doubts began to weaken under his father's booming energy and friendliness. Maureen sat where she was, staring at her hands.

While Roderick rummaged in the summer kitchen for bread and onions Lee went through the soft night to the spring-house. He found roast beef and butter in the metal well and he drew four brown bottles of beer from the icy water. On his way hack to the house he glanced once toward the Razors and the mighty pool of blackness that was Union Park. When he went into the house he saw that Roderick had taken off his pistol belt. He was slicing onions with a heavy knife.

"Women worry," Roderick said. "That first deal in

the park was hell on her, Lee." His voice was very low. "She's never been well since she took that spill." He flipped the onion slices on a saucer. "The reason I didn't come straight home from Kebler today was because I was ashamed to face her."

The frank admission of a fact already stated by Sam Harvey helped to still further the lingering unease in Lee.

They ate their food and drank the cold beer. Lee felt the last of his troubling uncertainty draining away. This was familiar security. For years his relationship with Roderick had been built on small things as strong and binding as this moment, their work together in the park, their target practice—all the remembered things that wove a tight effect and bound Lee powerfully to his father.

"Where'd you know Harvey?" Lee asked.

"We were lawmen together." Something pricked at Roderick's contentment, but he cast it off. "You could have stomped Alarid into the ground. How come you didn't?"

"I was sore at you for busting up the meeting."

"I sure did that." Roderick grinned. He took a great bite of onion and beef, wiping his lips on the back of his hand afterward. "Joe Emmet didn't like it but I've got him across a barrel. He wants to move his set into some of the timber in the park."

"Will you let him?"

"I guess so, when he gets around to asking again." Roderick grinned once more. "Did you see old Cantonwine's face when I shoved him out of the way? I thought he was going to swallow his teeth. They're all like that, Lee—afraid."

Lee would not say that Emmet had been afraid, or Bliss Rood or Chauncey Meeker either.

They finished their food. Since neither of them smoked they sat only a few moments longer before starting to clean up the mess they had made. Lee said, "Harvey found you tonight?"

"I met him at the twin cabins."

"He's going to run Houghton's stuff out?"

Roderick nodded. "It won't amount to anything. Some of the cattle will drift back later, but it was time to read the law about the park. Ever so often, Lee, when they think you're getting soft. You'll find out when I'm gone and you're running the place."

The thought of his father's ever being gone worked coldly inside Lee.

"Make your peace with Ann," Roderick said. "Better do it in the morning. She'll listen." He was sure. "Cal may snort around a little but he won't stand in your way." He wrapped up the roast and took the butter. He went out the back door, swearing mildly when he stumbled over loose stones Mrs. Vail had gathered for a new wall.

Lee went toward his room. His mother was still sitting where they had left her. "You feel all right?"

"Of course," she answered.

"You're just sitting there."

"I often do."

"Don't worry about the park and everything today," Lee said. "Nothing much will come of it."

"I have your father's word for that also." A bitterness sensed rather than apparent in his mother's manner made Lee eye her sharply; but he saw nothing and he guessed Roderick was right: women were worriers. He hesitated until Mrs. Vail said, "Good night, Lee."

He fell asleep at once but he woke up sometime in the night when he heard Roderick, half angry, half querulous in his efforts to be gentle, telling Maureen that she ought to go to bed. Once more the currents of things not understood worked in Lee, and he could not regain the relaxed feeling of a short time before.

"You won't start that wild riding business again?" Roderick asked in the living room.

"Probably not. Go back to bed, Roderick. I'm all right."

She was not all right, Lee thought. He kept seeing Harvey's small gesture when he was riding away that day; and he kept seeing his father's contorted face during the fight in Kebler.

"By God, I'm getting tired of this!" Roderick said.

"Are you? Then go to bed and leave me alone."

The force of Mrs. Vail's will sent Roderick back to his room and the house was tensely quiet and Lee did not sleep well.

CHAPTER FOUR

ON HIS WAY to the Teepees to see Ann Houghton, Lee met big Pete Kebler riding his thirteen-hundred-pound gray. Kebler's saddlebags were bulging. He was not a man content to let new merchandise sit on his shelves until someone came in to see it; instead he spent much time riding about the country with samples, and in the process he carried messages and mail and did favors for anyone who asked them. There was nothing servile in Kebler; he liked people.

His shrewd eyes brushed over the marks on Lee's face. "I'm headed for your place, Lee. Got some stuff here I think your mother might like."

Lee nodded. Mrs. Vail was always glad to see Kebler. Before his smooth expansiveness she loosened up and sometimes even laughed. It struck Lee that his mother was generally easy and natural in the presence of any man except Roderick.

"You just came from the Teepees, huh?"

"Yeah," Kebler said. "I was there a couple of hours."

"How's it look for me this morning?"

Kebler grinned. "I never predict the weather or the trend of a courtship." He unbuckled a saddlebag and hauled out Lee's pistol. "Happened to see it in the ditch. I took the liberty of cleaning it up and oiling it."

"Thanks." Lee thrust the pistol under his belt.

"Alarid was there when I left the Teepees." Kebler rode away.

Cal Houghton was a nephew of Cannon Ridgway and from him had inherited the Teepees when both the Ridgways died of typhoid fever. Like Diamond, the ranch sat at the head of meadowland. There were more buildings at Teepees, for Houghton's range was not largely in one place and so he needed twice the crew that Roderick did.

Lee rode into the yard and did not dismount.

Houghton came from a storehouse and crossed the yard with his rolling, choppy walk. His face was sour but neither bitterly hostile nor friendly until he saw the pistol under Lee's belt. Then he said, "Don't bother to get down."

"I came to see Ann."

Houghton might not have heard. "Tell your old man I won't have a crew on Cannibal Mesa to pick up my cattle. They can drift where they damn well please until I have time to gather them up in the fall."

"All right."

Houghton examined the mild answer with suspicion. He was anxious to quarrel but before he could get anything started his daughter came from the house.

Ann Houghton's eyes were green. There was lurking fire in the way she looked at Lee, but he doubted that she would ever break her reserve to quarrel violently. She came toward him unhurriedly. The sun brought out the blue squares in the pattern of her dress. Lee watched her quietly, thinking with a nagging sense of guilt of Iris Meeker, who was not reserved or careful in her manner.

Ann said, "Get down, Lee, if you wish."

"He's wearing a pistol like a damned tough," Houghton said. "He—"

"Get down, Lee, if you wish."

Houghton rolled his shoulders irritably. He chopped across the yard and went into the storeroom. Lee walked with Ann to the corner of a blacksmith's shop out of earshot of the main buildings. "Roderick might have been a little overhasty yesterday, Ann." At once Lee was annoyed because he had laid blame on his father, even though he had come here to apologize.

Ann glanced at the pistol. She gave Lee the sharp point of her expression. "You were with him."

"I was there." Lee would not say that it had been against his wishes, for that would censure Roderick more. "I think the whole thing can be smoothed out with no trouble."

"I'm sure it will be, as long as your father has his way."

"He had his side."

"Is that why you came here, to try to justify what you two did?"

"No, I came here to try to explain—" Lee's pride worked up in him and he was tired of trying to explain. Iris would not have asked him to, he was sure. "First, you'll have to admit that Roderick had a point."

"Perhaps. But no one has a right to make people feel small and afraid, to insult them publicly."

That was Lee's own thought, but it was different coming from someone else. Ann watched him as if he were a stranger. "Are you like him, Lee—or is it just that you try to be?"

"Am I like what?"

"Wanting to dominate everyone you meet. Riding high and mighty with a chip on your shoulder. I've wondered. You haven't grown up very fast, Lee, considering your age, and so it's been hard to tell." Ann watched him carefully. "You've been close to asking me to marry you, haven't you?"

"Yes."

Her even study was more disturbing than Roderick's had ever been. A doubt that might have been based on hurt touched the woman's eyes. For an instant she was on the verge of softening, Lee thought; and then she said, "I don't know you, Lee. I'm not sure. I do know that I wouldn't care for a life of building flower beds that I would tear up a week later."

The implication jolted Lee. "What do you mean?"

"Just what I said."

He grabbed her by the shoulders. "Speak up! What are you trying to say?"

Gravel crunched behind Lee and then, quite close, Tony Alarid said, "You finally found somebody you'd fight, huh, Vail?"

Even as he turned Lee knew it was a mistake to swing directly toward Alarid's voice. The blow caught him in the corner of the mouth. It hurt Lee worse than any of Roderick's punches, for it struck tortured flesh, and it was almost enough to send Lee rushing blindly into Alarid. But Lee caught himself in time. He raised his arms and with hands open he walked at the man. Alarid's smile was a cold streak across his dark face. He stepped back lightly, moving a little to one side before he stopped.

Lee walked straight at him, reaching. Three or four times Alarid's fists smashed into his battered face, splintering out a hell of pain that threatened to make Lee lose control. He knew Alarid was punishing him deliberately, not trying yet for a killing blow. Lee feinted a rush. Alarid set himself to strike and swing aside. Lee grasped his wrist and tugged as if he intended to drag Alarid close.

Alarid put all his wiry power into a countertug. Lee released his grip and Alarid staggered back, off balance for a moment. Lee followed into him then, smashing his shoulder against Alarid's chest. They crashed into the corner of the blacksmith's shop where the ax-cut log ends protruded raggedly. The impact of the logs against Alarid's spine made him gasp. His face lost color.

Lee chopped him once in the side of the neck and thought he had him. But Alarid was spring steel and fighting spirit. He knocked Lee back with an elbow in the mouth, slid along the building, and gained open ground. Alarid was white around the mouth and he held his back stiffly. He was hurt but still dangerous. He closed Lee's injured eye with a stabbing punch. He splattered blood from Lee's swollen lips.

Still plodding in, Lee twisted when Alarid kicked at his groin. The full force of the boot heel cracked on

Lee's hip-bone and sent pain racking through the joint.

Limping, spitting blood, Lee went ahead. There was no pain in Alarid's blows now, but each one was taking strength from Lee's legs and the day was growing dimmer. A step, a jolting impact that stayed him for an instant, and then Lee went on. Alarid tried for a clean knockout. Lee saw it coming, the way the man measured him, the way he marshaled everything behind his right.

Once more Lee caught Alarid's wrist. With his other hand he grabbed the man just above the elbow. Alarid jabbed at his eye with his thumb. The nail gouged into Lee's cheekbone beside his good eye. He pivoted, swinging Alarid. He took the lighter man around, Alarid's boots chopping as he tried to hold his feet.

At full swing Lee let him loose to crash once more into the building, so hard that chunks of mud daubing fell from between the logs.

Alarid hit on the point of his shoulder with his left hand slapping the wall as he tried to break the force of the collision. Lee was on him, crowding without mercy. He sledged Alarid in the side of the neck. The man's arms came down. His face turned a dirty gray color. Lee stepped back to get more force into his next blow.

The world became a white flash. Shock ran down Lee's body and his knees almost buckled. He stared numbly at Alarid, wondering how the man had reached him.

Ann said, "That's enough." She was holding a piece

of scrap iron in both hands, and it was raised for another blow. "You don't have to kill him." Her voice was strangely without passion, cold and authoritative.

Backed against the logs with his feet dug in to hold him up, Alarid stood with one hand on his injured shoulder. Only his body was defeated. His eyes sent out writhing hatred. He tried to move toward Lee.

It won't end here, Lee thought. He watched Alarid try to come to him. The man fell back, going down the building in little jerks. He sat on the ground with his knees jackknifed high and his eyes still burning with fight.

"Get out of here, Lee." Ann dropped the piece of iron.

Lee stumbled toward his horse.

Cal Houghton, running toward the scene, grabbed him by the shoulder and spun him around. "Stay clear to hell away from here, Vail—for good!"

Lee bumped against his horse and after a time he hauled himself into the saddle. Mrs. Houghton stood in the doorway and watched him leave. He heard Alarid say, "Never mind, I'm all right."

Three miles away, on Vail land, Lee stopped to wash at a spring. The surface of the water showed him the beaten features of a brute, and he kept remembering the cold disgust in Ann's expression when she told him to get out.

Still unsettled by the poison of the fight, he rode toward Union Park. He was a long way toward it before he wondered why he instinctively wanted to go there instead of to Diamond.

The park was a tremendous basin, running ten miles east and west and roughly five miles north and south, with the south rim resting against the heavy timber of the Razor Mountains. There were seven small streams in Union Park and a dozen trickles that ran all summer. For centuries the beavers had worked here, building ponds that retained the rich wash of the mountains; eating themselves out of a home in one place, and so moving on to where food was more abundant. It was a cycle that had made meadowland on silt eight and ten feet deep.

There were hills and ridges all the way through the park and small plateaus where spires of red sandstone had caught the first sunlight and held the last of it every clear day for centuries. Aspens grew in great sprawling patches and grass was everywhere.

Roderick Vail had chosen as his main camp the twin cabins before which he had hanged four men.

Lee rode up the east side of the park and came across Cannibal Ridge, a borderland of gray sage that lay between Vail and Houghton range. He looked east at the humped ridges where Teepees cattle were scattered in the wrinkles for twenty miles along the mountains. He looked at the brown hills far across the Sapinero; and then it was not too hard to give an edge of his mind to Roderick's belief that there were combinations of people and geography that threatened the Vails.

Yet, he could not truly believe the whole assumption.

He went to the holding corrals at the camp on Ballou Creek. There had been an old mine here once, and someone's intentions had been strong. Three stout log buildings still stood. In Lee's time one of them had had a sign: *Superintendent's Office.* Below the caved-in mine, on the creek, grass and willows almost obscured the stone foundation of a mill that had never been built. Roderick now used the office as a camp, and stored salt blocks in one of the other buildings.

Lee turned his horse into a corral on the creek and went to the main cabin. The last man to use it had left the water pail half full, so that now there was a ring around the metal and a stale odor in the pail. Lee scoured the utensil with sand at the creek. He swept the broad oak planks of the floor. He nailed a piece of tin over a corner of the door where a rat had been trying to gnaw its way inside. Roderick's camps were always tight, for he hated rats and the odor of them. Once he had threatened to kill a rider who tried to make a pet of one.

After a dozen small chores that helped release some of the tension in him, Lee cooked a meal and then he sat in the doorway, feeling the peace that comes from familiar quietness. Much of his life had been spent in the park; it was more home to him than the ranch on the Sapinero ever had been. Long ago Roderick had set the casual pattern of staying up here as long as it suited him, two days, a week, or a month at a time.

For the first time in his life Lee wondered if his

mother ever worried about the uncertain coming and going of her family.

Late in the afternoon Sam Harvey and Scott Murdock came in, driving eight head of Teepees cattle. Murdock was a blocky little man, nearly bald, with a face like an unhappy bulldog. He seldom spoke more than was necessary. He and Harvey ran the eight head of cows and steers into the enclosure on the Ballou, which was more a pasture than a corral.

"Slim pickings," Lee said.

Harvey looked at the fresh marks on Lee's face and said, "Timoney and Johnny Maxwell are working the east side. Altogether, we'll pick up thirty head, I guess."

"Houghton told me he wouldn't be on Cannibal Mesa to take them," Lee said.

Harvey shrugged. Murdock was riding around the pasture, looking at the fence.

"Then what?" Lee asked.

"Nothing. We'll hold the stuff on the mesa till Roderick gets tired of it, and then we'll turn them loose and they'll drift back here." Harvey gave Lee a queer, hard look. "Roderick has made his point. He's happy."

"Explain that, Sam."

"Ask Roderick." Harvey stripped the saddle and bridle from his horse, slapped the animal into the small corral, and started toward the cabins. Lee walked beside him.

"Where'd you know Roderick before, Sam?"

"We were lawmen together. A long time back."

"You knew my mother too, then?"

Harvey's intentness was like the stare of a gun muzzle. "Yes. Why?"

Under Harvey's quiet stare Lee was not sure why he had asked the question. "I just wondered."

Harvey was starting supper when he asked, "Who'd you mix with this time?"

"Alarid."

"Lick him?"

"I guess so. I threw him against the blacksmith's shop at Teepees until he was worn down."

"At Teepees, huh?" Harvey stared at the biscuit dough he was rolling with an empty whiskey bottle. "When you start, you go through with it, don't you?" Suddenly he was deeply angry. "Alarid will kill you with a pistol, Lee. Just because he's a show-off, don't think he hasn't got the guts."

"I guess he has."

"He damn well has!" Harvey shouted. He was more upset than Lee had ever seen him. "If your—"

Murdock came in. He put his saddle on the rack, fussing with it meticulously. He poured water and stared at it a moment before he began to soap his hands. "Fence is tight."

The two men ate in silence. Lying on a bunk, Lee watched them, puzzled. Murdock was habitually quiet, but a man content to be so. It was different with Harvey: he was, Lee thought, explosively still, holding thoughts that gnawed at him. The shadows of things that Lee did not understand kept moving across his mind. Two days ago his life had been most care-less and serene; but now he was plagued by a feeling that a blackness was edging in on Diamond and the people of Diamond.

CHAPTER FIVE

BLISS ROOD'S anger was as dangerous as fire that creeps slowly through a heavy forest mat, smoldering, crawling until it fingers out against barren ground—or erupts terribly against tall trees. He had been insulted. His whole life had been scorned. Each time he glanced at the Rood holdings, a patch of meadow on Cyclone Creek, drab hills beyond that would be burned crisp by fall, the insult was affirmed.

He sat on a block of wood before the small cabin where he lived apart from the rest of the Roods. Some-times the sight of them so disgusted him that he chose to cook his own meals rather than eat in the main house where Gramps Rood was forever yapping about the past; where the children of Jeremy and Buster, Bliss's brothers, whined about the food; where the women complained about things they did not have. Damnation on such a shiftless layout.

Bliss could say that, and frequently did, to the other Roods; but others had no right to hint at it, which was just what Roderick Vail had done.

At noon Jeremy came home from a two-day trip to the high range. He was a loose-limbed, tall blond man, generally in need of a shave. Bliss considered him a throwback to the maternal side, for Jeremy was content to raise kids and make a precarious living. Whenever Joe Emmet needed him for a few days at the sawmill, Jeremy hopped right over and worked twelve hours a day. He was pretty much of a damn fool, Bliss thought, his strongest point being that he was Bliss's brother, a relationship which had to be accepted patiently.

Jeremy rode near Bliss sitting on the block, sensed his savage mood, and almost did not speak; and then he said, "We need rain up high."

"Is that news?" Bliss jerked his thumb to the south. "They don't need it over there. They got all the water in the world cornered."

Jeremy was disturbed. "Now, Bliss, you're not thinking of anything to cause trouble with Roderick Vail, are you?"

"Hell no, not with everybody over here as spineless as you and Chauncey Meeker."

"There's nothing we can do about Vail. Let him blow off steam."

"Sure, sure."

"You take everything personal, Bliss. You always did."

Bliss surged up and strode away. He was disgusted with his life and therefore most sensitive to any criticism of it. There was a destructive recklessness in him, a dissatisfaction that grew enormously at the slightest touch.

He rode away from the ramshackle Rood place,

where everything was a reminder of weakness and failure. He crowded his horse until it was heaving, taking the steep trail toward Joe Emmet's sawmill on Gothic Creek. When the horse stopped of its own accord Bliss got down and looked across the bright distance at the green lands of Roderick Vail. Over there things were different.

A clear corner of Rood's mind told him that it was not covetousness that drove him; possessions would not quiet the burning unrest he felt. It was rather that others were getting something out of life that he could not find. He stood a long time on the ridge, a broad chunk of a man with heavy arms fitted awkwardly to his body. An odd expression lifted through the curdled sullenness of his features. He was perplexed without knowing it, but later the brutal, more familiar feeling of not being a part of the community of men rose in him once more. He pushed on until he came to the break above Gothic Creek and looked down on the sawmill.

Iris Meeker was there, standing by her horse as she talked to Emmet. The clear sound of her laughter came up to Bliss. He saw the shine of her hair and the bright green of her dress. Someday she would wiggle that big body at one too many men and then there would be a shooting scrape that would break her brother's pious heart. There was murky satisfaction in the thought.

From the timber Bliss watched for a while longer. He could picture the silly smirk Joe Emmet would be wearing. She had her guts, going back to torment Emmet, but if the man was fool enough to listen . . . Bliss went on down to the river road that led to the mill.

Emmet was not pleased to see him coming. The sawmill owner was a long-boned man who appeared thin, but those who had worked for him knew that his big frame and flat muscles were packed with tireless energy. His face was long, heavy-boned, his eyes brown and mild. His hair grew in crisp whorls and he kept it cut short.

"Just happened to be riding by," Bliss said.

Iris laughed. "Me too, Bliss."

After a time Bliss wondered if there had been a gentle hint in her words. She was twirling the knotted end of the reins, smiling at both men. She was a fine-looking woman, Rood admitted, big and strong, with the clear-cut features of all the Meekers. The vitality that poured from her was a challenge to any man. He kept staring at her until his interest brought counter-speculation to her eyes. A slow-growing thought threaded through his scrutiny, and he was startled to find it pleasant.

"Going up to look at your range?" Emmet asked. His voice was curt. It did not complement the mild-ness of his eyes.

"After a while," Bliss said. "You're getting to be a right pretty young lady, Iris." He was not given to compliments of any kind, so now he was surprised to discover how easily he had spoken this one. His quick side glance showed a hardening in Emmet's expression, and that pleased Bliss.

"Thank you, Brother Rood, thank you." Iris imitated Preacher Cantonwine so well that Bliss almost grinned. "I have to go on home now."

Bliss and Emmet bumped shoulders to help her up. She smiled her thanks at both of them, but her interest held a moment longer on Bliss with a casual warmth that brushed down the ragged points of his normal turbulence. She rode away, quite properly sidesaddle. Bliss watched until she crossed the road and entered the timber.

When he looked at Emmet the man's lean face was set in a warning cast. Emmet had it bad all right.

"I been thinking about last Sunday," Bliss said.

"I imagine."

"Are we going to do anything about it?"

"We?" Emmet shook his head. "I had my say."

Slowly Bliss swung his blunt features toward the ridges on both sides of the creek. "Your timber is just about gone."

"I know that." Emmet was curt. "It'll last till I cut it."

"And then?"

"Don't sidle around, Rood. I'm not figuring to get sucked into any scrap with Vail, not even if I wasn't planning to make a new set in his Union Park timber as soon as I have all my equipment running the way I want it."

"You think he'll let you move over there?"

"I think so," Emmet said.

"And Lee Vail—I suppose as far as you're concerned, him and Iris can lollygag and—"

"That's enough." Emmet's face was white.

The reaction was a sight stronger than Bliss had figured. Something to help get at the Vails could be worked out of it yet. Bliss started away. "It galls me when one man like Roderick Vail—"

"Anything galls you," Emmet said. He walked over to a circular saw lying on a ring of wooden blocks. He picked up a hammer and a heavy drift and went to work setting the teeth. From the edge of his eye he watched Bliss ride on west, and when the man was well out of sight Emmet stopped working.

He looked at his scarred hands with callus bumps like halved marbles. Hard work was nothing. He had done a power of it since he was ten years old, expecting little but the completion of the job at hand. Iris had changed his outlook, giving his labor meaning, giving his life a goal, so that for several months he had gone at his work with singing strength. Then she had turned toward Lee Vail, who properly belonged on the south side of the river . . . with Ann Houghton. Caste was even here in this remote land; Emmet's whole life had made him acutely aware of such things.

If Lee Vail did not know the fact, his old man would beat it into his head soon enough. Then Iris—there was no telling where she might turn. Today she had looked Bliss Rood over with careful interest. That was not, of course, Lee Vail's fault; but still Vail was the step that could unleash the fire in her and cause her to run full wild—after he learned that he should stay on his side of the river.

Emmet's hands were clenched on the tools he held. He dropped the hammer and the drift, rising to look around him. Life fell back into an old pattern. Secondhand machinery, a leaky boiler, a saw blade that was not quite true, the lack of tools. There were a hundred things he needed to make this a first-class outfit, but not long ago he had been unworried about temporary inadequacies that his strength and skill could conquer.

Nothing material was changed, but his incentive was threatened, and that was like a loss of courage.

She had been meeting Vail somewhere high on Gothic Creek. Today he must not have been there.

Emmet whirled away from tasks that were suddenly meaningless and onerous. He went into his cabin and dug a bottle of whiskey out of a cupboard that had not been tidy since Iris stopped visiting him regularly. He held the bottle a moment and then thrust it back. He drank whiskey when he was happy, in the presence of men, for companionship, for relaxation; and nothing could change that habit.

He stood in the doorway. The troubled expression turned bitter as he looked south to where the Vails and Houghtons lived. They had their differences, like Roderick's ill-timed outbreak Sunday, but over there was a happy land.

Since his first expanding joy in understanding and mastering the moving parts of things mechanical, Emmet thought he had never been truly happy. Happiness was always something that lay across a distant river, in another land. For a while he had thought he had cornered it here. He guessed it had been so, too, for a while.

He surged outside, a man made for working and not for thinking. He picked up an ax. The edge was sharp and well formed, but it irritated him. He sank the ax into a stump with one sweep of his arm. He watched the ridge where Iris had disappeared. If she came riding back, with a smile on her face. No, no . . . things never happened that way.

The words that he had told Bliss Rood not to speak came plainly to him from his own mind.

In the timber on the ridge west of the sawmill, Bliss half smiled when the sounds of Emmet's work died abruptly. A man could put on quite a show, maybe even mean it, but Emmet had his weak spot like any other man. Slow, patient work would make an ally of him.

That Iris—you couldn't tell what might run through a woman's mind. Bliss rubbed one hand across the coarse black stubble on his chin.

The big blue roan showed on the skyline for a moment before it plunged out of sight a quarter of a mile away. Why that was Cantonwine's stallion. The man was supposed to have started home from the Crawford place early this morning, and here he was ten miles west in the middle of the afternoon, holding low in a sand gully like he didn't want to be seen.

Rood's natural curiosity over a man's skulking was doubled because the man was a preacher. He kept watching. Cantonwine came into view, then dropped back into the wash once more. He was trying a thief's sneak, sure enough, sticking to the gully until narrowing rocks squeezed him out of it. Up this high the wash was a poor route, although near the river it was broad and easygoing.

A sneaking preacher . . . Him and Iris? Hell no. Why not? Bliss argued with himself. Cantonwine was a hot-eyed old hellion who might do anything if he got the chance; but Iris had settled the hash of younger and better men than him who thought she was easy. Bliss decided it wasn't what he had thought at first.

He went quartering in on the preacher, swinging down a feeder gully that grew deeper as it approached the main wash. Near the intersection he waited. Cantonwine's stallion smelled him out and snorted. The preacher said, "Easy there, Brigham! What the hell?" A moment later he came into view.

"Howdy," Bliss said loudly. It amused him to watch the greasy look of surprise that slid across Cantonwine's loose features. At first, mild shock, and then anger when Cantonwine realized that Bliss had waited here deliberately. "Well, well! Brother Rood, I declare." Cantonwine cleared his throat. He glanced across his shoulder, down the wash. He might just as well have said that some guilt lay behind him. An easy man to read, Bliss thought, because he carried a public conscience of sorts.

The wash led straight to a ford near the west side of Diamond. Bliss recalled Cantonwine's scorching, frustrated anger against Roderick Vail in the church grove. He cemented facts together with canny animal intuition that often outscores intelligence.

The stallion tossed its ugly head, sniffing at the odor of Rood's gelding. Hot sun pounded the two men. Bliss stared at the carbine in the preacher's saddle scabbard. It was always there, for Cantonwine was a good hunter, but Bliss continued to stare at it, and he used the weight of thinking silence like a lever.

"I sometimes grow tired of deer meat," Cantonwine said. "Today I thought to shoot an antelope on the mesas near the river." He shrugged. "But I saw none."

Rood's grin was a pulpy streak of triumph. "I didn't ask you where you had been, did I?" Some devilment had made the old sky-shouter edgy, but it would not do to anger him greatly. "Was it an antelope with long yellow hair?"

The barb struck deep and the nerves bunched around the wound, quivering. "You speak riddles, Brother Rood."

"I might be tempted by an antelope like that myself, Brother Cantonwine."

Cantonwine had balanced between anger and caution, but now his eyes grew somber. Fine dust and sweat lay in patches on his face, untidy islands on a sallow sea. "Temptation is a terrible evil. Yield not to temptation."

"It is ungodly. Awful."

"A despoiler."

"Ruinous," Bliss said. He glanced toward the river. "I never was one to get my game too quick, Brother Cantonwine. Take antelope, you pop up out of a gully and bust one and he never knows what happened. No fun in that."

"Punishment should be swift."

"It must be known. It shall be visited upon the children of sinners likewise."

"Are you a religious man, Brother Rood?"

"No. Are you, Brother Cantonwine?"

The question pierced all barriers that face the temporal world; it went through and sank at last to some hard bottom where truth looks at itself. There was a mauling of the outer surface only. Cantonwine was calm. "I do the Lord's work," he said.

"Vengeance is mine, sayeth the Lord."

"Nay, punishment for sins here done. Pride and arrogance topple before the holy storm, and the spirit is fierce—"

"Amen," Bliss said. "You didn't see any antelope then?"

Cantonwine's loose cheeks twitched as he swallowed. His eyes were brooding holes. "I saw none. I went but to look, Brother Rood."

Maybe. More likely he got it up in his neck when he was well started, but still the fact that he had gone near

Diamond to prowl made him dangerous. Bliss knew that he had found the same congenital cruelty which was inside himself. The branches came up in a puzzling manner, but the black, twisted mass of the roots was the same. "There are ways to hunt," Bliss said. "Two can do better than one."

"My work on the other side of the mountains slackens. It may be that I will have more time to visit those in this area who are in need of salvation."

"A good idea, Brother Cantonwine. Drop by when your work has slackened enough." Bliss wheeled his horse, the sand swishing as he turned. He heard the stallion crunching on up the wash.

He was not a queasy man, but something thready and writhing lived yet from the interview. The psalm-chanting bastard. He half believed some of the things he said. Punishment! Brother Rood, Brother Canton-wine. Bliss spat a bad taste from his mouth. Walk with the devil himself if the bridge ahead is bad.

Now it would be a good idea to ride back and have another word or two with Emmet. Maybe Iris had sneaked back after Bliss left. The thought shoveled around and Bliss did not like it.

He rubbed his hand across his chin.

The scope of country behind Cantonwine deepened into great distance as he sent the stallion surging upward on a rocky buttress of Shurfino Mountain. He liked the feel of power beneath him and the knowledge that he controlled it. When he was far above the range of any casual rider he dismounted and removed

71

his boots. He walked barefooted on the warm rocks.

In Pennsylvania when he was a boy he had seen an enormous, barefooted, bearded man in a dirty white robe preaching the gospel of doom one day at sunset. At once repelled and fascinated, Cantonwine had listened open-mouthed. The white-robed figure had been a brutal sword from the Old Testament, an awful shape of fear, a voice crying punishment upon a sinful world. Cantonwine had not slept well that night, for two-headed beasts crawled from his sea of dreams. The next morning when he saw the prophet walking out of town, his great bare feet slapping the dust, Cantonwine had followed as far as the bridge across Mill Run, and there the man had turned to point a finger at him and cry down a curse, and Cantonwine had run back to town as fast as he could.

Today the man in the white robe was formless in Cantonwine's mind; only the rioting fear of the incident was strong. He would not have allowed that there was a connection between his going barefooted now and the memory of the bearded man of long ago who had inspired such terror; but still the act was a secret ritual.

His feet were brown from sun, his toes long and spatulate. He strode across the rocks, looking to where he had been this morning. For a time when Roderick Vail was riding away from Diamond, Cantonwine had watched him down the barrel of his carbine. A scornful man who had told Cantonwine to be quiet, who had thrust him aside with physical force, humiliating him in the one position where Cantonwine held power.

There had been a feeling of strength in knowing that he held Vail's life under the pressure of a finger; but it was not enough. Power was pleasant only when those beneath it knew well who held it.

Even Bliss Rood knew that, a sullen clod who sniffed things out like an animal.

Cantonwine stood still, straight in his black frock coat. Through the sun-drenched air he looked to a green land flowing down from the Razor Mountains. His toes pulsed against the rock. His eyes narrowed. Spectral he was in his gauntness, Tartaric in his staring hatred.

CHAPTER SIX

THEY HELD the Teepees cattle on Cannibal Mesa, twenty-eight head, which was two short of what Sam Harvey had estimated. It was hot and dry in the full force of the sun, and the cattle wanted to break back to the cool green aspens.

Lee scrubbed dust scum off his lips and spat. "Houghton said he wouldn't come after them."

"Then he won't." Harvey had been curt all morning. "Roderick said keep them here. We'll wait for him."

"Suppose I say something else, Sam?"

Harvey measured Lee carefully. "I'm working for Roderick. Don't try to make it any tougher, Lee."

"What do you mean by that?"

"What I said."

A restless brindle cow that had been driven from the park without her calf bawled frantically and tried to make a break. Harvey wheeled his horse and beat her back into the herd so savagely that her commotion almost broke the bunch. It was needless, springing from some rawness in Harvey's thoughts, Lee thought.

Johnny Maxwell rode around the herd slowly. He was a beanpole of a youth, with a few blond hairs just sprouting on his chin. "They'd be a pile easier to hold, Sam, if we moved 'em back into that little park, instead—"

"I know that," Harvey said.

Maxwell closed his mouth on an unfinished thought. He rode back around the herd again and took his position. Scott Murdock removed his hat and wiped his bald head. Art Timmoney, the other Diamond rider, crowded a calf back into the bunch skillfully, without undue disturbance.

Foolishness, the whole thing, Lee thought. He was of a mind to force an issue with Harvey, but he decided there was enough trouble without starting more at home. If they turned the cattle loose, they would drift back into the park in minutes. They should be driven a few miles out on Houghton range. Like the others, he waited on Roderick. The bitter dust got into his healing cuts. It caked and burned.

Roderick came up from the park in the middle of the afternoon. He was in good humor. He glanced but briefly at the herd and the hot, disgusted men who held it. "Get things fixed up with Ann?" he asked Lee.

"That's a hell of a question, considering what we're doing right now," Lee said. "Houghton said he'd pick his stuff up next fall, as usual."

"That's like him." Roderick grinned. "Stubborn. Well, we'll hang on a while and see what happens."

"He won't be here," Lee insisted.

"I told him. It's up to him." Staring across the whalebacks, Roderick grinned suddenly. "You're wrong, Lee. Here comes Houghton now."

But it was not Cal Houghton. It was Alarid. He came in at a trot, and Roderick started out to meet him.

Harvey said, "Better watch this side of the herd, Lee." His tone was casual, but something bitterly significant had stilled his restless eyes. He fell in beside Roderick.

The brindle cow tried her break again. Lee had his hands full for a while. When he had a chance to look toward his father, Alarid was facing Roderick, saying, "Don't try to take it out on me. I've had all I want from any Vail."

Lee saw no marks on Alarid's face. Through the drifting dust he saw the shine of the man's belt buckles as Alarid rose in the saddle, set, waiting for Roderick to make his call. The scene tightened Lee's guts. Alarid's challenge would get him blasted from the saddle. He had been a fool to come here, urged on by his hatred of the Vails.

Harvey's horse twisted nervously. It sidled, jostling

75

between Alarid's and Roderick's mounts. The tall buckskin jerked its head, backing off; and then Roderick took it on around, turning. His face was blotchy, and fury ran along the tightness of his voice as he looked across his shoulder at Alarid and said, "Get out of here while you can!"

Alarid smiled, as if he knew a secret. He glanced at Harvey, whose horse was now under control. The smile settled into hardness. Alarid rode away.

Lee roped the determined cow when she made another run. He threw her hard and got down to tie her. Harvey rode back toward Roderick. His voice came with smoldering patience. "What about the herd, Roderick?"

"Shoot every damned one of them!"

Lee dropped his tie rope. "No."

On the far side of the herd Maxwell said to Murdock, "I ain't shooting no cattle for him." His voice was only normally loud but it fell across an instant when the noise did not cover it.

Roderick whirled his horse and rode toward Maxwell. Lee yelled, "Hold it!" He was too late.

Maxwell's Adam's apple jerked. Because of words he had not intended to be overheard, he was suddenly the focal point of all the afternoon's frustrations. He tried to stiffen both his pride and courage.

"What did you say, Johnny?" Roderick asked.

"I ain't shooting no cattle. I'm quitting."

"You can't do that," Roderick said. "Not until I say so. Get off your horse, Johnny."

76

Maxwell's chin muscles tightened. "What for, Mr. Vail?" He placed both hands on the horn. He glanced at Murdock and Timmoney, knowing that their judgment of him hung upon his actions now.

"Get down, Maxwell," Roderick said.

"No," Maxwell said. "No. I won't." He broke suddenly. He turned his horse and tried to ride away.

The tall buckskin went in with a lunge. Roderick drew his pistol. He stood high in the stirrups as he overhauled and crowded Maxwell. His long arm cut around and he knocked Maxwell to the ground with the pistol. The youth was all arms and legs as he sprawled into the sage. He staggered to his feet, his mouth open, his face shocked blank; but he turned to face Roderick when the man dismounted on the run and walked toward him.

"When I'm through with you, you can quit," Roderick said. He removed his pistol belt.

On the far side of the herd Lee stood beside the cow on the ground. This was a part of his father that he had seen before, but never so brutal and unreasonable. This was anger transferred from one cause to another and there was no honesty in it. He glanced at Harvey.

Harvey was watching him, not Roderick and Maxwell. Harvey was staring at him as if he were the central point of the incident.

"That's enough, Roderick!" Lee cried.

Roderick paid no attention. He kept walking toward Maxwell, who was backing away with his hands half raised.

Lee spoke to his horse. The animal let slack into the rope that held the cow. Lee freed the rope and ran. He went up into the saddle and wheeled clear just as the enraged cow hooked at the flank of the horse. Bawling, tail high, the cow then ran toward Union Park. Harvey made no effort to stop her. Lee rode into the herd, crowding, whacking with the doubled end of his rope. The cattle broke, bellowing, rocking through the sage in all directions. Timmoney and Murdock made only token efforts to stop them.

Both Roderick and Maxwell had to run for their horses, but even in the scramble Roderick stooped to grab his pistol belt.

Lee rode close to Maxwell. "Go by the ranch. Ask my mother for your money. Good luck, Johnny."

Maxwell stared at Lee. His lips quivered. "There never was a Vail that was any good," he muttered.

Roderick watched him ride away as if he had never had any interest in the man. Roderick's anger was gone, washed away by the brief excitement. Dust was heavy on the mesa. Most of the cattle had turned to follow the brindle cow back into Union Park. Over the break the sounds of their crashing grew fainter. Murdock and Timmoney had ridden after them, but Lee knew they would have little success in cornering any of that herd now.

"That seems to wind it up," Roderick said. Apparently he did not know what Lee had done. "Hell with them. There was only a handful anyway. Sam, tell the boys to let them go." He was blowing dust from his pistol. Most carefully he fondled the weapon before he put it away.

The pistol was too much of him, Lee thought. It lay too close to his thinking, to the gnashing emotions that made him ready to kill one moment and calm a few minutes later. It was no less an evil than his wish to hammer someone into insensibility with his fists. Lee did not know the basic reasons. It was best, he thought, to remember that Roderick had controlled himself enough not to kill Alarid when the man asked for it.

"It's good we're rid of Maxwell," Roderick said. "He was yellow to the core. I don't care for a man like that around me."

Sam Harvey sat his horse as if he had no thought of moving, as if he had deep personal troubles unrelated to anything here. He looked to where Maxwell's horse was raising a stream of dust on the mesa. The dark, restless eyes turned on Lee in a long, contemplative study that spoke of something raw and hurting inside Harvey.

"Tell the boys to let those scrubs go to hell," Roderick said.

It disturbed Lee that this was the pattern Harvey had predicted. He watched Harvey jog away. The back of his shirt was a dark patch of sweat. The set of his shoulders and head and the way he rode suggested a man who had driven himself too far into a bad bargain.

Obeying orders, Harvey disappeared over the break into Union Park.

Johnny Maxwell stood on the porch at Diamond with his hat in his hands and a hot shame in his heart because he had not fought Roderick. Mrs. Vail returned to the door. "I'm sorry, Johnny, there isn't twenty dollars in the whole house. Will an order on Mr. Kebler be all right with you?"

"I guess so. I'm going that way. I guess it'll be all right." Instantly Maxwell regretted his rudeness. Mrs. Vail looked tired, unhappy. She had asked him to come inside. She had treated him like a human being and seemed to understand his feelings. It was a shame she was married to a man like Roderick. "That will be fine, Mrs. Vail. It ain't a full month though. It was only—"

"It was most of the month. We won't worry over any objections Roderick has because of a few days."

Maxwell caught something in Maureen Vail's expression that seemed to join the two of them in league against Roderick. He took the note she gave him and fumbled it into his shirt pocket. The woman's understanding had pierced the shell of anger and brittle hardness with which Maxwell had faced the world since he was fourteen. He would have rejected violently any kindness coming from a man.

Awed and attracted, Maxwell lingered a moment longer, wanting sympathy and at the same time wishing to show that he needed none.

Maureen Vail looked at the youthful, dusty face yet unscored by the gravings of final character. She thought, *He can go one way or another from something as minor as being abused by men like Roderick.* She said, "I'm sorry about it, Johnny." She smiled with a gentleness she could show to anyone but Roderick.

A gush of emotion rose in Maxwell. He turned away and swaggered to his horse. "Nothing to it. I been riding since I was a kid. I can always find a job."

"I'm sure you can." Mrs. Vail noticed then that he was riding light. "If you can wait a day in Kebler, I'll see that your plunder is brought to you."

Maxwell's possessions, blankets, a warbag full of odds and ends, were still at the twin cabins. He had thought to leave them there to show that he didn't give a damn. "Well," he said, "I guess I'll be around a day or two in town at that." He was spurring away when he remembered to turn and call back, "Thanks, Mrs. Vail!"

The smile on the woman's face crumpled. Some of the Johnny Maxwells of the world would be driven and some would fight back and hammer out places for themselves; and a few of them, if they got the chance, would become Roderick Vails. It was really her own son she was thinking of with a terrible, compressing fear. Outwardly, he had followed Roderick so closely and had been so slow in maturing that the final stamp was not yet on him.

She thought that if she knew now the critical turning Lee would make, she would leave Diamond forever and the husband she had not loved for years. But she was afraid of her own integrity, far deeper than vows and spoken obligations. Its roots were entwined among the centuries of women fighting to preserve the human race in decent form, while men were often striving to destroy it.

Long ago she had lost her son to Roderick. Lee was not soft, compliant material that anyone could mold, she was well aware. What would happen to him now lay within himself; the development was there but the manifestation of it had not yet come. She had to know. If Lee was another Roderick, almost a quarter of a century of her life had been wasted, for her son was all that she had from marriage with Roderick.

She walked down the yard, her feet crunching in the white gravel. She picked up a five-pound hammer with a long handle. Her wrists were strong and brown, her fingers long and tapering. Until she was almost spent she knocked into pieces the mortared stones of a planter wall she had built ten days before, swinging the hammer with a fury that was like the strong, but pitiful, struggling of an animal held by the bloody steel jaws of a trap.

When Roderick came home he might, if he noticed, chide her about changing her mind so often about the walls. And that was all. He was insulated from Maureen Vail by himself. She stood with her breast heaving, looking at the wreckage of stones, the reddish spawls. What little release there had been in this before was eluding her of late.

There was another answer but she had long been fighting against it.

. . .

Johnny Maxwell presented his note aggressively to Pete Kebler. "Sure," Kebler said. He had paid off many such requests and knew the subsequent pattern well: Maxwell would drink, curse Roderick Vail, threaten to kill him if the man walked through the door, and then ride away like all the rest.

Kebler was curious but never prying. He was a rare man in that he liked people without straining to understand them, and thereby he did understand them to a remarkable extent. He put the note in his till and set twenty silver dollars on the bar. He brushed his hands across the great wings of his coarse sandy hair. When Maxwell ordered whiskey Kebler set it before him. He folded his arms on the bar, watching Maxwell with yellow-flaked eyes.

Maxwell took three drinks. "That dirty, goddam Vail. I should've killed him."

Kebler said nothing. The story came out as he knew it would, and he guessed it was close to the truth.

"I should've killed him," Maxwell said. "I don't know why I didn't."

They both knew why, but Kebler did not comment on the reason. He asked, "Was Lee there?"

"Sure he was there! Siding the old he-sow as always."

"What did he think of it?"

"Nothing! He don't think when his old man is around. He just jumps to Roderick's orders."

"I never noticed that particularly," Kebler said.

"You ain't been around them like me." Maxwell took another drink. "If the herd hadn't busted loose, I guess I'd 'a had to kill old Vail. It would be a good thing for his wife if someone did."

There was more stark truth in that than Maxwell knew. Kebler said, "I'm just before eating. Will you sit down with me?"

"To hell with eating. All you want to do is kill off the whiskey I've drunk so's you can sell me more afterward."

Kebler shook his head. "No, Johnny. You get one more drink from me and that's all." He poured the drink himself. He put the bottle away and held Maxwell with the level stare of his eyes.

"You and the Vails—you're great friends, ain't you?" Maxwell's unmarked face was flushed.

"It happens we're not. Do you want something to eat?"

"Save your grub, like your whiskey." Maxwell went to a table and sat down, staring at the door. The whiskey was raw inside him, biting the nerves that fed his hatred of Roderick Vail; and he was thinking, Kebler knew, that if Roderick came through the door, he would call him and shoot him.

Pete Kebler went to eat. He was called from his living quarters a few minutes later when Bliss Rood rocked into the saloon and ordered a bottle. Kebler looked thoughtfully at Maxwell, still at the table, still staring at the doorway. He put the bottle on the bar and went back to finish his meal.

Rood had one drink, watching Maxwell in the mirror. A can tied to his tail, sure enough. Bliss grinned to himself. After a time he turned around and spoke to Maxwell. "You quit, huh?"

"None of your—Yeah, I quit."

Bliss got another glass. He sat down with Maxwell and poured two drinks, studying the youth. Not a weak face or a strong face, either. The kid had some guts, at least; he had called Joe Emmet once at a dance in the Gothic Creek school-house, but Pete Kebler and Chauncey Meeker had broken things up in a hurry.

"That Vail—he's as quirky as a new rope," Bill said.

Maxwell used a stronger description of Roderick. He took his drink and reached for the bottle.

"That's all right with me," Bliss said. "But Pete is a little chinchy about a man getting drunk in here." He knew how that would rasp Maxwell's scraped sense of dignity and independence.

"Don't tell me how to drink," Maxwell said.

"I ain't, I ain't." Bliss shook his head.

"You can bet your boots you're not!"

Bliss sipped his whiskey. "I'll bet you told Vail plenty when you quit him."

"Like so much hell I did. I backed off from him, if you want to know the truth."

"Can't say that I blame you," Bliss said.

"He's not so tough. He's put the Indian sign on a lot of men around here, that's all, but he ain't so awful tough."

"No? I always figured he was."

"Tony Alarid backed him up," Maxwell said. "I saw it. That's what made Vail so mad at me when I said I wouldn't take his orders."

"Alarid called him?"

"I said I saw it! Vail backed up."

Maxwell was casting up anything to throw at Roderick Vail, Bliss thought. Alarid might be hard; Chauncey Meeker thought so. But Alarid didn't stand wide enough to make Roderick Vail go around him, not by any means. "Tell me about it," Bliss said.

He heard the story. The high point of it made him still inside, for he pictured himself facing those cold blue eyes. Alarid, the show-off, had been lucky, gambling on the strength of a story everybody in the Sapinero country knew: Right after Vail had killed two men in the yard at Diamond long ago his wife had told him she would leave him if he ever killed another person. So Alarid, gambling only a little, had set himself against the whole Diamond crew. Fools like Maxwell would spread the tale, and Alarid would brag about it.

Bliss said, "Tony Alarid can thank that stuck-up woman of Vail's for his life. She—"

Maxwell's arm shot across the table. His huge gaunt-knuckled hand clutched Rood's jumper. "Keep your filthy mouth off her, hear me!"

Bliss blinked. The drunken fool. "Sure, Maxwell." The man's intensity amazed Rood. "I was only going to say—"

"You called her stuck-up!"

"I didn't mean it. I was only going to say I don't know why she's put up with Roderick all these years. Have a drink, Maxwell. I didn't mean anything."

The bony fist relaxed its grip. "Never a bad word about her. Be damn sure you understand that."

Bliss nodded. He shrugged his jumper back into place. "I've always felt sorry for Mrs. Vail, a fine woman stuck out there with that cold-blooded killer. She must have led a hell of a life with him." He watched the thought crease into Maxwell's expression. Whiskey had reddened the youth's eyes. His anger gave him strength that was not apparent otherwise. His thoughts must be scrabbling around like a beetle in a box. Handle him properly and he was an ally.

"Where you headed now?" Bliss asked.

"Here and there. I had jobs long before I ever heard of Broken Diamond."

Rood's eyes looked out steadily, pin-pupiled beside his bridgeless nose. "You could come up to my place until you make up your mind."

"What for? You can't pay me anything."

Bliss set a stubborn wall against his slow-growing anger. "No, I can't. But we might figure out something to help Mrs. Vail. I feel sorry—"

"Yeah, I know. A fine woman stuck out there with a cold-blooded killer. Like hell you feel sorry for her. You hate her husband, you mean."

"Put it that way then. What's bad for Roderick may be good for Mrs. Vail. Know what I mean?"

87

Maxwell's hat was on the back of his head. His blond hair was matted down like old straw on his narrow brow, and his lips were scrolled away from his teeth as he stared at Bliss with drunken shrewdness that had a clarity of its own. "I don't think Vail is as tough as he's been made out."

"Maybe not."

The compact that developed in their gaze was strong enough to serve because it was based on their common hatred of a man; but still there was a shallowness in it that made Bliss wary. Walk with the devil himself . . .

The two men were going out when Kebler returned from eating. He watched them mount and ride away. A sense of responsibility that was deep and broad nagged him, saying that he should have tried to keep Bliss Rood and Maxwell from joining forces.

CHAPTER SEVEN

FOR A WEEK Roderick and Lee rode the park. They cruised the cool aspen thickets at dawn. The hoofs of their horses left long streaks in the dewy grass of the open places. They rode the dark timber where fern-lined streams boomed down from the Razors, and at sunset from the gray shelf rock of the mountains they saw the shine of countless beaver ponds.

The cattle everywhere were fat and wild. As always, the simple economy of the place appealed to Lee. In all the years he had been here Roderick had never trailed a herd out to the railroad at Buena Vista. Buyers came in the spring and fall, taking all the Diamond cattle he cared to sell.

On a gray ridge of the mountains late one afternoon Roderick dismounted and stood a long time looking at the great basin. "There's no place like it. I've never heard of a better place, Lee. Take care of it, never overcrowd it, and your grandchildren will see it as it is today."

Roderick was at peace with himself, quiet. There had been no driving hurry in him for a week. He leaned against his horse and looked down on the park, a man musing contentedly. And this was a part of Roderick's nature that Lee had seen almost as often as the brutal, driven side of him. He recalled that most clearly now.

When he and Roderick were alone in Union Park trouble seemed far away. It was when Roderick was among people, or at home, that he brooded himself into streaks of violence, as if he sensed then some failure that galled him and made him savage.

The aspen leaves were shaking to a sunset wind when they rode to the twin cabins camp, and Lee knew that this had been a beautiful, untroubled day, one of the rare days that lie serenely in the memory until there is no memory. They were cooking supper when Roderick noticed that Maxwell's possessions were gone from his bunk.

"He must have ridden back," Roderick said. "I didn't think he had the guts." He cursed Maxwell.

There was no reason to do so, Lee thought. He glanced through the window to where a yellow pine tree stood tall and strong in the dusk. The dying struggles of three men had gone up tight ropes and kicked along a limb to the heart growth of that giant tree, and maybe there were tiny tremors in the wood that would never end.

The quiet wonder of the day was lost. Not long afterward Roderick wanted to know again the details of how Lee had beaten Tony Alarid at Teepees.

Lying in his bunk that night, while a rat pattered on the roof, Lee said, "I think I'll go back to the ranch tomorrow."

Roderick cursed the rat irritably. "We may as well both go in for a day or two."

Maureen Vail did not come outside to greet them. Long ago, Lee recalled, her welcoming had been more than a casual duty for a while when he first started going to the park with Roderick, but as the periods away from home grew longer and Lee grew older, Mrs. Vail had learned to expect them when she saw them return and to accept their arrival without demonstration.

The first thing Lee noticed when he walked up from the corral was that a planter wall had been demolished; The wreckage had been wheeled away and a new wall started, but shards of bruised red stone still lay on the earth.

Once more Lee remembered what Ann Houghton had said about not wanting to marry him.

Roderick was silent during dinner. The restlessness and discontent that settled in him when he was home was growing.

Mrs. Vail said, "There's a dance at the schoolhouse tonight. Let's go."

Surprised, Roderick stared at her. Color stained her cheeks as she watched him quietly.

"It would do you good," Roderick said, "but it's a long buggy ride and you—"

"I'll ride a horse," she said. "I rode to twin cabins the other day, and then to town and back."

It was she, Lee guessed, who had picked up Maxwell's plunder. Sure, she had tried to soften Maxwell's anger against Roderick by doing so.

"If you're sure you feel all right—" Roderick mused. His eyes lighted up. "Remember the dances in Hays? We cut quite a figure. Put on your best silk dress, Maureen. We'll show those northside clodhoppers a thing or two."

"I haven't worn a silk dress in fifteen years," Mrs. Vail said. "I'll go just like the rest."

Roderick did not hear her. "You hike over to the Teepees, Lee, and ask Ann—"

"It's too late to be doing that," Lee said. "Besides, I told you what happened between us the last time I was there."

"Ah, she didn't mean it!" Roderick said. "Women never mean anything by those little spats, do they, Maureen?"

"I'm not sure." Mrs. Vail walked out of the room.

Her expression said that the prospect of going to the dance had dimmed already, but Roderick did not notice. He winked at Lee. "See what I mean, boy?"

He was completely blind in some respects, Lee thought.

The schoolhouse, an enormous, raw board building, was on Gothic Creek just above the lower falls. The windows were aglow with light. A gobble of voices bulged the walls. The grove of cottonwoods behind the structure was full of horses and wagons and children who ran among the trees, screaming like Indians. Over near the creek Lee heard a group of men talking. He took care of the horses while his parents went inside.

Someone at the creek—he thought it was one of Houghton's men—said, "That's real forty-rod! You could use a cupful of that to keep the pitch off your saw up there at the mill, Joe."

"Old Joe—he uses sweat," Jeremy Rood said, and there was a comfortable laugh.

A boy, scooting through the gloom, collided against Lee's legs, bounced off, and resumed his chasing of another boy. Lee walked toward the creek. Joe Emmet came slanting into the light, going toward the building. He nodded at Lee, seemed on the verge of stopping to talk, and then went on.

"Who we got here?" somebody asked, as Lee walked up to the men beside the water. "If that's Mell Crawford, hide the jug quick."

A moment later Jeremy Rood said, "Oh, Lee Vail," and then there was silence.

Lee said, "Hello, boys." No one answered him. He could make out Jeremy Rood, Bliss, Johnny Maxwell, a Houghton rider named Sandy, and two or three dark shapes standing under a cottonwood. The stark silence was like a blow in the face. Lee stood there, his embarrassment coloring toward anger but he knew no way to knock aside a wall of bristling hostility with words, and so he went back toward the schoolhouse. *To hell with them,* he thought, but it was not a satisfying answer.

The room was already crowded. Desks were piled in one corner of the room, benches set against the walls, and women were coming and going from the teacher's living quarters. Roderick was standing near the stove with Pete Kebler and Chauncey Meeker. Roderick was talking, using his hands. His teeth flashed as he grinned. Kebler seemed to be attentive, but his gaze strayed around the room. Meeker nodded, watching Roderick with the serious expression of a man whose work is always two jumps ahead of him.

Lee's quick survey of the room stopped abruptly when he saw Preacher Cantonwine bent forward a trifle, hands clasped behind his back, listening politely to the rapid talk of Minnie Rood, Jeremy's wife. Cantonwine's thin, dark hair was carefully combed. His sallow face took a yellowish tinge from the lamps overhead. Between nods to Mrs. Rood, he raised his eyes to study Roderick.

"Hey, sobersides!" Iris Meeker brushed Lee's arm,

smiling up at him. Her cheeks were shining, her hazel eyes bright with interest and mischief.

"Hello, Iris." Lee glanced across the room. She had just skipped away from Joe Emmet, he guessed, judging from the way Emmet was watching him.

"You don't come to our dances very often, Lee."

"And you never miss one."

"I have fun. I don't intend to miss one." She lowered her voice, still smiling. "I was up on Gothic Creek the other day, Lee. At the old place."

"I've been busy lately."

"Fighting?"

"One thing and another," Lee said. Her eyes searched for facts behind his careful expression. She was a flirt, a vigorous one, but there was no sneaking or evasion in her. She did as she pleased, and Lee thought she was not one to regret any mistakes she might make. It was he who suddenly felt a sense of guilt; and then a narrowing jealousy as he wondered about other men in whom she had shown interest.

Her gaze flicked away and then it settled on him again with new intensity. "There's Ann," she murmured. "Her dress is pretty too." There might have been wistfulness in her voice but here was no malice. "Dance with me sometimes during the evening, Lee." Iris went back to Emmet, moving gracefully across the rough floor.

Caught entirely by his own thoughts for a moment, Lee stood still. *I wonder,* he thought. *It might be that I'm the only one who's been with her.* The sensation of guilt was stronger. He felt the back of his neck warming, as if everyone in the room was staring at him. He turned to look at Ann Houghton. The room was full of noise.

Ann, at least, had been watching him. She nodded with cool civility, and he made a soundless hello with lips that moved stiffly when he tried to strengthen the greeting with a smile. Her dress was pale green, puffed at the shoulders, with long, tight sleeves. Her hair was like burnished copper.

Tony Alarid was with her. The smile stayed on his lips when he met Lee's gaze, but a quick opaqueness in his eyes spoke clearly of unfinished business.

Ann and Alarid came across the room, headed for the corner where the wraps were hung on hooks along the wall behind the stove. Lee moved aside to let them pass. Tall and calm, Ann spoke to the women on her way. It struck Lee that there was something unbending in her manner. He heard Caroline Dewhurst say to Landon Crawford's oldest girl, Laurel, "Muttonchop sleeves—on a gingham dress!"

An instant later Cal Houghton and his wife came in. The talking in the room took a down curve, and eyes went back and forth between Roderick and Houghton. Houghton ignored Roderick after one sharp glance at him. He took his wife's coat and stumped toward the corner, and afterward he poked his head into the room where women were trying to bed down fretful babies. He said something in a joshing manner to Ben Meeker's tired wife.

Maureen Vail came from the teacher's room, and Houghton stood back to let her pass. Her voice carried clearly as she smiled and said, "Good evening, Cal."

Houghton bowed like a bear and answered her. The talk went up again. Lee watched Mrs. Houghton working her way across the floor and he observed how readily she was accepted by the other women. There was another pause in talk when she came near Roderick. No one in the room missed their exchange of greetings as Roderick bowed in a courtly manner.

A great deal of the surface tension was gone then, but Lee was still in the grip of an uneasy undercurrent. He saw Cantonwine smiling mechanically at Mrs. Houghton and watching Maureen Vail with a brooding, spiteful look as she stood beside Roderick; and Lee saw Tony Alarid staring at him steadily before the man turned to answer something Ann said. Outside, some of the group by the creek were probably getting drunk.

Pete Kebler announced the first dance. Gramps Rood, his bushy white beard stained yellow around his mouth, began to tune his violin, making the most of the attention that would be on him. Ben Meeker was telling Tinsley Dewhurst a tale of suffering in the Civil War. "If I wasn't shivering wet I was dying of heat. I tell you, them fellows didn't know no more about running a war than old Crumple, my milk cow."

Kebler called the dance. The floor had been dampened, but now, under the pounding, dust came up from the cracks and drifted in a fine sheen toward the lamps where moths were committing suicide. Lee stood against the wall. He watched his parents for a while. His mother seemed to be quite happy and Roderick was a gallant partner. Lee thought there was a stiffness in the way Ann danced.

Joe Emmet, his solemn face beginning to break down into pleasant lines, was having a time with Iris. She was full of life, laughing, and on every turn she glanced at Lee. In the back room some of the babies that had gone to sleep woke up and began to scream. Ben Meeker's wife and two other women left the floor to see about them, Little Ben, a comic, whooped and went on dancing with an imaginary partner.

Lee's mind kept drifting to the hostile group outside.

He danced once with Iris, and Emmet did not like it. He asked Ann Houghton for a dance, and she said that she might find time later.

One of Ben Meeker's grandsons came in and tugged at Lee's sleeve. "Somebody's cutting your saddle all to hell, Lee." The boy ran out before Lee could say a word.

On his way to the door Lee met Cantonwine. The preacher inclined his head. "Good evening, Brother Vail." There was a sly expression in his eyes.

After the lighted room the outside seemed like total darkness for a time. Lee stumbled over a rock on his way to the tree where he had left his saddle. He cursed softly. The saddle was there. He knelt and ran his hands over it. There was nothing wrong.

They came out of the darkness in a semicircle, walking slowly. Lee jumped up. He could not tell one form from another, but he could hear the breathing and smell the odor of whiskey. There must be five or six of them, he thought. They stopped, waiting.

"Well?" he said.

Someone shifted his boots, cracking a dry stick. No one answered Lee. "It's a bum joke," he said.

They stood in the darkness, shapeless figures that gave menace through their silence. Lee knew it was a gag, but still it rasped his nerves. He walked close to the nearest man and reached out, feeling a bony shoulder. The man struck his arm away. "Keep your stinking hands off me!" It was Johnny Maxwell.

"What's the idea, Maxwell?"

The man was silent and all the others were silent. They were making a fool of him, Lee knew. They wanted him to lose his temper. He walked back toward the schoolhouse, expecting laughter to jeer him. That would be the natural ending, even if there was no humor in the laughter. But the silence held on in the cottonwoods, and the final run of it, more than anything else about the incident, shook Lee and told him how sly and cruel must be the mind that had directed the little game.

Bliss Rood. It must be him. Lee remembered the greasy expression on Cantonwine's face. He paused a moment on the steps before he went inside. From the corner of his eye he watched Cantonwine look at him slyly. The man's loose lips pursed out as if he was subduing a smile; his slashed cheeks pinched in, and then he turned to watch Roderick.

Roderick was dancing now with Iris. She was studying him with the keen, unfeigned interest she gave any man, and he was looking down at her with an expression that bothered Lee. He glanced at his mother, paired with Emmet. He could catch nothing from her face; but the expression of the married women sitting along the wall confirmed his opinion that Roderick was making a fool of himself.

Pete Kebler called the dance. His face was broad and pleasant. Anyone could see that he was enjoying the duty as much as Gramps Rood liked to play the violin; but Kebler missed nothing in the room, for people, more than merchandise, had always been his major interest.

Like the married women, he saw all the little byplay between the dancing couples, but he observed on a much broader basis because, unlike the married women, he had no limited, narrow field to protect. Kebler saw the rising warmth in Roderick's eyes and the appreciation that Iris Meeker extended toward it.

That was natural. The spirit of the girl was as much alive as her fine body. She would be questing about, exploring until she was married. There was no mystery in her. The mystery would develop after she was married, for then she would be fiercely devoted to one man, if she got the right one. No man would ever own her, because she would have her youth to look back upon and, more lasting, the certainty that she could attract men all her life if she cared to.

The right man. Kebler did not know who it was. He doubted that Emmet could hold her. After the first great surge died away, Emmet would go back to building things, to working with machinery. Lee Vail had the marks of a man, and the actions of a man, but still he was untried in Kebler's estimation. Maybe Lee wouldn't do either.

Allemand left and swing the girl
With a rat in her hair,
For she's the belle of the parlor!

If Lee turned out like his father, he would never hold any woman. Maureen Vail had stayed with him, and that was all. Roderick Vail was a man Kebler did not understand beyond certain surface ripples. He guessed it was that men who were killers had wide areas in them where nothing warmly human could live, and maybe they never knew the fact. Kebler watched the gleam in Roderick's eye as he danced with Iris. That much he did understand, and he wondered how long Roderick and his wife had slept apart.

Now turn to your right
And once around!
Step like a cougar,
Bay like a hound!

Kebler smiled at Ben Meeker's antics. Some would say that Ben was a failure and so must gain his share of attention by showing off. Kebler disagreed. The failures were those who knew it, and Ben did not. Alarid swung past, dancing lightly with Mrs. Houghton. There, besides Roderick Vail, was the true show-off in the room. Alarid had been quiet all evening, but before the dance was over he would find a way to make himself the center of all attention.

Three steps to the right
And make 'em high

Ben Meeker ran into the wall. He held his nose as if he had broken it. Kebler watched Lee. Lee was stony-faced. He had come from the outside like that. Trouble was growing out there. Bliss Rood working on Johnny Maxwell, probably. Kebler shot a glance at Canton-wine. That old buzzard, gloating over something as he watched Maureen Vail. Why had he come back so soon? *Folks in need of salvation . . .* People in need of hell, he really meant.

Kebler called the final step. The sets broke and milled around the room. Iris walked to Lee. Kebler saw the half smile touch Lee's face, but there was no real breaking away from something that was bothering him. Mrs. Vail came over to her husband. She gave him the first full, direct glance since he started the dance with Iris.

Cantonwine drifted past Kebler, carrying a cup of

water to someone. "A fine evening of neighborly plea-sure, Brother Kebler," he intoned.

So help me, Kebler thought, *he leaves a shadow like a carrion bird.* Salvation . . . Salvation under Canton-wine's direction would be a dip in boiling pitch to purify the soul. Kebler's thoughts were unsettled for a while.

When the next dance started Roderick was once more paired with Iris. Joe Emmet went outside. Mau-reen Vail sat down with Nettie Houghton and made great work of talking. Cal Houghton, who had danced once, sat in a corner smoking a cigar and talking seri-ously to Chauncey Meeker.

Caroline Dewhurst, a rawboned, awkward girl, six feet tall, watched Lee Vail wistfully.

Outside, Bliss Rood and Johnny Maxwell stood on stumps, looking through the windows at the dance. Sandy Macklin, two other Teepees riders, Bur Harris, who worked for Chauncey Meeker, and Cliff McLeod were having a noisy drinking session near the pony shed. Bliss had roped them all in for the trick on Lee Vail.

"Lookit him!" Maxwell said. "Dancing with that young girl all the time, and his wife just sitting there looking miserable!"

"Well, that's the kind of stuff she's had to put up with ever since she married him." Bliss laughed deep in his chest. "There's nothing we can do about it, I guess."

"It ain't funny!" Maxwell's voice was wire tight. "The no-good sonofabitch."

"I won't argue there, Johnny," Bliss said. "But let's not get too heated up about it." Maxwell's brittle, unpredictable temper might send him splintering off in a wild direction. Bliss did not know quite how to handle him.

"Don't get heated up! All you've done for a whole week is work on me to kill Roderick Vail, and now you say don't get heated up. Goddam you, Rood, do you think I'm dumb?"

He was altogether too smart, Bliss thought. At first it had appeared that he would be a good tool to use, but his cutting edges were hard to manage. Bliss said, "I suppose you want me to go bring him out here?"

"Yes! Tell him—"

"Roderick would take you apart in about one minute, Maxwell. He'd turn you every way but loose."

"Would he!" Maxwell said viciously. He slapped his pistol. "You think so, huh?"

"You had that kind of chance once. You didn't care to take it. Houghton and Chaunce Meeker and a few more in there would hang you high and dry for the birds to pick if you shot even Roderick Vail while he was coming through a lighted doorway."

Maxwell mouthed the bitter taste of Rood's words. The truth increased his wish to act against Roderick, but it also strengthened his fear. Roderick was a monster. Mrs. Vail was an ideal, beautiful and suffering, a combination mother, dream sweetheart, and friend, none of which Maxwell had ever known. He was her defender. Maxwell had been kicked from childhood into adult life so abruptly that some of the strings binding him to immaturity had not withered.

The most hopeless part of all was his undiminished fear of meeting Roderick fairly. A week of drinking with Bliss, of listening to his prodding, knowing what it was all the time, had not overcome Maxwell's fear.

So all he could do now was grind his helplessness into rage and curse Roderick Vail.

Bliss was trying to make something out of the situation but he could not settle on an idea. The little stunt against Lee had not been much. It seemed childish now. What Bliss needed was something to set the Vails still farther apart from the rest of the country.

A man bumped down the steps and started across the yard toward the creek.

"Emmet!" Bliss called.

Joe Emmet had made up his mind to join the non-dancing drinkers for the rest of the evening. Iris had come with him, and now, as usual, she was making a fool of him over a Vail. Emmet strode over to Bliss. "Where's the jug?"

"We'll find it directly," Bliss said. "Looks like you lost your girl again. Them Vails—"

"Shut up!"

"Just friendly joshing," Bliss said. "I—"

"Well, cut it out!"

"Sure, sure. I didn't mean anything, Emmet. Did

you happen to ask Roderick about letting you move over into some of his timber?"

"No. That's more of my business, Rood."

"Damn, you're touchy tonight. I just thought—"

"Where's the jug?" Emmet demanded.

"Over by the pony shed."

Emmet walked away quickly. Bliss munched slow thoughts and watched Johnny Maxwell. Maxwell shifted his run-over boots on the stump but he did not take his gaze off the room.

"A fine, cool evening, I would say." It was Canton-wine, speaking from behind Bliss and Maxwell. He had drifted up silently. In spite of brutish nerves, Bliss felt the coarse hairs on the back of his neck stiffen. Maxwell jerked his head to give the preacher a quick look.

"May I speak to you for a moment, Brother Rood?" Cantonwine asked.

Looking down from his stump, Bliss saw the light lying in dead gray patches on Cantonwine's thinly haired skull. The man's head was not clean but that did not bother Bliss, nor did Cantonwine's soundless approach trouble him too greatly now. It was, rather, a disturbing feeling that something warm and moist was shifting, sliding around in Cantonwine's mind.

"Yeah." Bliss jumped down from the stump. He gave Maxwell a worried look. The fool was crazy enough over Mrs. Vail to throw a slug through the window at Roderick. Because he knew trust of no man, Bliss was uneasy about his own feelings. His goal had been to ruin the Vails because of an insult, but now he was all tangled up with a crazy kid and a preacher the devil wouldn't have.

He walked toward the creek with Cantonwine. In the dark the man's presence made Bliss more uneasy.

"In matters of this sort," Cantonwine said, "there should be some ultimate objective."

"Yeah? What's that?"

"A goal, a vision, Brother Rood, something that can be reached by patient steps and courage."

"I don't want no sermon." Bliss almost said Brother Cantonwine. At the wash that day, when he had had the upper hand, Bliss had found a pleasant mockery in the term; but here in the dark, with Cantonwine's presence getting under his skin, Bliss did not care for mockery.

"Man lives by vision," Cantonwine said. "If he does not include service to his fellow men in his vision, he fails. Now I have that in mind. Just before I returned I checked on the title Roderick Vail holds to his land. It is, I'm afraid, imperfect, except for one homesteaded tract on the Sapinero. Union Park is—"

"I know that," Bliss said. "He doesn't own it."

"He holds it." Cantonwine cleared his throat. "Very desirable range, Brother Rood."

"What are you getting at?"

"If the Vails fall of their own errors, through the Lord's punishment, of course, almost all of what they now control would be open ground."

Rood's breathing was heavy. "You and me, huh?"

"Oh, no," Cantonwine said quickly. "You misunderstand. There are many over here who could share the use of land on the south side of the Sapinero, dwelling in harmony—"

"Harmony, hell." A wide field had been opened up momentarily to Bliss, and then the old mealymouth had gone pious. Mere possession of land was not a dazzling goal, but it did have its points, especially Vail land, for loss of it would mean greater injury to Roderick than death.

"I have at times considered going into the cattle business," Cantonwine said. "It has its rewards. Now if it were known that we were going to find means to dispossess Roderick Vail, we would have support. Wouldn't we?"

"Yeah." Even straight-backed people like Chaunce Meeker might change some of their principles under the lure of Vail range. "What's the means you're talking about?"

"Don't hurry, Brother Rood. Let me state the case. The Vails are wayward and will not be warned to leave the path of arrogance and sin. They are covetous and bold. Roderick lusts for the flesh of a pure young maiden, while—"

"Say what you brought me down here for." This ranting in the dark was getting on Rood's nerves.

"They are sinful," Cantonwine said. "Punishment follows sin as night must follow day. If Roderick Vail is dispossessed through our efforts to serve the Lord and mankind, then it is fitting that we should receive the first share of that which is taken from him. As it is written—"

"What's the first share?"

"Union Park."

All that talk to get to the point. Rood's mind backtracked through Cantonwine's hypocrisy about the people north of the river sharing Vail land. What he meant was that they could scramble for a few hundred acres of hayland on the Sapinero—if he was honest even to that extent. Bliss had an uneasy feeling that he was getting in too deep, that he was being handled by a superior intelligence. His own thinking had been muddy and his goal, beyond revenge, uncertain. He was not sure that he cared to have everything mapped out for him by someone else.

"The means will be slow steps, well planned," Cantonwine said.

"You weren't planning very slow the other day when you sneaked across the river to pot Roderick."

"You showed me the error of my ways, Brother Rood, with your apt dissertation on hunting antelope." Cantonwine waited for his flattery to sink in.

Bliss was unimpressed; any kind of buttering always made him suspicious.

"Now," Cantonwine said, "what is there to Maxwell's tale that Roderick was afraid of Alarid?"

"Nothing." It was a contemptuous grunt.

"Lee Vail did fight Alarid and best him?"

"So I hear," Bliss said. "But I see more marks on Lee's face than Alarid's. He ain't got none, in fact."

"Even so, we will make our first steps." Cantonwine talked on, his voice low, even. Bliss glanced now and then toward the building. Maxwell was still on the stump. Each time Bliss turned back to face the dark form before him he had an eerie feeling that Cantonwine's eyes were set and beady, that venom was dripping from the corners of his mouth in amber drops.

Gramps Rood's violin ended suddenly. Lee Vail came to the door, standing in the light an instant before he turned back inside. Over by the pony shed someone spoke a rapid sentence in a drunken voice. Joe Emmet laughed, forcing unnatural recklessness into the expression. Caroline Dewhurst came out on the porch and called for the boys to come inside to eat. There was a whooping in the cottonwoods, and a dozen youngsters came racing into the light.

Cantonwine said, "And perhaps we will learn something of value, Brother Rood. As you said about antelope hunting—"

Bliss was of a mind to tell Cantonwine violently to cut out the brother stuff and keep his mouth shut, also, about antelope hunting. "May the Lord be with us," Cantonwine said. He put his hand on Rood's heavy shoulder, and Bliss felt the coldness of it seeping down through his shirt. He pulled away quickly and walked toward the building, feeling better when he came into the light.

Maxwell glanced around. "Lookit him, bringing that girl a cup of coffee before he even goes near his wife!"

"I wish you'd shut up about Mrs. Vail," Bliss

growled. "Let's get a drink." He looked over his shoulder toward the darkness near the creek.

"I'll shut up when I get ready," Maxwell said. "Don't give me no orders, Rood."

"All right, all right." Bliss had another angry, bewildered moment when he wondered why he had ever started anything at all. The feral stubbornness in him overwhelmed his doubts. The larger idea that Cantonwine had suggested was slowly gaining strength, but still he distrusted it because it was not of his own making.

Stunned by food and tired from their romping in the grove, some of the boys began to fall asleep. Although there was no fire in the big-chested stove, habit grouped the boys behind it, sprawled on the floor or sitting on the woodbox. Their mothers roused them sufficiently to walk them into the teacher's living quarters, or their fathers picked them up bodily.

Many of the younger girls were already sleeping on benches along the walls. Now the dancers would take a break to eat and drink strong coffee, and then the party could go under full steam until dawn. Preacher Cantonwine moved about the big room, visiting here and there, carrying food to some of the older women, helping mothers with their children.

Lee took a plate to his mother. She saw him glance to where Roderick and Iris were talking. She murmured, smiling faintly, "It's all right, Lee."

"No, it isn't."

He walked across the room, deliberately slow. He shouldered in between his father and Iris. His voice was low and rough when he said, "I'll do the dancing with her now, Roderick."

Hell came to Roderick's eyes. The blotchy red rose in his flat cheeks, but he smiled thinly and held his temper before the watching eyes of the room. He went back to his wife. Lee sat down beside Iris. "What's the idea?" he asked.

She studied him thoughtfully. "He's not like you at all, Lee. I wanted to know."

"I'm tired of those comparisons."

All the mischief was gone from Iris' face. "Ann, too? I suppose she's wondered."

"Have you got anything to think about except me and my father and yourself and Ann Houghton?"

"That's quite a bit, Lee."

He had never seen Iris so seriously intent. The feeling of guilt crept into him again.

"Your mother is not very happy, is she, Lee?"

"She's all right," he said sharply. "Why shouldn't she be happy?" He tried to stare Iris down, but the lie would not stick; and the woman would not quarrel.

She looked away from him, watching Cantonwine. It was a time of relative quiet when most of the people in the room were busy with food. Cantonwine sidled up to Roderick, now talking to Pete Kebler. The preacher's voice was strong.

"I understand, Brother Vail, that you're giving Joe Emmet a timber lease in Union Park."

Roderick looked upon Cantonwine with obvious dislike. "I hadn't heard about it."

"My mistake," Cantonwine said. He seemed abashed, but his voice was as strong as before when he went on, "It would be a neighborly act. I understand Brother Emmet has almost exhausted the timber where he is presently working, and for the good of the whole—"

"What business is it of yours?" Roderick asked.

"I have nothing but the welfare of the whole area in my heart, and—"

"I can damned well imagine that," Roderick said.

"You mean you would not give Brother Emmet—"

"I mean nothing!" Roderick looked around him. Everyone was watching and listening. "Let him do his own talking."

"I see that I should have," Cantonwine said. "Of course, I thought that friendly intercession between your refusal—"

"I haven't refused him! He hasn't asked—not lately!" For once Roderick started to control his temper. He turned back to Kebler.

"Then you have refused him," Cantonwine said. He shook his head. "I regret that my wish to be helpful has made it difficult for Brother Emmet. He has suffered enough and he deserves better." He looked then directly at Iris Meeker with a significance that was clear to everyone.

Roderick drew back his left hand. Kebler grabbed his arm. Roderick wasted no effort in struggling. With his right hand he slapped Cantonwine across the mouth, a blow that struck sharply through the silence of the room.

Cantonwine's head jerked back. A drop of blood blossomed on his upper lip. His eyes were hell's own pits. "May God forgive you, Brother Vail," he said humbly. He walked away with bowed head, and several women rushed forward to comfort him. He patted the air with spread hands. "It is nothing, Sisters. He knows not what he does."

"The hell I don't!" Roderick said. "Get out of my sight!"

It was, Lee thought angrily, the foulest bit of goading he had ever seen, deliberate and sly; but if Roderick had held his wicked temper, he could have turned the incident aside before it developed. Lee saw Ann staring across the room at him.

Tony Alarid's laugh fell in the brittle silence. "Big man with his fists."

Chaunce Meeker said, "Cantonwine brought that on himself." But he looked accusingly at Roderick and then when he saw that his own wife was one of the women giving Cantonwine sympathy, Meeker's expression said that he wished he had kept his mouth shut.

Roderick hooked his arm away from Kebler's relaxed grip. He glared about him, knowing now that Cantonwine had made a fool of him, and that, of course, increased his temper. Resentment against the Vails, temporarily submerged because of the occasion, was once more a working force. Mrs. Vail came up beside her husband and took his arm. "You should apologize, Roderick."

"Apologize! To hell with him and Emmet too!"

Iris said to Lee, "Since he went that far, he should have knocked Cantonwine stem-winding. All the preacher wanted to do was set Joe against your father, and now he's done it. Why, Lee?"

Startled by the depth of her quiet question, Lee said uneasily, "I don't know." He watched his mother lead Roderick toward a bench. Kebler announced another dance, and then he had to go looking for Gramps Rood, who was outside having a drink.

Alarid sat lazily beside Ann Houghton. He began to roll a cigarette, smiling to himself. When he licked the paper he looked at Lee with a narrow, deadly interest; and then he studied Roderick, tainting his expression with cold speculation.

Gramps Rood came hurrying in with importance bulging his whole manner. He walked directly to Roderick and said loudly, "Man outside wants to see you, Vail."

"Who?" Roderick asked.

"He didn't say. He just sent the message."

Lee surveyed the room quickly. Alarid, Cantonwine, Houghton were all here. He saw too that Bliss Rood was inside for the first time tonight. It must be Johnny Maxwell then, curdled with drink, waiting out there in the dark.

"Maxwell?" Roderick said the name contemptuously.

Gramps Rood shook his head violently. "Last I see of Maxwell he was sleeping off too much forty-rod. I don't know who it was. He eased up out of the dark and sort of kept his face and voice hid from me. I don't mind saying the way he asked for you kind of chilled me."

The old man could be building things up a little, Lee thought; it was likely that he was, but still Gramps Rood was no liar and he knew everyone in the country, so this must be a stranger outside. Nameless, faceless, waiting in the dark. In view of Roderick's background, the man took on deadly significance.

"Joe Emmet?" Roderick asked.

Gramps Rood wagged his head irritably. "I don't know who, I said!"

The room waited on Roderick. His glance slid away from Gramps Rood and fixed on the doorway, a big rectangle that framed light which went out into the yard and died away in the shadows at the edge of the trees.

"Why don't you go find out, Vail?" Tony Alarid said.

"No, no!" Cantonwine said. "We want no gunplay here. There are women and children. Let the man come inside if he has honest business." He spoke to the whole room but he watched only Roderick.

In a tight voice Maureen Vail said, "It would be foolish to go out there, Roderick."

Alarid walked across the room to the big chest where textbooks were stored against rat spoilage. The few men who wore pistols when they came to a dance checked them voluntarily into the chest. Alarid found Roderick's pistol and carried it to him; standing with the belt lying across both hands.

Roderick made no move to take the pistol. Mrs. Vail snatched it from Alarid and held it at her side.

Heads jerked around when footsteps struck the porch. Pete Kebler came through the doorway, stopping when he saw the fierce attention on him.

"Who's out there, Pete?" Roderick asked.

Kebler was puzzled. "No one—now. The bunch that was drinking at the pony shed loaded Johnny Maxwell on his horse and they all lit out for Emmet's sawmill."

"There is too a man!" Gramps Rood cried. "I talked to him, I tell you!"

"Go find out, Vail," Alarid said.

"Why don't you be quiet and sit down, Mr. Alarid?" Maureen Vail appeared ill, as if something she could not bear was churning inside her.

Roderick stared at the doorway. He glanced around the room with a hot-eyed, trapped expression. "I'd be an idiot to go through that light," he muttered.

Lee was of the same mind. He felt revulsion against the faces turned toward Roderick with expressions of deadly curiosity. Lee strode toward the door. His mother cried, "No, Lee!" An instant later he was on the porch. Kebler joined him. They looked at each other a moment. They stared at the silent blackness of the grove, and then they walked down the steps side by side. A man watching from the night could see they

116

were unarmed, and if he knew Roderick Vail, he could see, also, that neither of them was Roderick.

Together they walked from the pony shed to the creek, seeing nothing, hearing nothing. Still, they knew a man could be within ten feet of them, or he could have faded away into the night.

"What do you think?" Kebler asked.

"I don't know." This had the same odor as the trick that had been played on Lee. "Gramps! Gramps Rood!" Lee saw the old man hesitate in the doorway, with the light playing on the edges of his white beard. "We can't find anyone out here. Where was the man when you saw him?"

"Right smack at the pony shed, after the others loaded Maxwell on his horse and left." There was no doubting the old man's sincerity.

A nameless man, clothed in the hatred and menace of Roderick's past. Lee fought against the idea; but he could remember the crashing guns on a night long ago when Roderick had been called out of bed.

Alarid was among the group of men who came from the schoolhouse and started across the yard.

Kebler said, "He seems to be gone now. I'm not disappointed."

"Neither is Vail." Alarid laughed.

Lee walked out of the darkness and jarred Alarid to a stop with a palm against the man's shoulder. "You were told once to shut up and sit down, Alarid. Now I'm telling you." He knew by the man's instant tenseness that he had waited, and played, for this moment.

It had been in his mind all evening. Perhaps bringing Ann had been a part of it, a move to help irritate Lee.

Alarid spoke deliberately, so sure of himself that Lee knew he must have been running over the lines in his head. "You Vails, both of you, big men with your fists. Why didn't you wear a pistol here tonight?"

"I'm not going after one, if that's what you want me to say."

"That's exactly what I want you to say," Alarid said. "But I know you lack the guts. You're all bluff, just like your old man."

"You keep building it up, don't you, Alarid? You asked for a fist fight in Kebler and I refused you. You started it at Teepees and I might have killed you if it hadn't been for Ann. You're still walking stiff-backed from that one. Now you want—"

"Get a pistol, Vail."

"No. I'll just smash your face again."

Pete Kebler stepped solidly between the two men. He drove his shoulder into Lee. He thrust Alarid back three flying steps so that the man almost fell. "That's enough for both of you. We came here to have a good time."

Without speaking Alarid turned and went back into the schoolhouse. Lee let out a long breath but nothing inside was relieved. He stood there with the frustration of the whole evening rankling in him. Cal Houghton spoke angrily to Alarid and followed him inside.

"Well, let's look for that man," Ben Meeker said.

"Now that we know he ain't around." He and some others went threshing through the grove. Ben fell over a dead limb and ripped his pants, yelling so loudly about the accident that some of his companions thought for a time the unknown man was grappling with him.

The dance went sour soon afterward. Ann Houghton quarrelled with Alarid because he had tried to start trouble. She went home with her mother and father. Ben Meeker's wife said she was worn out, which was the truth. She dragged Ben home and half the family went with them.

Maureen Vail disappeared not long afterward, It was a half hour later before Lee and Roderick found out that she had saddled her horse and ridden away toward the Diamond. Some of the women left at the dance eyed Roderick accusingly and then they glanced at Iris. Roderick strode out angrily, saddled up, and drummed away after his wife.

Too many men tried to question Gramps Rood about the man he had seen in the grove. Their doubt enraged him. He put his violin into the case and stalked out. Alarid made one more play. He asked to take Iris home. She refused. He gave Lee an insolent look and rode away alone.

Bliss and Cantonwine and Kebler were helping some of the women tidy up the room. Cantonwine kept murmuring his regrets over the ruination of the evening. Kebler watched him shrewdly, making no comment.

Lee started to take Iris home. Chaunce said he guessed he'd go along. When they came to the forks where the road led toward Chaunce's place, he remembered that he had to see his father about something.

Lee was irritable by then. "Since you suddenly remembered what you couldn't think of all evening, I may as well go on back from here. You can see Iris home as well as me, I guess."

"Maybe even better," Chauncey said evenly. "Good night, Lee."

The cold stars made a shadowy mystery of the land as Lee rode toward the Sapinero. Far away the Razors hulked over Union Park like guards. The park was a refuge when problems bothered a man. Tonight Maureen Vail would wander quietly in the house again or sit in the living room until daylight. In the morning Roderick would be bitter and edgy.

"Let's get out of here," he would say to Lee. His mood would lift when they entered the first aspen thickets on the way to the park. It occurred to Lee that he and Roderick might have been running to the park for a long time in an effort to escape from something.

Even in the face of the realization, after he crossed the river, Lee wanted to go on to the park. Life up there was simple. He hesitated before he swung toward Diamond. When he entered the yard he saw the low-burning light and the motionless figure of his mother in her chair. Doubts sank their fangs into him. Diamond was not threatened as he had once thought.

Diamond was only a place, a name. It was the people he loved who were living under a disquieting cloud which had nothing to do with outsiders.

He went on to the corral. Once more the urge came to ride straight to the park. After a moment he swung down and began to slide gate poles. Tonight would be a good time to talk to his mother about things he did not understand.

When he went inside Maureen Vail was gone. For an instant he wondered if she had slipped out the back door to take a ride. Old memories and fears no better understood now than in the days when his mother was wont to whirl away from home in the dark worked up in Lee. And then he heard Maureen moving in her room. No light showed beneath the door. He hesitated before he knocked.

"Lee?"

"Yes. I want to—" To talk about what? Lee had not known his mother for so many years that now he had no simple approach. "I was wondering if you're all right."

"Of course."

"You're sure?"

"Of course."

Lee stood a moment longer at the door. He said good night and turned away.

His own room seemed strange. There were things here he had cherished as a child, a rock collection, bird feathers, a piece of rusty Spanish armor he had found after a flood in Arroyo Seco. The house had been home then. He sat down and pulled off his boots. Now it was a place to eat and sleep between trips to the park.

Even when he was in bed there was no sense of familiarity. Maybe Roderick felt that way too. Perhaps they both had lost or overlooked something here that once, at least for Lee, had made Diamond home.

CHAPTER EIGHT

AT BREAKFAST Roderick said, "Pick out something besides that steep-rumped bay, Lee. I want to cover the whole west end of the park today."

"I don't," Lee said. He had set himself. "I'm starting the new roof on the storage shed today." The lumber for it had been hauled to Diamond six months before.

"Never mind that shed." Roderick pushed his chair back. "It can wait another winter."

"I'm starting on it today," Lee said.

Roderick appealed to his wife. "All he ever does lately is argue."

Maureen and Lee watched Roderick quietly. He rose with a burst of impatience. "All right, we'll roof the damned shed! No use for me to go to the park alone." He strode out.

Mrs. Vail was studying Lee thoughtfully. "Why did you want to go to that dance?" he asked.

She shook her head. "It was a mistake. I suppose I had some idea of meeting people on their own terms again, but . . . It was a mistake."

"Maybe not. We'll try it again. We're not big enough to live our own lives out here alone. There's been too much of that already, and you've got the worst end of the whole deal."

As Lee walked out he saw Maureen watching him with an odd expression. When he hesitated she smiled suddenly, and it was a warm joining of understanding.

Roderick wrecked the old roof as if it were a personal enemy. He smashed through shingles and sheeting with a heavy bar, pitching the wreckage of rotting boards down to Lee, who burned them. Square nails screamed in the plates as Roderick wrenched the rafters loose. Rebuilding, Roderick was a different man. He held a blue-sheen nail in his teeth and hummed to himself.

His long fingers managed a square and saw with dexterity that amazed Lee. He helped his father make two quick measurements and then Roderick cut a rafter pattern without hesitation. Doubtful of such swiftness, Lee threw a plank between the rafter plates and went up and tried the first two roof members. They fitted as neatly as a handsaw could cut them.

"Where'd you learn this stuff?" Lee asked.

"I built everything here."

"I know, but—"

"I used to be a carpenter," Roderick said curtly.

Lee had never known the fact. He wondered why. "Were you ashamed of the trade or something?" He grinned. "Did you build a house that fell down the next day?"

"I loved the trade. There was a time when I thought I'd never want to do anything else. I got away from it, that's all."

A quick leaping savageness in Roderick's manner made Lee drop the subject. He carried more two-by-sixes, red spruce lumber that was already settling into a hardness that would last a century. The top pieces of the pile were twisted, but underneath the lumber was surprisingly true. Joe Emmet had cut and hauled the pile.

Lee said, "Emmet does need a new timber lease."

"He can't get it from me—now."

"That's what Cantonwine was playing for. Just—"

"People would think I'm soft!" Roderick said. "They'd think I'd been forced into doing something."

There again was the weak side of Roderick, the fear of what others thought of him, the fanatical adherence to a belief in strength and independence. All the creed had ever brought him was trouble.

"Emmet needs a new set for his mill," Lee said.

"I know it, but people in hell need ice water too. Emmet let Cantonwine talk for him. If he—"

"Cantonwine probably butted in on his own hook."

"Forget it," Roderick said. "I'm not giving Emmet anything."

Lee dropped the subject.

Maureen was rebuilding a planter wall. After a time Roderick gave over the cutting of the rafters to Lee and went to help his wife. It occurred to Lee that he would have been an unhappy man if he had ever been wholly aware of the tensions between his parents; but while growing up he had been on his father's side so completely there had been no problem in his mind.

When he had cut all the rafters he wandered over to where his father was helping Maureen. Roderick was mixing mortar and carrying stones that Mrs. Vail laid with a deftness Lee had always admired. After a while she scoured her trowel shining clean in the earth and laid it aside.

"Time for dinner. Steak, I suppose?" she said.

"It'll do." Roderick put his arm around his wife. "I wish you wouldn't always be tearing up your walls, Maureen. You'll ruin your health."

"There's nothing wrong with my health." Maureen looked up at her husband with an expression touched with wistfulness and longing, and she seemed to be running down the past, reaching for something lost, striving against a hopelessness she would not admit.

When she passed Lee on her way into the house she squeezed his arm and smiled at him.

"Twenty-six years ago we were married," Roderick mused. After a few moments he glanced at Lee. "Got 'em all cut, huh?"

Lee nodded.

Roderick had forgotten the question as soon as he asked it. "Twenty-six years. The whole town turned out for that one." He laughed. "There were some who were afraid not to be there."

He always ruined everything he said, Lee thought.

Lee and Roderick stayed home for two days. They

finished the shed and caught up chores that had been long neglected. Late the second afternoon they went behind the springhouse to practice shooting. At fifteen paces Roderick could knock a small tin can spinning and hit it with three out of four shots afterward. At the same distance Lee's first shot at the stationary target was good but he could seldom hit a rolling can more than once before it came to rest.

"You're always awful close," Roderick said. "You just lack the practice I've had. Now let's see you draw and shoot."

Lee's actions were deliberate. He drew his pistol and fired with both eyes open, his shooting then being no better or worse than when he started with his pistol in his hand.

"Draw faster," Roderick said.

Lee could not hurry the motion.

"You're fairly fast, at that," Roderick mused. He frowned and his voice was curiously tight. "Suppose it was a man—would that throw you off?"

"I don't know and I never intend to find out."

"Alarid," Roderick said. "You'll have to meet him sometime. Don't forget that, Lee."

"Not with a pistol."

"You'll have to! He's called you."

"No, I won't have to. I've told him so."

Roderick juggled a can that was nothing but ripped edges.

"You're not afraid?"

The question burning out of Roderick's eyes. The

probing that had always bothered Lee. "I don't know. The thought of having to face a man with a pistol doesn't scare me—now. If it ever happened—I can't say what it would be like."

Roderick was not satisfied. "There's Alarid."

"To hell with him!" There was a trap in this thing. It started with a fist fight, once refused. If Alarid had won he might have been satisfied, but he had lost, so he must carry his challenge to a more deadly level. Lee tried to reject the inevitability in the proposition; but there was Roderick, weighing him, trying to assay the color of his backbone for pistol fighting, for killing a man. There was Roderick's record and his life to prove that violence was not a settlement of anything.

"I'll not meet Alarid unless he forces me to," Lee said, and that, he thought, was a compromise of weakness. He put his pistol away.

"It's no crime to be afraid," Roderick said.

"All right then! Let's not talk about it any more."

Roderick nodded. He gave his son a haunted, doubting look.

They started back to the house, silent, with the pleasure of the afternoon turned sour. It was then they saw the riders coming from the direction of the river.

There were five of them. Lee identified Pete Kebler's big gray and Cantonwine's blue roan stallion. The men came on in a solid group, as if they had a unity that would suffer if anyone straggled.

Roderick looked at Lee uneasily. "If that's trouble—"

"Is trouble all you ever think of?" But Lee was

127

uneasy too. The group came closer. He made them all out. Cal Houghton, Bliss Rood and Chaunce Meeker were the other three. It was a strange assortment; it was trouble, all right. Everyone but Kebler was armed.

Lee and Roderick walked to the edge of the yard to wait.

Five faces heavy with individual seriousness, the group as a whole bearing a solidarity of grimness. Cantonwine's eyes strayed around the ranch as if he were counting something. Bliss Rood was a great sullen lump. Meeker's square-jawed face showed reluctance that had been overborne by necessity. He spoke first. Spittle caught in his throat and slurred the words. A brief flash of annoyance crossed his features. He cleared his throat and spoke again. "Howdy, Roderick, Lee."

"You fellows have a hanging look." Roderick laughed. The sound fell into a hollow silence.

Pete Kebler rested both hands on the horn. "We've got a problem, Roderick. You two won't mind a few questions, I hope?"

Houghton's face was flushed. He cocked his head, with his little eyes squinting wickedly. "Just ask the questions, Kebler. Don't be so damned polite."

"This is not an inquisition," Cantonwine said gravely. "Let us remember that." He pursed his loose lips. He stared at the house until Lee turned to see if his mother was on the porch. She was not in sight.

"Ask your questions!" Roderick said.

128

"When you left the dance," Kebler said, "your wife had gone on ahead. Do you mind telling us where you caught up with her?"

"What business is that of yours?" Roderick said angrily.

"We'll have to know," Kebler insisted.

"To hell with you!" Roderick's cheeks were blotched red and white. "You don't have to know anything about my personal life."

"It's no longer personal." Kebler's will was a solid force.

"Try the other one," Cantonwine said. "Perhaps there is more reason in him."

The five men eyed Lee, but after a moment Cantonwine's gaze shifted away to the buildings.

"You left Chaunce and Iris where the road breaks down to Ben Meeker's place," Kebler said. "Now how did you go home from there, Lee?"

"I crossed the river at Island Ford," Lee said. "And then I came on in. Why?"

Kebler licked his lips. "You heard or saw no one else that night?"

Lee shook his head. The five pairs of eyes fell on Roderick, who started to curse.

"Be quiet," Lee said. "Let's hear what they have to say." The calmness of his voice surprised him. He was more surprised when Roderick held his tongue.

"Where did you catch up with Mrs. Vail, Roderick?" Kebler asked.

"Below the bluffs on Dry Creek," Roderick said.

"Stony ground." Bliss Rood looked at Houghton.

"You caught up on this side of the Sapinero, below the bluffs?" Kebler asked.

"Yes."

"Stoniest ground in the country," Bliss grunted.

Meeker spoke slowly, "Can I look at your buckskin, Roderick?"

"What for?" Some of the fire was going out of Roderick, a change that puzzled Lee.

"Look at the buckskin and look at my horse too," Lee said. "If it will help you to get around to the point."

Meeker swung down and walked to the corral.

Cantonwine said, "Do you always go armed around your own home, you two?"

"We happened to be target shooting when we saw you coming," Lee said.

"Practicing with pistols," Cantonwine murmured. It was condemnation.

"That will be enough," Kebler said. He kept studying Cantonwine after the man no longer met his eyes.

Meeker was not long at the corral. He came back and stood beside his horse. "Can't say. The calks are the same, worn down, maybe, about alike; but all the shoes in this country come out of the same kegs at your store, Pete. I just can't say.

Bliss Rood started to swing down. "I'll look."

"Stay in your saddle, Rood." The authority in Kebler's voice hung on after the words were gone. Bliss put his right foot back into the stirrup.

"Let's have the rest of it." Lee glanced at his father. Roderick's silence still puzzled him.

"First, we'd like to talk to Mrs. Vail," Houghton said. "Shall I go in, Pete?"

"Stay where you are, Houghton," Roderick said. "Nobody's bothering my wife." He gave Lee a quick side glance.

"Can't she come out here a minute?" Meeker asked.

"No!" Once more Roderick glanced at Lee.

It hung suspended, a deadly weighted moment. Lee was cold and hot by turns. These were neighbors, men he had known for years; and a preacher wearing a gun under his waistband. He saw Cantonwine watching Roderick with an expression that was moist and licking.

"We won't bother my mother," Lee said.

Kebler broke the tension. "The night of the dance someone waited for Tony Alarid at the buggy crossing to the Teepees. The man killed him. Houghton found the body against some willows in a backwash a mile downstream the next day."

After the first swift shock Lee passed to condemnation of the act.

"Too bad," Roderick said. He seemed relieved.

Responsibility gave Kebler a heavy, thoughtful appearance. "The country is pretty hot about it. If we all rode back to town and talked it over with the people gathered there, it would be good, I believe. It would help a great deal if Mrs. Vail could come too."

"What kind of an outlaw court are you fellows trying to set up?" Roderick asked.

Kebler shook his head. "No court. You know better than that. We've sent a man to report to the sheriff in Buena Vista. Maybe next month a deputy will be over, and you know what that'll amount to. In the meantime, to prevent bitterness and misunderstanding that could go on for years, we think the three of you should come to town to tell your story." Enormous patience came from Kebler.

He was, Lee thought, doing his best to be fair and honest; but his determination was not lessened. The visit was far from being finished.

"I have enemies on the other side of the river," Roderick said. "You're weaseling around with words."

"If you have enemies there, you've made them yourself," Kebler said. "I'll admit there's a bunch of hotheads stirring up things. They wanted to ride over here and take quick action. To prevent that we promised that you'd come to town and state your case. If you don't do so, both yourselves and we who made the promise have thrown away the right to be trusted."

Roderick said, "To hell with sticking my neck out among people who hate me!"

"What happens if they don't believe us?" Lee asked.

Still watching Roderick, Kebler said, "Then you have the right to go by yourselves to the sheriff to keep the record clear. As a former lawman Roderick ought to recognize the sense in that. In my opinion there is no evidence for any of us to pass judgment, but still—"

"No thanks," Roderick said. "Keep your kangaroo court." His arrogance was returning.

"Can't you see we're trying to do the best we can over a dirty thing that's got the country buzzing like a hornet's nest!" Chauncey Meeker was half pleading and half angry.

"Let it buzz," Roderick said. "We're not going to town with you or anybody else."

"We'll have to insist on it." Kebler spoke with quiet assurance. He wore no pistol. He was without anger and yet he was the most dangerous of the five, for he held their purpose together.

Lee watched them all and tried to weigh his thoughts. Kebler would be out of it. Meeker was not a violent man, but he had come here and so he was ready to go through with it. Houghton was explosive. Bliss Rood was slow but once he started he would go to the end; although right now it appeared that he wished to be out of the situation.

It was Cantonwine who held Lee's attention more than any of the rest. A preacher with a pistol in his waistband. A scared man, but with the kind of fear that drives to sudden, desperate action. Cantonwine's eyes were steady now, glazed with concentration. The rotten core of true hate was in him, and Lee saw it clearly.

"Will you go with us?" Kebler asked.

Roderick glanced at Lee with quick appeal. Not to

make the decision, Lee thought; that was already made. But to stand and fight it out. So this was how it felt the instant before death leaped from pistols. The tightness of the tongue, the coldness of the stomach, and the terrible clarity of small details that bore no weight upon the main proposition.

Almost together Roderick and Lee said no with brief movements of their heads. Their stubbornness and the pride of those who faced them blotted out the last instant for further talk.

In his mind's eye Lee was already going for his pistol when his mother's voice bit through the silence.

"There will be no shooting!" She was standing at one corner of the house with a rifle against her shoulder. Her line of aim quartered across the yard. Her face was white. "I will kill the first man who touches his pistol."

Lee and Roderick backed away slowly until Kebler's group was clearly isolated, alone in the bare yard against the unwavering rifle. Cantonwine's mouth fell loosely open. He raised his hands chest high.

"All right, Maureen, all right," Kebler said. He waited until his delegation had turned and was riding away. He shook his head. "It's a mistake, Roderick. Now the whole country will think someone here killed Alarid."

"Get out!" Roderick said.

Kebler turned and rode away. Bliss and Cantonwine were looking back over their shoulders. Cantonwine said something in a low voice, and Bliss answered, "The hell she wouldn't!"

All the outer tension left Lee. Inside it was worse than ever. He watched his father walk over to Maureen. "We could have handled them, Lee and me," Roderick said, "but that was good work, old girl."

A deadness lay on Maureen Vail's face, frozen there with her pale look. She lowered the rifle, holding it in both hands. She threw it against her husband's legs. "'Good work, old girl.' You said that once before. Goddam you, Roderick Vail."

The angry spots whirled up in Roderick's cheeks. Then for an instant he looked at his wife with a hollow, shamed expression that left him without character. He spun around and walked away, not seeing Lee. He went straight toward the corral. Mrs. Vail walked slowly toward the house. She bumped against a planter wall. She caught a porch post with both hands and clung to it, staring at nothing.

Her thoughts rallied from some distant place when she looked at Lee as he put his arms around her. "You're all right?" he asked. "I thought you were going to drop."

"Fainting is a luxury I gave up long ago." Mrs. Vail grabbed Lee by the shirt with both hands. "You were going to kill men you've known all your life!"

It was a miserable thought now. "They were going to shoot us down if they could. They forced—"

"Forced!" Mrs. Vail flung away from Lee and went inside. He stood on the porch indecisively. A few minutes later Roderick burst from the corral and sent his buckskin pounding toward Union Park. He rode like hell drove him and he did not glance at the house in going.

Maureen Vail was calmer when Lee went inside. She was sitting in the kitchen.

"Roderick's gone," Lee said.

"Why didn't you leave with him?"

"It's too much like running from something. Didn't you and Roderick ever get along together?"

"For a very short time—until I learned what he was."

"You knew he was a pistol fighter when you married him!"

Mrs. Vail nodded. She gave her son a level look. "Yes, I knew that." She hesitated. "You would have shot these men. Were you afraid?"

"No. Not at the very last moment. I admit it was a mistake. We should have gone to town with them. I think I'll do that yet. We owe that much to Kebler."

"You told them the truth?" Mrs. Vail asked.

Puzzled, Lee said, "Of course. I came across Island Ford that night. I never saw Alarid after we left the dance." Lee thought he saw doubt in his mother's expression. "You don't think I'd shoot a man from the dark, do you?"

Mrs. Vail said, "We should know each other so well that your question, and mine too, need not have been asked." Her manner was musing, preoccupied—and lonely. She shook her head. "No, I don't believe you would do that, Lee."

136

If it was not doubt of him, then where was the doubt directed? A thought twisted up dark and terrifying. "Roderick did catch up with you where he said?" Lee asked.

"Yes."

"You're sure?"

"Yes." Maureen answered so quickly and watched Lee with such intentness that his doubt kept growing. "Tell me the truth!" he said.

"You don't think Roderick would—"

"No! You're the one who's doubting him, Maureen." Her attitude had confused Lee. It threw an ugly color on Roderick's behavior at the dance, when there were men who thought he was afraid to go outside to meet an unknown man; it left doubt that she was telling the truth about Roderick catching up with her near the bluffs.

"Come to town with me," Lee said. "Tell them that Roderick wasn't within miles of Houghton's crossing that night."

Maureen shook her head.

"Why not?"

"Because my going won't prove your story."

"Mine is already proved. I went clear to Ben Meeker's turnoff with Iris and Chauncey. They know I couldn't have got to the buggy crossing in time to wait for Alarid."

"But still they asked you where you'd been."

"They had to ask both of us," Lee said impatiently.

Mrs. Vail still shook her head. "Don't go to town.

Even if they believe you they may try to take out their hatred of Roderick on you."

"We both should have gone when Kebler asked us."

"Wait for Roderick, Lee."

"The whole country might be down on us for good before he comes out of the park again." On his way to the door Lee turned. "Would you have used that rifle?"

It came from deep in her, like a wash of nausea the will cannot overcome. Maureen stared at her son and she was deathly ill. "I don't know, Lee. I—" She rested her head on her bent wrist and would not look at him.

Lee saddled his horse, still wondering if his mother had told the truth about Roderick's overtaking her the night Alarid was killed. Of course she had. Roderick had no need to take unfair advantage of any man in a pistol fight.

CHAPTER NINE

LEE'S SHADOW was falling before him in a long slant when he reached the sagebrush mesas west of Kebler. He kept looking to his right, to where the foaming green of Union Park held the sunset. Roderick would have reached one of the camps by now. He would build a fire and sprinkle spruce needles on the stove to kill the odor of staleness in the cabin, and then he would go striding down to an icy creek with a water bucket.

After that there would be the companionship of a well-remembered room, with the evening wind running gently outside and the dusk coming down on the strong security and peace of the mighty basin. Union Park was a barrier against all unpleasantness.

But there was a falseness somewhere in the idea. Lee had to wrench the thought up and grapple with it to keep it from escaping, for even now he had an urge to turn back and join Roderick in the park. Up there, they could ignore the rest of the country and let the excitement over the killing of Alarid die a natural death. Still, the idea would not stick.

Lee kept on toward Kebler.

The rider came toward him at a steady pace, stringing thin dust far toward town. It was Ann Houghton. The last of the sun caught the burnished copper color of her hair. There were dust streaks on her face, dust on her lips and teeth. She reined in deliberately. She took a handkerchief from her pocket and wiped her mouth. Even in her urgency there was reserve in the way she looked at Lee.

"Don't go into town," she said.

"How bad is it, Ann?"

"They're getting ready to ride to Diamond. Kebler and Chauncey Meeker have been trying to hold them but they can't." She saw a question in Lee's eyes, or thought she saw one. "My father went home on the way back from Diamond. He's not involved in it now."

"Who's stirring it up?"

"It hardly needs any stirring. Your highhanded attitude, the way you and Roderick have acted—"

"Somebody has to be the leader."

"Well, Bliss Rood and Cliff McLeod, mainly, I guess, and Sandy Macklin."

"Macklin works for your father."

Color came to Ann's face. "He was a close friend of Alarid's."

"The only friend Alarid had—until somebody killed him," Lee said. "Who sent you?" Lee was blunt.

"You mean I wouldn't have come unless someone sent me?"

"I didn't mean that. I'm sore about the whole thing. Neither Roderick nor me was even close to your crossing that night. I didn't mean—"

"Chaunce Meeker sent me, if you have to know."

"Thanks to both of you then." Lee started on.

"I said you couldn't go there!"

"I heard you." Lee hesitated. "Would you go stay with my mother until this is cleaned up?"

Ann was angry, but she nodded.

They met him at the edge of town. Kebler was the only one who did not have an ugly purpose stamped on him. Cliff McLeod seemed to be the leader. He was a bearded, hot-eyed little man who did little but hunt and fish. He had a cabin on the Sapinero, with a still in a cave behind it. Roderick had talked violently of running him out of the country on general principles.

Swaying drunk, his eyes glazed, Johnny Maxwell said, "Well, we got one of the back-shooters anyway!"

The wicked feeling of the group came hard against Lee. He saw Cantonwine, staring, working his fluid lips. Bliss Rood was a dark chunk of brutality. Sandy Macklin, gray-haired, lean, stared from hooded eyes. He, too, was drunk. Lee had heard conjecture about the color of Macklin's past, but the man had been a long time at Teepees, and he had no greatly violent record in this country. But now he was staring at Lee as if he would kill him on the spot.

Joe Emmet was along too, a man who kept his own counsel, a man of deep independence. He did not belong with this bunch, Lee thought; but here he was. He was not as drunk as some of the others, and he kept frowning as if he felt some uncertainty. Still he was here.

His presence brought home to Lee the full sickening charge of enmity raised against the Vails. He knew they must have been cursing and raging a few moments before, but now they were silent, puzzled at the ease of their first conquest.

Kebler grasped the moment. "Give me your pistol, Lee."

Lee passed it over, and he saw Macklin consider every tiny movement with an eye to finding an excuse for killing him.

"You're not in charge, Kebler," Rood said. "You had your chance and missed. We'll take care of him now."

"We'll put Cantonwine in charge then," Kebler said. "He's a preacher, a man of God. He's a fair man—and he's your particular friend lately, Bliss."

It was a shrewd shift. Cantonwine gave Kebler a wicked look, but he could not decline and he could not deny what had been said about him.

"Just remember this is no trial," Kebler said. "Lee came in voluntarily, no matter what happened before."

McLeod growled, "We ought to hang him now. His old man never balked at hanging people."

There was a mutter of assent, and then Kebler raised his voice. "How about that, Cantonwine?"

Reluctantly, Cantonwine said, "We must be fair. We must hear what he has to say." He looked sidewise at Bliss Rood.

"Let's go up to the church," Kebler said.

"That is not the proper place," Cantonwine said. "It is more fitting to hold the hearing in the saloon."

"The saloon is locked. It stays that way," Kebler said. "We'll go to the church. What better place is there to hear the truth?"

Violence ripped across Sandy Macklin's brown face. He shoved his horse in toward Kebler. "You're using your mouth altogether too much, storekeeper! You're—"

"Make something of it." Kebler balanced Lee's pistol in his hand. The chips in his yellow eyes glinted coldly. He stared Macklin down.

"We can put this man under guard," Cantonwine said, studying Lee. "We can then go after the father."

"Roderick is in Union Park," Lee said. "Sam Harvey is there and two other men who might like to look down rifles at a drunken mob floundering through the aspens."

142

"Don't boast," Cantonwine said. "You're here."

"And if anything happens to me, Roderick will remember that you were in charge, Cantonwine." Lee waited for fear to claw Cantonwine's features, but it was merely caution that rippled across the man's face. The strength of the mob was in him, Lee thought.

There was no more talking of going after Roderick.

Kebler rode beside Lee on the way up the street. For the first time in his life Lee felt a weakness in being unarmed. Men came out of Kebler's store, from Crawford's harness shop, from the blacksmith's building behind it. Chauncey Meeker stood at the gate of Mrs. Crawford's house, his heavy jaw hanging loose. Kebler looked at him and nodded toward the church.

The crowd was surging through the doorway when Lee swung down. He saw Bliss and Cantonwine and Maxwell in heated conversation near the steps. Maxwell kept shaking his head, drunkenly stubborn. Cantonwine was furious.

A warm hand slipped under Lee's arm when he touched ground. Iris Meeker said, "You're in a nice stew, aren't you?" Her grip tightened. "Why didn't your father come along?"

"Busy." Lee watched the steadiness in the woman's eyes. She gave him her opinion of Roderick without saying a word.

McLeod gave Lee a hard shove from behind. "Come on, come on! We got no time for you to be having cozy talk with a fly-up-the-crick!"

Lee cracked his elbow into McLeod's mouth as he

143

turned. He tried to hit the man, but Kebler grabbed Lee's shoulders and hauled him back. McLeod staggered into Chauncey Meeker. "Back-shooting sonofabitch!" the little bearded man cried, and grabbed for his pistol.

Meeker's bony left wrist came around and slammed across McLeod's throat. He clamped down on McLeod's gun hand and forced it away from the holster, twisting the mans' arm behind his back. "Take that pistol," Meeker said to Landon Crawford.

Crawford hesitated an instant and then he lifted McLeod's weapon.

"A few of us have got to keep our heads," Meeker said. Close to McLeod's ear he whispered hotly, "I'll stand no remarks about my sister, little man." His accusing gaze lay on Lee a moment and then Meeker released McLeod.

Inside the church, Iris turned to Kebler. "I'm trusting you, Pete."

"He'll be all right," Kebler said smoothly, but Lee saw the hard worry behind the words. Kebler motioned for him to take a seat in a front pew.

Habit sent Cantonwine toward the pulpit, and then he decided to stay on the main deck. He raised his arms for silence, standing with a pained expression on his face. His eyes were narrowed. Something that was at once thoughtful and cruel came between the lids at Lee.

While the room was quieting down Lee tried to weigh his chances. There were too few men like

Kebler and Chauncey Meeker here, too many like McLeod and Bliss Rood; and Cantonwine was in charge. Honesty told Lee that coming had been the right act, but still he wished now that he had not done so.

"Let us start with a prayer," Cantonwine said. He bowed his head. The pistol under his belt caught his attention. He removed it slowly, staring at it. "The hand of the Lord is never in such an instrument, but sometimes we are carried away by worldly thought." He cast the pistol aside and stood with head bowed once more in humility before he started the prayer.

His action was most effective, Lee thought. From the edge of his eye he glanced at Kebler and saw that Kebler, too, was uneasy about the preacher's attitude.

Cantonwine spoke quietly. "Tony Alarid, a well-beloved and respected member of our group, was killed at Houghton's crossing at point-blank range by someone with a pistol. We think the man approached the place from the river, and we know that he rode into the stream afterward. You have Brother Meeker's word that he could not match the shoes on either Lee or Roderick Vail's horse with what we think are the right tracks.

"Because the Vails had words with Alarid at the dance, some of you have assumed that one of them killed him. There is no evidence to this effect. Roderick says he was with his wife from Dry Creek on that night, and although the committee which you selected to go to Diamond and inquire about certain facts was not privileged to speak directly to Mrs. Vail, it is my personal opinion that she will bear out her husband's statement."

Completely surprised, Lee studied the gaunt face. Cantonwine was a spectral image of justice, of fairness; and Lee was still deeply suspicious of him. But the words were there. *Perhaps I have held a mean opinion of this man,* Lee thought.

Cantonwine cleared his throat. "Lee Vail says that he went home from Ben Meeker's turnoff by way of Island Crossing. We know that Alarid went to Cliff McLeod's cabin after the dance, where he stayed at least an hour, drinking and talking. Unless he dallied, and there seems to be no reason that he would, he would have been, even with his hour at Brother McLeod's, at the crossing long before Lee Vail could have arrived there." Cantonwine let this elementary bit of geography sink in. "So there it stands: Roderick Vail was with his wife, and Lee, at about the time we think Alarid was killed, was just leaving the company of Brother Meeker and his sister."

Sandy Macklin leaped up. "We don't know where Roderick was! His wife never said he was with her."

"She will, I am sure." Cantonwine's gaze strayed across Lee's face with an expression that stirred a terrible doubt. As a self-appointed friend, the man might be more dangerous than he was as an enemy.

"I will call attention to one more fact," Cantonwine said gently. "Lee Vail came unarmed to the dance. He left unarmed. Now, let those with whom Brother

Kebler and I rode in an effort to prevent violence at Diamond speak up."

Joe Emmet said, "We were going to check Roderick's story with his wife."

"You had violence in your hearts," Cantonwine said. "There were some of you would have killed Lee Vail when we met him riding, courageously and voluntarily, to meet with us."

Cantonwine had broken the backbone of the affair before it could get well started. His reversal, if that was what it was, left Lee confused. He knew by the silence, by the moody expressions of the men avoiding each other's eyes, that he was all right now. It was difficult to appreciate how close he had been to death.

"Since we have no further business with this young man," Cantonwine said, "I suggest the meeting be closed."

Macklin rose angrily. "I'm not satisfied about Roderick Vail, not by a heap." He stared at Lee. "I'm not sure about him either." He and McLeod went out together. Now there was only the after-buzz, the minor arguments, and the talk of those who said they had known all the time that Lee was guiltless.

Lee thanked Cantonwine, "I serve as best as I can," the preacher said. He put his hand on Lee's shoulder, and afterward Lee still felt the coldness of his touch. "May I suggest that you be careful about going home in the dark? Someone with an ungodly spirit is abroad in our land." Cantonwine watched to judge the impact of his words.

Lee nodded absently. He saw Iris rushing toward him. "I'll be careful." And then Iris was beside him, smiling.

On the way out she said, "He switched horses awful fast, didn't he?"

Behind them Kebler murmured. "Go home, Lee. Go straight home without any fooling around."

"What's the hurry, Pete?" Lee asked.

"I don't know." Kebler paused on the steps. He glanced inside the church. He looked down the street at the crowd headed toward his saloon. The first of dusk was settling. The tall cottonwoods Kebler had planted long ago were motionless. Heat lightning flicked across the sky above the Razors. "I don't know." Kebler's face was hard and thoughtful as he followed the crowd.

Now it was dark and a coolness was coming across the land. The lights of town did not show behind the church where Johnny Maxwell lay in drunken slumber on a plank table. Bliss Rood stamped back and forth, as close to bellowing anger as he ever got.

"We had him!" he said. "We could have seen him hanged, and you had to let him off. I don't like that kind of pussy-footing, Cantonwine. Business like Sandy Macklin wearing your coat the other night and pulling his hat down and telling my father he wanted to see Roderick. Who'd that fool?"

"It scared the very soul in Roderick Vail," Cantonwine said. "I saw the cowardliness deep in him."

Bliss cursed. "Cowardliness! Tackle him sometime and find out. Did you expect him to go stand in a lighted doorway when he thought—"

"No. But I wanted to see inside him. I did. He is not to be feared. I know now that his son is the one we must fear. He is more dangerous than five Rodericks, and before he realizes it—"

"Hell!" Bliss said. "He's never had a pistol fight in his life."

"That can be arranged." Cantonwine had moved, for his voice now came from near the table where Maxwell lay, but Bliss had not heard him change position.

"Arrange, that's all we do!"

"You yourself advised slowness in our first meeting," Cantonwine said.

"Maybe I did. I'm sick of the whole thing now. We had Lee where we could have handled him, and you—"

"He didn't kill Alarid. Roderick did. Besides, there was doubt that we could have raised the crowd to the proper pitch. Kebler was there, Meeker, others who would have fought for him. It was also necessary that my position did not become obvious."

"You made a hero of yourself," Bliss said.

"That rankles, does it? Perhaps you had better pull out. Macklin or McLeod, I'm sure, would be happy at the prospect of sharing Union Park with me."

"If that ever happens, I'll be there," Bliss growled.

"I thought it would get into your blood in time. Vengeance is not enough, Bliss. There must also be rewards." Cantonwine came toward Bliss, making no sound. It gave Bliss a creepy feeling, the man moving in the dark like that. "Go to Macklin and McLeod, Bliss. Do what I told you."

"You give a lot of orders," Bliss muttered. Once he had been in charge. He did not know how the leadership had slipped away from him. Out of a great natural discontent he had sought vengeance for an insult; no more than that at first. Then Cantonwine had introduced a material goal. Never greatly desiring material things but merely wishing for them, Bliss had been hooked almost against his will; and now the hook was deeper because of the thought that someone besides him might share Union Park. Maybe it was only bluff with Cantonwine.

"Go on." Cantonwine had moved again. He must be pacing, Bliss thought. It was eerie that he could do it so silently. Rood left the grove. He felt better when he saw the lights at the lower end of the street.

Cantonwine began to rouse Maxwell. The drunken cowboy made miserable noises and that was all. Cantonwine rolled him over and let him fall to the ground. Maxwell groaned.

"Whiskey. A curse, Maxwell."

"I don't want any of your sermons."

"You recognize me then?"

"I'd know that voice in hell. Leave me alone."

"Hell is where you've been. Now you are back and must be made whole again."

Maxwell got to his feet. He staggered into the table and fell across it, cursing. "What happened? I remember starting to Diamond. What happened there?"

There was a long silence. "Nothing," Cantonwine said. "Both Lee and Roderick forced Mrs. Vail to lie. One of them had beaten her. The marks were on her face, but she stood before us and said her husband had been with her the night Alarid was killed, and so—"

"That's enough!" Maxwell pushed the table over. "I told Bliss to send Roderick out to me at the dance. He wouldn't do it!"

"Lee is here now."

"He's a whipped pup! I want Roderick!"

"That a son should strike his mother, force her—"

"Shut up!" Maxwell yelled. "How do I know he did?"

Even when his mind was sodden with drink, his streak of stubborn shrewdness held. It gave Cantonwine pause. He said, "Restrain your evil temper, Maxwell. Perhaps Lee did not strike his mother after all. But nonetheless he is a dangerous man, and you are hopelessly drunk—"

"Don't give me orders!"

"Keep away from him. Stay away from the saloon."

Maxwell's wildness crossed the line of sanity. He could not be egged directly but he could drive himself beyond fear. With the filth of his drunkenness on him, he stumbled from the grove.

He ran down the street until a thumping in his temples sickened him. Whiskey ripped his nerves. He stood in the dark fumbling with his pistol, and then he lurched to a water box. He slopped water on his face and chest, gasping from the coldness. When he rose the lights were steadier. He went down the street, leaning forward, taking long strides.

Cantonwine went toward the church. He would light a lamp. He would be inside when the shots rocked out. Maxwell was a vicious child. Bliss had been a fool to enlist him in the cause. There were the other two, Macklin and the little whiskey maker. They were valuable, for one had vengeance on his mind and the other was a natural malcontent. It was possible that one of them might be lost, but that would have to be. Bliss had orders to stay out of it after he had done the preliminary work.

But one of the other three would get Lee Vail. Roderick then would be obliged to seek revenge. He was a coward; Cantonwine was sure of it. But even cowards must act. It was altogether possible that two Vails would be eliminated without any direct involvement of Cantonwine.

Cantonwine was on the porch before he realized that he was barefooted. The knowledge hit him like the cold turning of the public eye upon a vice. He ran back to the grove and began casting around for his boots, and when he found them he could not remember taking them off. But no one had known, no one had known.

In the quiet church he waited, with the light of a lamp on the pulpit reaching but dimly to where he sat. He looked like ancient evil, driven once into the misty forest, returned by darkness to crouch in a sanctuary of man.

Cleared of guilt in a roughly legal manner but still resented, a Vail, a man whose name had been linked with murder, Lee did not take Kebler's advice to leave at once after the meeting. Stubbornness and his own resentment held him in town. Now it was well after dark. Most of the ranchers had gone home soon after the high point of the excitement dwindled away. Kebler, not in the saloon at the moment, had warned Lee to wait a while longer.

Sandy Macklin and McLeod were close together at the bar. Soon after the meeting they had tried to edge into a fight with Lee, but Kebler had stopped it quickly. Kebler was not here now. Lee figured he would, from now on, take care of his own shooting trouble if it came.

Jameson was behind the bar, a tall, blond man. It was obvious that the quietness was making him nervous. He jumped too quickly when Macklin or McLeod or any of the few hangers-on wanted service.

Bliss Rood came in the side door. He talked briefly to McLeod and Macklin, glancing only casually at Lee in the back-bar mirror. When Bliss went out McLeod sauntered after him.

Minutes later Kebler came in, crossing directly to Lee. "You're welcome to that spare bed in my back room, Lee." He spoke in a normal tone. Lee had refused the bed once but now he went along with the hard intentness behind Kebler's casual manner, nodding his thanks. "A hard day." Kebler sat down, yawning. Softly he said, "Get out of her—now!"

He had been scouting around outside, Lee thought. For the moment the way must be clear. But running was no good. The same men could be in town the next time he came, next week, next year; or they could meet him anywhere. It was a thought that closed like a trap but it had to be met. If Bliss and the other two thought they had a settlement coming, let it be now.

Macklin was walking slowing down the bar, toward the front door. A gray-haired man with a corded neck. Alarid's only friend, Cal Houghton's oldest employee. It seemed long ago that the trouble began against Houghton, the day Roderick and Lee rode into the grove. Now Houghton was home in bed and Roderick was not here either. But the disease of trouble was still spreading.

Watching Macklin, Lee shook his head at Kebler.

Kebler went across the room and locked the side door. "I'm closing up, boys. Let's go."

From behind him, from the doorway of his living quarters, McLeod said, "Stand quiet, Pete." The little bearded man's eyes were bright with malice as he stepped into the room with a pistol in his hand. "Against the bar, Pete. You can't do one more thing to help him."

Bliss Rood came in behind McLeod, following Kebler's retreat as far as the end of the bar. Macklin was at the other end, making the base of a triangle, the sharp apex running straight to Lee, still seated in his corner.

The few drinkers caught between Macklin and McLeod bunched together. They had no place to go without crossing someone's line of fire. Jameson turned white and sank out of sight behind the bar.

Sandy Macklin's face was a brown death's-head. His words came thickly. "No matter what that preacher said, we got our own ideas, Vail. You killed Alarid. Get up."

They gave Lee that much. He put his hands on the table and rose slowly. He could not watch all three of them and he had no way of knowing who would start it. McLeod had a pistol in his hand already. Lee's stomach was pulled in tight, his mouth was dry, and the barbing run of fear was in his spine. But he had no terror and no cowardice and his mind did not go numb.

There was Macklin, waiting. Macklin first, and then if he had any luck he would turn to the other two.

"Well, Vail?" Macklin said.

It went awry. Someone threw the front door open. Lee's nerves jumped. The sudden action at the door was almost enough to drive him to his pistol. And then he saw Johnny Maxwell, a gray-faced apparition, mouth clamped tight, with twigs and dead leaves in his matted hair, his face gleaming wetly as the light struck it.

"Vail, you bastard!" Maxwell paused an instant in the doorway. He saw no one but Lee, and straight at

Lee he came in a dragging, short-stepped walk.

The coldest voice Lee had ever heard sliced through the sound of Maxwell's shuffling boots. "Drop it, McLeod."

Roderick! It was Roderick, Lee thought. He heard McLeod's pistol bump on the floor.

But it was not Roderick; it was Sam Harvey. He came from Kebler's living quarters like a cat. He slid along the partition in one swift motion until he had Bliss and McLeod and Sandy Macklin all under his pistol.

If Maxwell heard or saw him, he gave no sign. Maxwell was still inching toward Lee and his mind was set like a cocked pistol.

Harvey said, "Hold it, Maxwell." It had no effect.

"No, Johnny!" Lee said. "Stop there!"

Maxwell stopped. His body stiffened. His eyes were staring. Lee thought he was coming to his senses. And then Maxwell drew his pistol and shot. He peered through the bloom of smoke and when he saw Lee still on his feet, he put both hands on the pistol and aimed again.

That was when Lee's bullet struck him, twisting him out of shape, smashing him back, dropping him to the floor.

Harvey's voice was still in command. "Get their pistols, Kebler."

Kebler turned to Rood first. Bliss was staring sullenly, shocked, with all the animal instinct in him stilled. Kebler took his pistol, and then he scooped up

McLeod's weapon, and then he went behind the bar, stepping over the crouched Jameson, to walk down the room to disarm Sandy Macklin from behind.

McLeod went over to Maxwell. "Shooting down a drunken kid." His voice was loud and bitter. "That's the Vails for you."

Kebler looked thoughtfully at the bearded man, and it was hard to say what lay in the merchant's mind, until he picked McLeod up and threw him toward the front door. The disgust and terrible anger that can overcome the most patient man sent Kebler walking purposefully toward Bliss. "Rood—" Kebler said, and then he knew that words were useless.

Bliss backed away. He threw up the bar on the side door and leaped into the night. Sandy Macklin did not run when Kebler started toward him.

"Wait a minute," Harvey said. He put his pistol away. "Macklin thought he had an honest reason, at least. He was running with mongrels but he thought he had a good reason." He allowed Macklin that much, and then he said, "Of course he played it three to one."

Shame darkened Macklin's features. He glanced at Lee, now kneeling beside Maxwell. He was remembering that Lee Vail had risked his life to keep from shooting at Johnny Maxwell, a searing test that Macklin doubted he could have stood himself. Lee had shot only when he had to. That did not fit Macklin's idea of a man who would ambush from the dark. Macklin remembered, too, that he had been a little drunk. The coppery taste of sudden soberness was in his mouth now. McLeod and Bliss—he couldn't have joined up with two sneakier curs.

He walked over to the bar and took his pistol from where Kebler had left it. He put it in the holster. "Where do you want to carry him?" he asked, and that was his admission that he no longer thought Lee had killed Tony Alarid.

They carried Johnny Maxwell into Kebler's bedroom. The wound was high in his chest. Kebler cut the bullet out under the skin on his back.

"Will he live?" Lee asked.

"Who the hell knows?" Kebler said, suddenly unreasonably angry.

"A doctor—" It seemed to Lee that Maxwell was dying now.

"The bullet's out," Kebler said. "A doctor won't do him any good, one way or another, even if we could get one within a week. Go home, Lee. I told you to a long time ago."

If you had listened this would not have happened. That was what he meant, Lee thought. But if Roderick had not fired Maxwell unfairly, it would not have happened either. Lee buried both thoughts; there was no help in the past, no use in trying to shift responsibility.

Lee walked out to the bar and poured himself a drink. He was almost unaware of the few men who had been spectators, of Mell Crawford and others who had come running at the sound of the shots. Macklin came up beside him.

"I was dead wrong, Vail. I know I was."

Lee looked at the weathered features, a hard, tough face that had stared death at him a short time before. "It's all right, Sandy. Let's forget it."

Macklin poured himself a drink. In the voice of one who has just discovered something startling he said, "You're more of a man than your father ever was."

CHAPTER TEN

RIDING BACK to Diamond with Harvey, Lee asked, "How'd you happen to show up at the right time, Sam?"

"I'd been there for a half hour, sizing things up. For a while, it didn't look like anything was going to come off." As if he knew what Lee was thinking, Harvey added, "Yes, I could have gone in and taken you out of Kebler's before anything popped, but I knew you wouldn't like that." He paused. "I didn't even know Maxwell was around. What did he have against you, Lee?"

"I don't know, beyond the fact that Roderick ran him off. He was drunk, too, of course."

"Yeah," Harvey said.

"When you told McLeod to drop his pistol, I thought you were Roderick. Did he send you, Sam?"

"No. He told me about the bunch that came to the ranch. I figured you'd go into town, after you had time to think things over."

"Why didn't Roderick know that?" Lee asked.

"I don't know."

159

They forded the Sapinero. The suck of dark water around the legs of the horses and the crunching of rocks in the stream bed made lonely sounds. The animals surged up the incline to the meadows, and then the lights of Diamond showed far away across the flatness. Lee thought of all the nights Maureen Vail had been there by herself.

"Did you stop at the house on your way, Sam?"

"Yes. Your mother was worried about you."

"Roderick didn't send you. You came on your own. Why didn't he come with you?"

"I don't know."

"You do know. You know all of us better than we know ourselves. You can guess what Roderick will do before he does it, and now you're doing the same thing with me."

"All right, I do know. I've been around you a long time," Harvey said. Stubborn silence would have been a better answer.

After a time Lee asked, "When you shoved your horse between Alarid and Roderick on Cannibal Mesa, who were you protecting?"

"I'm against useless pistol fights."

"That's no answer, Sam. How long have you been standing between Roderick and the trouble he asks for? Was it like that when you knew him a long time ago?"

"Ask Roderick these things, not me." By the tone of Harvey's voice Lee knew this was the final word.

They were several hundred yards from Diamond

when they saw the light break in the doorway. Mrs. Vail came out on the porch. "Lee?"

"I'm all right, Maureen."

When he swung down she put her arms around him briefly. It was the greatest display of affection she had shown him since he grew up; and most miserably he recalled that he had shown her no love since he was a boy.

"Where's Ann?" he asked.

"She went on home. I didn't need her."

Harvey started to ride on.

"There's not that much hurry, Sam," Maureen said. "Come inside."

The maple furniture of the living room was dark from age and much polishing. Lee stared at the diamond design in heavy drapes, undrawn across a window that looked out on the dark land. He saw the dull shine of brass trivets on the wall just inside the kitchen doorway. The odors of the house, the feeling of it, were strange to him all at once.

Roderick and I have left no mark upon this place, he thought. *We've been visitors here, that's all.*

"What happened?" Mrs. Vail asked.

Harvey stood just inside the door, a tired man with a troubled expression. His dark eyes turned to Lee and put the responsibility for answers on him.

What indeed, had happened? Lee felt a great sag of futility. Events poured through his memory, and the sharpest of all was the remembrance of Maxwell twisting and falling. Lee found it difficult to meet his mother's questioning look. Too much, it seemed, depended on his answer. He told her slowly about the meeting, about his refusal to leave town. He wanted to hurry over the affair in Kebler's saloon, but he forced the details out with deliberate honesty.

"Johnny Maxwell—that angry, half-grown man. . . . You shot him?" Maureen Vail's fingers were twisted in the neck of her dark dress. "You had to do that?"

"I—Yes, I had to." Lee looked at Harvey.

"He had to, Maureen," Harvey said. "He waited—"

"I didn't ask you, Sam." Mrs. Vail walked toward her son slowly. "You had to?"

"If I had been a better shot, I would have tried to shoot him in the arm. Maybe Roderick—"

"Roderick!" Maureen hit Lee with the name. He saw a disgust and fury that astonished him. "Don't tell me what your father might have done!" She looked accusingly at Harvey. The gray in Harvey's reddish hair, the bleakness of his tired face, made him old and hard and bitter. For one stark moment he threw all of Mrs. Vail's accusation back at her.

His voice came out with a grinding patience. "If I had tried to stop Maxwell with a careful shot, Macklin would have had his chance, and McLeod and maybe Rood, and then it would have been another Trail's End deal, Maureen. I am not as young as then, and Lee took care of himself."

Some significance beyond Lee crossed between his mother and Sam Harvey. Lee was a stranger in the room then.

He said, "I had no quarrel with Johnny. I don't know why he hated me."

Mrs. Vail shook her head slowly. "He didn't hate you." Her manner toward her son softened.

"Good night." Harvey went out quickly. His going caught at something in Mrs. Vail. For an instant, although she was looking steadily at Lee, she did not see him; and a few moments later it was the same, the sharp arresting of all her attention at the sounds of the hoofs going south.

"How long have you been in love with him, Maureen?"

"Possibly before I married Roderick."

His mother's calmness angered Lee. "That's a hell of a thing to admit!"

Her temper flashed back at him. "You asked me!"

"You loved Sam and you married Roderick. What—"

"It isn't simple to explain, Lee. I didn't know at the time. Of course I thought I loved Roderick, or I wouldn't have married him. And then I found out that he didn't need me, that he never really wanted me."

"After a quarter of a century, you found that out," Lee said bitterly.

"You make it sound very long, Lee. There were times when I was happy, I suppose, and there were other times when I could not admit that I was unhappy. I—"

"Then Sam came back. Did you send—"

Mrs. Vail shook her head. "Roderick sent for him,

Lee. Roderick has"—she searched for a word—"depended on Sam a great deal."

"Everybody in the country knows what I couldn't see for myself."

"No, not everybody. Pete Kebler knows, I'm sure, but not everybody."

"Ann Houghton told me she didn't want a life of building flower beds that she would rip apart a week later!"

Mrs. Vail nodded. The corners of her mouth pinched in. Her resignation, her regret whipped across Lee's mind and cooled his anger. His mother had never been meek or whining, and he sensed now the pounding of a woman furiously alive. He saw the stark image of thoughts long hidden behind the gray eyes, and his mind leaped back to the days when he had been closer to his mother than to Roderick, to the memory of laughter that had died, to changes that had grown tremendous when he could not see them.

Something was torn inside him; part of him was lost to his mother and much of him was still fiercely loyal to Roderick. He said, "You've thought of running off with Harvey, of getting a divorce?"

"Of course I have!" A passionate fire blazed in Maureen Vail's eyes, and then it dulled away. "But I never will."

"It's no good having Harvey around."

"When he leaves this fall he's not coming back," Mrs. Vail said. "I made him promise."

"How far has it gone with you two?"

"No farther than anything you've seen. Why?"

Lee faltered under his mother's steady look. "I wondered."

"Now you know. Does it relieve that overbloated sense of ownership you men feel?"

"If that's what you call it—yes."

"How about you and Ann?"

"That isn't the same."

"Did she ever unbend enough to be kissed?"

Lee blinked. "Yes."

"I'm surprised. Now, how about you and Iris?"

Lee felt himself reddening. "That's different. We were talking about—"

"Don't be so ashamed of yourself." Mrs. Vail separated her words with flat emphasis. "Iris isn't. She's a remarkably honest girl, for all her flirting. You have many things to learn, Lee, other than standing up well when three men with pistols corner you."

"We were talking about you and Sam."

"So we were, and you got your answer."

Lee knew that he had been knocked out of position when he thought he held the offensive.

Mrs. Vail started toward her room. "Will you saddle a horse for me, please."

"Where—"

"I'm going to town. Pete Kebler has carried the woes of this country for years, so there is no reason why he should have to nurse a wounded man."

Lee stared darkly. "You're blaming Roderick, aren't you? You're thinking that—"

"I blame no one any longer, Lee. I merely try to pick up the loose ends. *You* shot Johnny Maxwell, although it was not your fault."

Still, Roderick had brought it on. Lee started out to saddle his mother's horse. He wondered how it was he could admit to himself Roderick's weaknesses but refuse to lay them before anyone else, even Maureen.

He helped his mother up when she was ready to go. She was a strong, active woman who went into the saddle easily. She leaned down and slapped him gently on the cheek. "Don't worry, Lee. You'd better go to bed now."

Suddenly Lee Vail was proud of his mother. He felt a bond, a partnership, that was apart from the accident of kinship. "I'll take a wagon in and we can bring him back here, if you think that will be better," he said.

"You think Roderick would stand—"

"Yes," Lee said, "he'll stand for that."

Mrs. Vail was silent for several moments. "I'll no longer worry about you."

He did not know what she meant and he had no chance to ask. She started away. "From what you and Sam have said, I doubt that Johnny Maxwell can be moved for a long time. Good night, Lee."

For one of the few times in his life Lee was alone at Diamond. Habit was strong. As tired as he was he thought of taking a fresh horse and riding to the park, for it seemed that all problems would vanish then. But he turned and went wearily toward the house.

Something had broken the magic power of Union

Park. It was no longer a place where everything but simple living could be shut away. It would never be that again.

The hoofbeats of his mother's horse died away. Lee went into the silent, empty house.

The street of Kebler was quiet now, back to its shady, drowsing aspect. A dead man was a cause but a wounded man was a burden without excitement, and so the few who had rushed to town on hearing about Maxwell had heard the story and gone back home, believing the truth but more resentful of the Vails.

Kebler and Maureen Vail took care of Maxwell. He was not doing well but he did not know that. His bitter sharp senses dulled by fever, Johnny Maxwell was close to contentment, as well as close to death.

Preacher Cantonwine came to pray for him.

Kebler said, "I think he can get along all right without it, Cantonwine."

"No man can live without the Lord. Evil has struck down a youthful spirit. It would be compounding evil to deny him grace when he lies at death's door."

Washing glasses behind the bar, Kebler paused to give Cantonwine the same still expression that had been on the saloonman's face just before he threw Cliff McLeod across the room.

From a back room Mrs. Vail called, "Send the minister in, Mr. Kebler."

Cantonwine slanted a sly, triumphant glance at Kebler. He bowed his head and clasped his hands behind his back and went to where Mrs. Vail sat beside the wounded man. "Unfortunate," Cantonwine murmured, searching Maxwell's face for the signs of death. He wondered how much memory had threaded back through the swirls of drunken remembrance. "You are a good woman, Sister Vail." Cantonwine saw faint amusement color the woman's expression.

An impotent fury crunched through him as he knelt. He spoke of the evil that had struck down Maxwell, of punishment that must follow. Maxwell looked only at Maureen Vail. Cantonwine then spoke of a wasted life, of a hell waiting for those who did not repent when the Reaper was poised above them. A tiny dent showed in Maxwell's cheek. He kept looking at Mrs. Vail. *Goddam the man,* Cantonwine thought. The words had been fear and fear was power, but Maxwell was laughing.

Cantonwine rose, frustrated.

"Thank you," Mrs. Vail said.

Cantonwine looked down at her gleaming black hair, into the quiet gray of her eyes. She was not mocking him. A beautiful woman in her prime. Cantonwine felt an urge to have and at the same time to destroy. He laid his hand on Maureen Vail's head. The soft warmth of her hair was like a shock. "You are a good woman, Sister Vail."

Maxwell's fever-bright eyes burned in his narrow face. "Take your stinking paw off her!"

"You are very ill, my friend, but I shall pray for your recovery," Cantonwine said. He walked through the saloon with his head bowed. Kebler watched him coldly. When he went out the front door Kebler, frowning, walked in to see Maxwell.

"How you feeling, Johnny?"

"Fine."

"Can you remember yet how you got it in for Lee so bad?"

Maxwell shook his head.

"Where were you after the meeting in the church that evening?"

"I don't know. I remember I fell into a water box, I think. I washed my face and drank some water. I seem to remember that." Maxwell was puzzled and ashamed. "Lee was always fine to me, Mrs. Vail. I just don't know what happened."

"It's all right." Kebler shook his head as if it did not matter greatly.

Listening just outside the front door of the saloon, Cantonwine nodded. His purpose in going to see Maxwell had been obstructed by Mrs. Vail's presence, but now he knew that fortune was with him. Of course, fortune ever smiled on the bold. His toes were clutching at his boots and in his mind was a picture of himself, barefooted, clothed in white robes, striding on rocks that commanded a great area; and at his feet, garbed in gleaming samite, lay Maureen Vail looking up at him with mingled fear and adoration.

Suddenly he glanced about him guiltily. The moments of dreaming were growing more powerful each time they came. They were killing his fears of earthly things, but he must be careful lest someone peer in on his thoughts. He went to saddle Brigham, for he had to see Bliss and Emmet at once.

Maxwell lived three days before he coughed up his life. While he still had a grasp on this world he watched Maureen Vail with a rapt expression, and it seemed that he was dying a completely happy man, which is a privilege granted few. Desperately Kebler tried to get something from him of events just before he came into the saloon to kill Lee, but Maxwell could not remember, for the compressing hand of death is no great clarifier of the memory.

An understanding of each other's thoughts ran between Kebler and Mrs. Vail when they turned away from the bed. They both were in revolt against circumstances, and both of them were hard losers. Having seen much of human beings, Kebler still expected much of them; but now he had a rare moment of blackness; he cursed the world because of what the people in it did to each other.

"You'd better send for Cantonwine," Mrs. Vail said.

"To hell with him!" Then Kebler nodded.

"I'll take Johnny back to Diamond." A deadly anger colored the woman's tone. "Roderick will understand."

Kebler considered her meaning and was unsure of it, except that she might be blaming Roderick for Maxwell's death; but there seemed to be something deeper than that. They walked outside. Lee Vail was riding into town. "Remember," Kebler said quickly, "Lee couldn't help it."

"I know."

Before Lee dismounted, he asked, "How is he?"

Kebler and Mrs. Vail glanced at each other. "Dead," Kebler said. "Just a minute ago, Lee." He watched the splintery shock of regret and self-blame lay a grayness across Lee's face. He saw Lee Vail grow older in the few moments between the news and when he swung down.

"What can we do now?" Lee asked.

He'll he all right, Kebler thought. *He's outgrown the useless, heated attitude that cripples reason and he's trying to hang to the thoughts that serve future living.* "Come have a drink with me," Kebler said. He turned to Mrs. Vail. "We'll be ready with the wagon and all in an hour."

They watched Maureen Vail go up the street to Mrs. Crawford's house where she had stayed when she was not with Maxwell. "I wish I'd met her before she ever saw Roderick or Sam Harvey, either." Kebler challenged Lee with a hot look.

"The past cannot be helped." Lee's calmness shamed the older man.

They went inside to get the drink.

Maureen insisted that the word be sent around the countryside. It was not a large funeral for a land where death always exerted the strong attention of people living far apart. Ben Meeker came with his wife and Chauncey and Iris. Sandy Macklin rode over with the

Houghtons. When Kebler asked Cantonwine pointedly where Bliss Rood was, the preacher said Brother Rood was ill with stomach trouble. Sam Harvey rode down from the park when Lee went after him. Roderick was somewhere on the east side, Harvey thought, so there was no time to go after him.

When Harvey learned where the grave was dug, beside the graves of the two men who had come by night to Diamond when Lee was a boy, a brittle stillness caught his features. He glanced quickly at Maureen, who was waiting for his expression; and then they both saw Lee watching them. The frozen moment passed, leaving its unpleasant mystery with Lee.

Cantonwine did not talk long. Kebler had been curt, almost brutal, about his insistence on shortness when he made the arrangements.

From across the grave Lee saw Ann Houghton weighing him. Afterward she came to him, and he was sure then of the sympathy in her eyes. "Don't blame yourself," she said. She glanced at Iris and then she went toward the house with her parents.

Macklin, hard-bitten, scowling, came over and said, "I'm sorry, Vail." He clumped away toward his horse, awkward on the ground.

Iris stood beside Lee for just a moment. She gave him an odd look. "You'll be all right, Lee. You're like your mother, hard to break."

Maureen and Harvey and Lee were walking toward the house together when Roderick came out of the willows on the south meadows. The tall buckskin was gleaming in the sunlight. It broke into a gallop as Roderick rode high in the saddle, swinging his head toward the groups straggling from the low hill.

Mrs. Vail stopped. "I want three crosses on that hill, Lee. We've neglected those first two graves too long."

"I wouldn't do that, Maureen!" Pain twisted Harvey's face. "Don't do that!"

Roderick came in and dismounted on the run. He had shaved that morning. His face was sharp and bright, his blue eyes flashing. "What's going on?"

"We buried Johnny Maxwell," Mrs. Vail said.

Roderick kept looking toward the hill. "Up there? Up there beside those two?"

"Yes," Mrs. Vail said.

The blotches came to Roderick's cheeks. "By God, Maureen! What are you trying to do? I won't stand—" He stopped. "What happened to Maxwell?"

"I killed him," Lee said.

"I'll tell you about it, Roderick," Mrs. Vail said quietly. She motioned for Lee and Harvey to walk on.

Lee looked back and saw Roderick standing with a stunned expression, with his shoulders sagging.

Harvey said, "I'm going to leave right after roundup, Lee—for good."

"We'll talk about that later, Sam."

Maureen and Roderick were still talking when Harvey rode away. Sandy Macklin was already a long distance toward the Teepees, and Cantonwine had left also. Lee saw the stallion stop and turn as Cantonwine sat for a full two minutes looking back at Diamond.

No one had gone inside. People were waiting near their horses or their wagons. Politeness bade them say a word to Mrs. Vail before they left, but the awkwardness of the situation was fretting them. At last Ben Meeker's wife, looking toward Roderick and Maureen, said to Lee, "Tell your mother to come over and see us when she can." Ben Meeker and his wife left.

Maureen Vail finally came toward the house alone. As casually as they could those remaining said goodbye, skirting the edges of a sympathy they felt for Mrs. Vail but could not state before her son.

Maureen asked Chauncey, "I wonder if Iris could stay with me a few days?"

"Sure, if she wants to," Chauncey answered quickly, looking directly at Mrs. Vail, avoiding Lee's eyes.

"I'll be glad to stay," Iris said.

Leaving with her parents, Ann held her head high, apparently unaware of both the invitation and acceptance; but Lee knew she had missed nothing. He went down to the corral to talk to his father.

He had never seen Roderick so subdued; it was almost as if he had been badly frightened. Roderick was rubbing down his buckskin but he had not put his rig away, and that was an indication that he would go back to the park before long.

"I shouldn't have fired him," Roderick said. "That started the whole thing." He looked at Lee as if he seriously wanted the answer to a question. "Why did I do that, Lee?"

"You were sore at Alarid."

Roderick nodded. "Now Alarid is dead too." He looked up the hill toward the graves. Something seemed to have snapped his spirit. "It's hell how things turn out."

Looking at his father now, Lee could not find blame in him for Maxwell's death. He saw a dejected man, a man who could not find the reasons for his own behavior.

"Did Maureen blame you?" Roderick asked.

Roderick shook his head. "That's the hell of it. She just told me the facts and let it go at that."

But she had insisted that Maxwell be buried beside two men that Roderick had killed; so there was no need to speak her blame. Lee's sympathy ran toward his father, but he had a question to ask and it could wait no longer.

"The night of the dance, Roderick—where did you catch up with Maureen?"

"I didn't. She was home long before I got here. I thought she was off on another of her wild runs and I went ten miles west looking for her."

"You told Kebler and the others that you caught up near the bluffs."

"Sure I did. What right had they to question either of us?" Anger began to build in little steps on Roderick's face. "You're not hinting that I killed Tony Alarid?"

Lee's gaze was bleak. "Why didn't you tell the truth then?"

"Damn it! It was nobody's business! If I had to explain why I rode west looking for Maureen, then it became a personal matter. If we have any family trouble here, Lee, it's our own." Roderick's face was growing red and white; he had replaced his dejection with anger.

The change was easy for him, Lee thought; and Lee believed the explanation. Roderick's vanity had outstripped his reason when Kebler's delegation called.

"Let's get out of here," Roderick said. "There's work for us in the park. We'll get something to eat and beat it." He glanced again toward the graves on the hill.

"No." Lee walked away. It was incredible that his mother would believe Roderick had killed Alarid, but yet she had lied to him; and maybe the reason she had refused to go to town was because she was afraid to repeat the lie to Kebler and an angry mob. Lee was pacing aimlessly near the creek when his mother called to him from the back door of the house.

"Tell Roderick we'll have dinner in a half hour."

Lee motioned to her to come to him.

He asked, "Why didn't you tell me the truth about Roderick the night Alarid was shot?"

"Roderick told you the truth?"

"Yes."

"All right then." Mrs. Vail's eyes did not waver.

"But you still think he killed Alarid."

"No." Mrs. Vail was either deliberate or reluctant. "Not if you don't think so."

"That's no answer!"

Mrs. Vail sighed. "You're right, it isn't. I suppose I

was badly upset the day the men came here. When Roderick lied to them I jumped to a bad conclusion." She studied her son quietly.

Lee was certain now that she was telling the truth but he found no relief in it. That she had doubted Roderick in the first place left a great void unexplained.

"Would you have told the truth the day Kebler's bunch was here if they'd had a chance to ask you?" Lee saw Iris come to the doorway of the kitchen for a moment.

"I don't know," Mrs. Vail said. "I suppose not. After you live a lie for so long, refusing to believe it—" She shook her head. "Why don't you go on to the park with Roderick after dinner? I'd like to talk to Iris alone."

"I will." Lee turned away dissatisfied, still tight inside. When one dark shadow was explored and found to be nothing there was always another.

The meal was a strained affair. Just once Roderick spoke. Looking at Iris, he said, "I made a fool of myself at that dance, didn't I?"

"Yes." Iris glanced at Maureen Vail. The two women seemed to understand each other perfectly.

Roderick dropped at once into a sullen anger. There were times, Lee thought, when Roderick could speak the truth of himself with startling frankness, but he could not stand agreement with his statement afterward.

Soon after dinner the two men rode away, Roderick still sullen; but when they reached the aspens and began to climb to the north edge of the park his mood changed. "Women can give a man a lot of grief, Lee." After another mile he was humming and his face was set eagerly toward Union Park. And then he wanted to know the exact details of how Lee had shot Johnny Maxwell.

CHAPTER ELEVEN

THEY STARTED the search at Houghton's buggy crossing where the Sapinero was wide and shallow. Cliff McLeod's place was about a mile upstream on the other side of the river. Island Ford was two miles downstream, toward the Diamond.

Sandy Macklin looked at the pools of spring seep in the willows. "Right here was the only tracks we could be sure of that day and they wasn't much even then. This should have been done long ago when we were getting drunk and wanting to hang the Vails."

"Since it wasn't, we'll do it now," Ann Houghton said.

Her calm insistence was getting under Macklin's hide. She asked, "Don't you want to find out who killed Tony?"

Macklin's rutted brown face was grim. "I'd like to awful well." He was a simple man. He did not know that he had always been more of a friend to Alarid than Alarid had ever been to him. Secure in her understanding and ability to handle most men, Ann had judged him rightly.

"We know who *didn't* do it." Macklin stared glumly at the water in the willows. Someone had sat his horse right here, shooting when Alarid came from the river, probably getting down afterward to drag him back into the current of the river. There was nothing to read here now. Coming home at dawn after a drinking party at Emmet's sawmill the night of the dance, Macklin had crossed here himself, too foggy and tired to notice anything.

"Who didn't do it, Sandy?"

"For one, Lee Vail, and neither did Roderick."

"How do you know that?"

Macklin stared at her. "You been acting like you wanted to prove one of them did." It was a funny thing; Ann and Lee had been pretty close and then Lee had got mixed up with old Ben's youngest daughter. . . . Macklin's thoughts ran on and made him uneasy, and Ann kept waiting for his answer.

"Not Lee," Macklin said, "no matter what I was thinking when Rood dragged me into a mess. I was three-fourths drunk but I sobered up in a hurry. Not Lee. He stood up to all three of us, Ann. And then he let a crazy man shoot at him before he was forced to protect himself. He wouldn't kill a man from ambush. I know."

"That isn't very good evidence, Sandy," Ann said calmly.

"It suits me. I'll take it."

Ann nodded. "I see. What makes you say Roderick didn't do it?"

"He was with his wife."

"She hasn't said so."

"Why, hell, she will if anyone asks her. Besides, Roderick don't need to shoot from the dark. If he wanted to kill a man—" Macklin shook his head. There was no way to convince a woman of facts that were clearly beyond her understanding.

"All right," Ann said. "What do we do first?"

Macklin stared across the river at the broad gap in the cliffs where the road came down. "We think it was somebody who was at the dance, so—"

"We think nothing of the sort, Sandy. We're trying to find out without any prejudgment involved."

A cold-blooded way of going at things, Macklin thought. If Ann tried to do everything like that she'd make it hell on the man she married. A calm sort of lass she was, but still Macklin was willing to bet there was a hot temper underneath. She acted like she was depending on him, but Macklin had an unhappy feeling that she was merely using him.

He said, "Tracking is no simple thing, especially when the sign is as old as this. If we don't want to guess where the man came from, then all we can do is try to find out where he went."

Ann nodded. "Into the river, Chauncey said."

They both looked downstream. From here to Island Ford there was no crossing because the cliffs stood hard against the river on both sides. Macklin did not like the looks of the water below the ford and he knew that farther down it was worse. He could not swim, and a good soaking always left his legs aching for a week afterward.

"That's a poor way for a man to go at night," he said. "Now if he went upstream—"

"He could come out only at McLeod's," Ann said. "McLeod is a suspicious man and he has dogs that raise the very devil even in daylight."

Macklin kept staring at the water where it came narrowing back between the cliffs downstream. "No horse ever foaled could live through to Island Ford. He came out somewhere between here and there. You ride the south side on the cliffs—"

"I've ridden both sides already and I found nothing, and before that Chauncey Meeker found nothing." Ann put her red roan into the river, turning downstream to where the water broke into whitecaps.

Macklin muttered a curse under his breath and followed her.

"Take the north side, Sandy!"

Before he had gone a hundred yards Macklin was out of the saddle, clinging to the loops of his lariat. The icy water hammered his breath out in gasps and the whitecaps slapped him across the face and once he thought he was strangling. His horse slanted over to a mud bar under a vertical stand of brown rock a hundred feet high. Macklin scrambled up and stood there shivering.

Across the river Ann had put in against willows at the base of a chimney which ran up toward blue sky. She left her horse belly-deep in the river and climbed into the crevice of the chimney. Her clothes were tight against her body, and the sun put a sheen on them as she turned and shook her head and pointed on downstream.

Wearing a man's clothes and going into a place like this! Good Lord. Macklin worked his toes in his boots. He looked downstream and shuddered and then he forced his horse away from the cliff and set out again. They were into it for fair then and there was no going back. Macklin was dragged through a place where the tug of the boiling current sent fear hard into him. He came out in deep, black water that moved slowly. Here the canyon was so narrow there was no sun.

He did not have to direct the horse. It swam to a sand bar where the water lapped shallowly against another cliff. Macklin staggered out, looking up. The horse shook itself violently, and one of the stirrups bounced off Macklin's hip with a rapping pain that made him curse.

Ann was exploring her side. She walked along a ledge, searching the sides of a cliff that would have given small purchase to a chipmunk. She was overlooking nothing, Macklin thought. She had a stubbornness that was neither from her father nor her mother, some solid determination that was all her own.

Her ledge ran out and there was deep water at her feet. She tried to force her red roan into it and the horse backed away. She signaled Macklin, pointing downstream, and then she mounted and jumped her horse from the ledge. When she hit the water in a shower of sullen spray she left the saddle and swam beside the animal.

For two agonizing hours Macklin fought the river and his fear of drowning. The cold was deep into his bones. His horse was bruised and limping. He wanted to know who had killed Alarid, but it was easy to tell himself that this was a crazy way of trying to find out.

He found twisting passages in the cliffs where dry stream beds came down. They were choked with debris and a horse could not have got up them unless the rider spent an hour or two moving logs and brush. He passed the cascades of Silver Creek. Not far downstream was the place where he and Houghton had seen Alarid's body from the south cliffs. It had taken ropes and five men to get him out of there.

Each turning back into the river became more difficult, but every time Macklin hesitated Ann waved him on downstream. Her horse was limping too. Macklin could not leave her. He wondered how far her stubbornness would take them.

They coursed through a rapid where the bump of rocks staggered the horses and then they came into a great rocky cup where the water swirled in slow eddies. Macklin found no way up on his side. His teeth were rattling and he was rubbing his hands together when Ann called to him.

"Come here, Sandy, and look at this!"

Macklin forced his numbed body back into the water and let his horse tow him across.

"Are you all right, Ann?"

"Of course I am. Look here."

She was on a wide, sloping ledge that ran up to stairsteps of rocks where a small stream came down. The break went clear to the top, steep and twisting, narrowing up there where cottonwoods showed on the rim.

Macklin hauled himself out of the water. Ann was pointing to a place on the ledge that had been scored as if by steel. She walked to the first stairstep. It came against her waist. On it the stones had been chipped and scored as if a well-shod horse had leaped and skidded as it held its feet.

They went up on foot. There were fallen rocks on the ledges and tight-clinging brush that tore at their clothes. After ten minutes Macklin said cautiously, "A horse came up this way all right, but—"

"But what? What other horse could it have been?"

"That first ledge—I don't know how he got up it."

They went back to the river. Their horses were standing close together, weary, dejected. Macklin studied the first step that rose above the sloping rock at the edge of the stream. He shook his head. "He couldn't have let it. No horse can climb like a cat. It's a straight jump."

"He jumped it." Ann mounted. The shoes of her red roan clattered as she turned. She put the horse straight at the first ledge. It balked and swung away. She tried again. A second time the animal refused the leap. "You try it, Sandy."

"Not room enough. I can't make it."

"Someone else did."

"His horse jumped straight up like a cat then. Mine won't."

"Do you have a better horse than Lee Vail?"

"Yes," Macklin said, "but—"

"Put him up there, Sandy."

"He can't— Why'd you ask about Lee Vail's—"

"Try it, I said!"

Macklin scowled. The woman's will lay on him harshly. Some horses, yes; maybe a powerful, elk-legged one like Roderick Vail's, if a man were driven by murder. The ledges were white quartz and there had been starlight that night so that the jump would have been clear enough. He shook his head. "It was done, I've no doubt, but my horse is cold and skinned up—"

"So was the other one. Jump him up there!"

"It will prove nothing, Ann. My God, girl—"

"Do as I say, damn you!"

Macklin met her gaze a moment. He swung up and backed his horse to the edge of the water. There was very little room. He walked the horse to the ledge, then turned and went back to the water and made his run. He felt the animal put everything it had into the leap, a bunching of hindquarters and a surge. The horse crashed short and a foreleg doubled. Macklin heard the snap and it was like the breaking of one of his own bones.

He jumped clear and fell, grinding the skin off his

palms and elbows and knees. He got up white-faced and with a drenching rage he could not speak. His horse had fallen side-wise, its broken leg flopping as it tried to roll and paw up.

Ann's coolness was a stunning slap. "No," she said, "he couldn't make it. I think you were right, it was a better horse than Lee's bay." She weighed something very carefully in her mind and then she looked fully at Macklin as if he were an afterthought. "Are you hurt?"

"No," Macklin said bitterly. He had no pistol. He thought of his pocket knife and the idea revolted him. Sick at his stomach, biting his lips against a green bile taste, he cast around until he found a jagged stone that weighed about fifty pounds.

His horse struggled up to a sitting position with its one good foreleg. It was bowing its head up and down, trying to rise. Macklin walked forward. He raised the stone in both bleeding hands. Ann turned her back.

They piled rocks against the first step until Ann could lead her red roan up the passage. Macklin's wet rig was lashed on the saddle. He was silent while they made the brutal climb out. Stiff brush stubs and clutters of sharp rocks on the ledges ripped the legs of the horse in a dozen places. When they came to the first soil near the top Macklin found faint impressions where the horse before them had made the last lift.

They came out on top and lost the marks on the sod of Teepee's western meadows. Macklin could see the dark pool far below. From here it appeared that no horse could have come up the crooked slot.

Ann got down and walked along the grass. "What happened to the tracks?"

"Somewhere down below he tied gunny sacks around the horse's feet," Macklin said.

"How do you know?"

"What little sign there is ain't clear. It's all smudgy. Your father and me missed it when we came by here the day after Alarid was killed."

"How do you know it was gunny sacks?" Ann asked.

"Canvas, gunny sacks, anything like that." Macklin was curt. He kept thinking of the dead horse down there by the river. He'd been a damned fool to listen to a woman. His legs were aching. He thought of Alarid and the cold stream and how he must have bumped along over the rocks, rolling, turning as the river bore him on. Sandy Macklin was ready to kill somebody.

"You're sure Lee's horse couldn't have made that jump—the horse he rode to the dance, I mean?" Ann watched Macklin intently.

"Damned few horses I know of could make that jump. Why do you keep harping on Lee? Even without the things I learned about him, he couldn't have been at the crossing. He was with Iris and her brother."

"Yes." Ann nodded. "But Tony stopped at McLeod's place that night. For about an hour?"

"That's what Cliff said."

"He's sure it wasn't longer?"

Macklin knew what she was thinking. If Alarid had spent forty minutes longer drinking with McLeod, then Lee Vail would have had time to be at the buggy crossing ahead of him. Her insistence, her suspicious mind deeply angered Macklin. Among other things, she was the same as telling him he was no judge of men.

"Why don't you ask Lee straight out about all this?" Macklin growled. "You rode to warn Lee not to come to town when we were after him. You didn't think he was guilty then. You—"

"I don't think he's guilty now. It's only that I must know beyond any doubt."

Macklin muttered a curse under his breath. God help the man who married Ann Houghton.

"I'll go talk to McLeod now," Ann said.

"Go ahead." It was a long walk back to Diamond, but Macklin was willing to make it just to get away from this driving woman.

"You're coming with me, Sandy. You know McLeod. He might not want to talk readily to me."

"I don't want to walk over there."

"My horse will carry double. We'll leave your saddle here. It can be picked up anytime."

It displeased Macklin to ride double behind a woman. He got down and walked when they came to the patch of level ground under the cliffs where McLeod lived. Four mongrel dogs boiled out to meet them when they approached the house. A little later McLeod stepped out of the brush from the direction of

188

the cliffs where he had his still in a cave. He walked forward with a rifle in his hand, a bitter, alert little man with no welcome in his look.

"What do you want?" he asked.

"I want to know how long Tony Alarid stayed here after the dance," Macklin said.

McLeod considered the question. "Told you once, about an hour."

"You're sure of that?" Ann asked.

McLeod paid her no attention. He spoke directly to Macklin. "Maybe a little less. That all you want?"

"How do you know for sure?" Ann asked.

Dogs jumped clear as McLeod strode into the cabin. He came out with his rifle still in one hand and a clock in the other. He held the clock up, looking at the woman insolently.

Macklin glanced at Ann. She nodded. She seemed satisfied.

"Could you lend me a horse?" Macklin asked. "I'll bring it back tomorrow."

"You came double. Go back the same way. The Houghtons never loaned me nothing."

"To hell with you, Cliff McLeod!" Macklin turned and limped away. A fellow Scot, too, the onery sonofabitch! Macklin wondered how he'd ever got tangled up with him when Bliss Rood framed up to kill Lee Vail in Kebler's saloon. Then, before that, all the silly business at the dance. Just plain damned-fool drunkenness, that's what it was.

Ann rode up beside him. "I saw a stack of gunny

sacks in the lean-to behind McLeod's cabin."

"Where ain't there gunny sacks around a house?" Macklin grunted. McLeod had brought three jugs of whiskey padded in gunny sacks to the dance. Macklin plodded on, refusing to get on the horse as long as he was in sight of the cabin. Anger and a feeling of guilt made him cast up a stray thought that had been bothering him for some time.

"There wasn't anybody out in the trees that night at the dance when old man Rood told Roderick a man wanted to see him. That was me. I put on an old coat we found in the preacher's saddle pack and pulled my hat down. Bliss and the rest of 'em was hiding out, watching."

"What in the world was the idea?"

"I don't know. Bliss thought it up. Said he wanted to see if Roderick had any guts. I could have told him, if I hadn't been so drunk."

Ann showed only passing interest. Her mood had softened. "I'll walk a while, Sandy." She swung down. "Now please don't argue about it." She was asking now, not ordering.

"You satisfied about Lee Vail?"

Ann nodded. She had changed from a determined woman to a beautiful woman. "I had to know in my own way."

It was a strange, unsettling sort of way, Macklin considered. If you had to base your trust in anybody on facts dug out the way they had done this day, then you were in for a lifetime of making things unhappy for people close to you. Macklin's estimate of Lee had come in one sharp moment of intuition, not by hours of getting half drowned and climbing cliffs and losing a good horse and taking insults from a renegade Scot.

Ann's quiet, pleading expression began to confuse Macklin. He tried one more shot. "Roderick Vail's buckskin might have made that jump."

"That's possible, but I'm not interested in Roderick."

She had not been interested at all in who killed Alarid, except to prove to herself that Lee was not the one. The thought made the day a failure for Macklin. He had been used, sure enough.

"I'm awful sorry about your horse, Sandy."

He could see now that she really was.

"Pick out any one you want at Teepees. It's yours. I was crazy to try to make you try that jump. Will you forgive me?"

She was sincere. She was close to tears. It threw all Macklin's thinking out of gear. He guessed she was so much in love with Lee Vail that she had to do things her way. Maybe her way was not as cold-blooded as he had thought. Maybe he just didn't know what a woman would do.

"Forget it," Macklin said. "It was me that tried the jump." Therein lay his philosophy: every man was responsible for his own mistakes. "Anyway, I'm glad you're satisfied about Lee Vail."

"I should have known all the time."

"Well, now you do," Macklin said. "Get up. We can

ride double." He saw how tired Ann was. He thought he saw humility in her bearing too. He must have been all wrong about her.

But by the time they reached the buggy ford and he looked downstream at the racing water, the little sharp points of the day were digging at him and his native simplicity surged up through sentiment. Damn it, if she had trusted Lee at all she should have trusted him all the way. Then too, Macklin could not get it out of his mind that another horse, no matter how good, would never make him forget how he had lost the sorrel. And something else jabbed at him: the whole day's performance hadn't given him any idea about who had killed Tony Alarid.

By the time they reached Teepees, Macklin was a dour man. He decided a woman could throw you off the track quite as easily as whiskey. Maybe he ought to tell Lee Vail a thing or two for his own good; but he knew he wouldn't.

Cal Houghton came rolling down to the corral where Macklin was opening a gate. "What did you find out?"

Macklin told him.

Houghton glared at Ann. "A crazy stunt, going into the canyon!" He looked at the legs of her horse. "The river did that, huh?"

"Some," Ann said. "Most of those cuts came from the climb out."

Houghton's tight little eyes jerked toward Macklin. "Wasn't the Vails, Sandy. Chaunce looked at their horses. If one of them had had its legs chopped up like that, Chaunce would have said something. He never overlooks much."

"I didn't think of that!" Ann was smiling. The last link was in place and she was pleased. Macklin watched her uneasily.

"It's something to go on," Houghton said. "Got any guesses, Sandy?"

Macklin shook his head. Bleakly he watched Ann going toward the house. She didn't give a damn, now that Lee was out of it.

"McLeod?" Houghton said. He cocked his head. "Maybe him and Tony had a quarrel while they were drinking at his place."

Macklin thought about it. McLeod had gone home soon after he sold his last jug at the dance. He was good for a quarrel anytime, with anyone, a murderous affair if he was pushed hard enough. But Macklin shook his head. "McLeod's old crowbait couldn't make that jump down in the canyon. He never owned a horse that could.

Macklin watched Ann run into the house.

CHAPTER TWELVE

HIGH ON Gothic Creek there was a pocket in the rocks where pinion trees grew thickly. It was an off-trail spot, hardly worth the climb to see. Once Cliff McLeod, trapping the wolf and coyote range below the Fossils, had built a lean-to here, although water was two hundred yards below at the creek. Not given to sociability, McLeod preferred to camp where people were unlikely to find him.

Lee Vail and Iris had been meeting here for several months. She was waiting this afternoon when Lee came up the long sweep of land and dropped into the pocket. He was both surprised and pleased, but yet he knew that he had expected to find her. He spent a long moment looking at her as she stood beside a rock, strongly shaped, quiet. She was all woman, but sometimes there was a searching, childish curiosity about her. She wore a brown riding skirt and a shirtwaist that was very white against the light tan of her face.

"Hello," Lee said. He felt self-conscious all at once as he swung down and walked toward her.

"You didn't stay long in the park this time."

"You knew when I'd be here. You can always guess that pretty close."

"Yes," she said, without possessiveness, almost without any shading of meaning at all.

They kissed and the reaction swept through Lee the same as it always did after a separation, a blurring of sharp thoughts, a driving from his mind of things that worried him, a desiring for more. She returned his love-making for a short time and then she drew away, watching him with a puzzled sort of curiosity.

"Somehow, the park isn't what it used to be," Lee said, wondering how the thought had intruded. He sat down on the springy needle mat.

"Did you quarrel with Roderick?"

"No. We never quarrel—up there."

"Oh?"

Lee grinned. "What's the matter, Iris?" He caught her hand and tried to pull her down beside him, but she shifted away and remained standing.

"Nothing is the matter."

She had been at Diamond with Maureen for three days. Lee wondered what they had talked about. Recalling his mother's frankness about a thing or two, he guessed he wouldn't ask. "Come here," he said.

"No, Lee."

"What's the matter?"

"Nothing."

"Well, then?"

She studied him gravely until he grew self-conscious and irritated.

"It's a long ride up here, Iris." Lee knew instantly that he had said the wrong thing. "I didn't mean that like it sounds."

"What did you mean?"

"What's the matter, Iris? You've changed."

"So have you these last few weeks." The hazel eyes kept studying Lee.

"All right," Lee said. "What do you want me to say?"

"That's your business."

Lee got up. "You're talking in circles. Why'd you come up here today at all?"

The longer the question ran unanswered, the more the echoes of it marred the brightness that had been in all former meetings with Iris.

At last Iris said, "I came here to tell you that I'm not coming here any more."

"I see."

"You can come to the ranch or to my brother's place when I'm there."

"You mean from now on everything must be nice and proper?"

There was little change in Iris' expression. She held herself as if she had been fortified well in advance of this moment by acceptance of what might happen. She said, "If that's the only way you can think of saying it—yes."

"Maybe you think I should have proposed a long time ago?"

She had a right to grow angry then, and Lee expected that she would. He saw her eyes darken and he saw some of the color go out of her face, but she spoke calmly. "Did I ever hint at that or try to force you into anything of the sort?"

Lee stared at her, ashamed. He could not say anything right today. She gave him time to answer and then she walked to her horse. The sidesaddle was an awkward rig, but she went up easily, handling herself with graceful strength.

They rode side by side, not speaking, until they came to the last cutting of Joe Emmet's timber where a skid road broke down toward the creek. Iris stopped. "I have to talk to Joe a few minutes." It was clear that she meant alone.

Lee watched from the ridge until she disappeared,

and only only then did it occur to him that she might be playing on jealousy, withdrawing much, promising little, trying to make him unsure. But none of that had been in her manner when she looked squarely at him a few moments before.

Lee stared across old slash piles that led down to the silent mill. He tried to judge exactly what kind of man Emmet was. After a while he went toward home with one more major worry on his mind.

Joe Emmet was doing nothing when he saw Iris coming. For some time he hadn't been worth a damn and he knew it. It was not just that his timber was gone, either; he thought he had lost the will to fight against obstacles that always grew faster than he could overcome them.

About noon he had been on the ridge when he saw Iris heading for the pinions where McLeod used to camp; and then he had seen Lee Vail's bay headed in the same direction. Emmet left the ridge then, driven deep into the savageness of despair.

But still the sight of Iris made him aware of things he had forgotten in the last month. He knew that he was unshaved and that his clothes were more torn and dirtier than he ever allowed them to become. He had even let his shoulders slouch, tired not from work but from his thoughts. He straightened his back. He stood by the mill shed waiting, a tall man with tight curly hair and a heavily boned face that had never known much youth.

Maybe she had quarreled with Vail and broken away from him for good. Emmet had no pride in the matter: he would take her on any terms if she gave him the chance. *Just once,* he thought, *just once something ought to come out right in this stinking world!*

But when Iris came closer he saw there was no hope. Something was tormenting her and behind that was a determination based on an unpleasant thought that made her look at him intently, as if not meeting his gaze might cause a faltering in her purpose.

"I've got to tell you something, Joe."

"I'm here." For an instant Emmet thought she was going to dismount and he stepped forward to help her, but she settled back in the saddle.

"I've misled you, Joe."

"Go on."

"It didn't mean anything, you understand? And you shouldn't let it mean anything to you."

Emmet's mouth tightened in bitter lines. "It's a little late for that, ain't it?"

"Yes, but I had to come and speak the truth."

"Yeah." Emmet nodded. "I can thank you for that, at least." He saw the appeal in the woman's eyes, a waiting as if she wanted him to say he understood and that everything was all right. But a blackness was curling around inside him. He walked to his cabin and went inside and he did not look out until he knew Iris was out of sight.

The grinding feeling of defeat was gone then; he was filled with explosive anger and there was nothing to vent it on, nothing but a distorted vision of Lee Vail. It was so strongly before him that when he heard a horse in the gulch he grabbed his rifle from its pegs on the wall.

Pete Kebler was riding toward the cabin.

Emmet put the rifle back on the wall. He stood a moment looking at his shaking hands before he stepped out to greet Kebler.

The big merchant had seen Iris riding away from the mill. He had, in fact, waited several minutes before coming on. Doing what seemed sensible and right was one thing; pure meddling was another. Kebler was not sure at the moment just what his position was. It was evident that Emmet was in a bad mood for a talk. All the better to find out what was inside him, Kebler thought.

"Pretty busy?" Kebler asked.

"That's a fool question, Pete. Get down."

"It was for a fact." Kebler got down and stretched his legs. He took a long time flexing the saddle kinks out of his heavy body and all the while he was studying Emmet. The man was on the edge of hell. All men must have their moments when they feel that they have failed, or else they have lived lives of smug uselessness. Perhaps Emmet had walked the black vales more often than less sensitive men.

Kebler said, "Just wanted to talk to you about something."

"You're the second one today."

Bitter as gall. Kebler concealed his own thoughts

behind a mask of shrewdness. For some time he had been worried about Emmet and when Kebler worried he tried to do something about it. "Well," he said, "don't just stand there with your bare face hanging down to your belly button. Put on some coffee and then we'll see if we got any business to talk about."

"I don't know what it would be," Emmet said, but he was interested nonetheless.

Pete Kebler guessed that he'd made a fair appraisal: Emmet was a fighter. He was at a very low point now and a lot of stuffing had been knocked out of him, but it might be that a good kick in the tail and some encouragement would start him up once more. It was lucky that Kebler had blundered in at the right time, before someone like Bliss Rood got in his licks.

Iris Meeker was still crying when she approached the ridge from the slanting trail that led east of the mill. She stopped behind a jungle of granite boulders to shake away her tears and dab at her face, and then she went on to the top of the ridge.

She had hoped that Lee would be waiting there; she had half expected that he would. But his horse was raising dust a half mile toward the river. At first, the sight was a dull blow and then she was steadied by it, for it served as full realization of what she had set herself to accept: she could lose him for good. Mrs. Vail had said the same thing when she brought Iris to the understanding that Lee was unsure of himself, that a continued drifting with him in the old pattern might wreck both him and Iris. Maureen Vail had not said a word about right and wrong; she said she was no judge.

Deep within her Iris still believed that she had taken the correct course, but she watched the dust and said, "To hell with you! Go on!" Lee had not seen the beaten look on Emmet's face when Iris spoke bluntly to him; Lee didn't know how much it had hurt Iris. Lee Vail thought *he* had been hurt.

"To hell with you!" Iris said, but it was a thin cry running into an emptiness as big as the land. She was crying again when she rode on. She held her shoulders straight and faced the trail. She was much older than she had been a few hours before. She had learned that even within safe limits, limits sometimes confused with decency, there is no honesty in playing with the emotions of other human beings.

She rebelled at the thought of going home. Her mother was too tired and defeated to help her; old Ben, her father, was helplessness personified. Her brother Chauncey! Chaunce, with his big-jawed face and grave, worried look; he would listen to her and give her comfort, even if she didn't want his advice.

Sandy Macklin was making the rounds of the north-side ranches, asking casual questions, sizing up horses as he went. He had left the Crawford place and was headed to Chauncey Meeker's when he saw Lee coming down the mill road. Macklin swung down through the scrub oak and the two men met in a sandy wash where a few broken boards still lay from the time Joe Emmet had turned over with a load of lumber.

Lee was sore about something. His disposition did not improve when he saw Macklin studying the legs of his horse.

"I've been wondering," Lee said, "why you were asking Art Timmoney and Murdock questions about Roderick's buckskin a couple of days ago."

"I had reasons." Macklin respected Lee but they were not friends yet. "Just to keep things straight, Art and Scott didn't tell me anything."

"What do you want to ask me about my horse?"

"Nothing," Macklin said. "He passes with me, in case I had any doubts."

"That's fine, Sandy." Lee's manner toward Macklin eased. "How's Houghton these days?"

"Same as ever." Macklin remembered that there was something he might say about Houghton's daughter, but it was merely a thought. "How's your mother?"

"Fine, thanks."

"Be seeing you." Macklin rode on. The brief meeting had served to reaffirm his opinion of Lee; he liked the man. Macklin hoped that nothing he found out about Roderick would upset his attitude toward Lee.

A quarter of a mile farther on he was startled when he ran head on into Ann Houghton on a trim claybank. "Well, the whole southside is over here today."

"What do you mean, Sandy?"

"You and me and Lee Vail—"

"Where'd you see Lee?"

"Just a minute ago, on the mill road. Where you been, Ann?"

She was scarcely paying Macklin any attention now. "At Chauncey Meeker's. Papa was right. Chauncey said there were no fresh marks on either Lee's or his father's horse when he and Kebler and the others went to Diamond." She rode around Macklin and went down the trail at a trot.

Once she had been satisfied about Lee, Macklin thought; but she had to make another check after she kept thinking. It took a hell of a lot to convince her. If a man had, to put up with a lifetime of that . . . Macklin shook his head and rode on.

Iris Meeker ran to the door when she heard the horse in the yard. She was unsettled about something, Macklin observed, watching the life in her expression fade as she saw who he was. She turned away and Chauncey came outside. Macklin had a careful look at him. Everybody over here was having trouble today, it appeared. Macklin put several things together and thought he had a picture, and without losing stride from there decided it was strictly none of his business.

"Come on down to the corral," Meeker said. He strode away without looking back, a man showing vast patience in the face of many difficulties. "Houghton's kid was here a while ago. Are you after the same thing?"

Iris' little mare, still saddled, was nosing at the corral bars. Chauncey slid the poles back, slapped the mare inside, and began to unsaddle. "I'll get this much done today, at least," he said.

"Yeah, I'm after the same thing," Macklin said. "Only on a little bigger scale. I ain't stopping when I find out about one or two people."

"That's all she wanted to know, sure enough—just about Lee and Roderick. I'll tell you the same thing, Sandy, the legs of their horses, the two horses they rode away from the dance, wasn't hurt a bit."

"That's good." Macklin looked around the ranch. The way the buildings were set, the solid way everything was put together, pleased his sense of thrift and order. He knew Chauncey was a man to be trusted; the appearance of his place seemed to bear that out. "This horse had skinned legs. He was a powerful horse that could take a pounding from the river and then make a jump up a ledge that"—Macklin looked at Chauncey's meager stock of riding horses—"nothing you got, or this new buckskin of mine, could do."

"So?"

"There ain't many horses in the country like that, Chaunce."

"No." Meeker was wary.

"That big gray of Pete Kebler's."

"Kebler!" Chauncey gave Macklin a startled look. "What are you talking about, man?"

"I'm after a horse, first. Then I'll have a man. I don't care who it is." Macklin was wickedly quiet.

Meeker shook his head. "I don't know your ledge, Sandy. Pete's horse is powerful, sure enough."

"The preacher's stallion."

"Cantonwine? Oh, hell!"

"Big brute of a horse, Chaunce."

"You ain't getting anywhere," Meeker said.

"Jim Dewhurst's blue roan."

"Dewhurst hardly knew Alarid. Jim was one of the first ones to leave that night, with his family."

"I ain't overlooking anybody." Macklin named the owners of three more horses, and Meeker kept shaking his head until he finally came as close to anger as he ever did.

"You're holding pretty tight to this side of the river, Sandy. There's a few big, powerful horses at Teepees."

"I ain't passing them up, either," Macklin said evenly. "Now, you rode out to Diamond with both Kebler and Cantonwine a couple of days after we found Alarid. How about the legs of their horses?"

Meeker opened his mouth and closed it. "I never noticed."

"You noticed the Vails' horses and how their legs was, Chaunce."

"That was a damned sight different! We were all wondering about the Vails' horses, not looking for skinned legs on each other's horses."

Macklin nodded. "I ain't crowding, Chaunce, I'm just trying to take little steps."

The Rood place was closer than any of the others left on Macklin's list. He went there. Bliss was not at home. Cantonwine, who had been staying there, was in Buena Vista, Jeremy's wife said.

Macklin went to town. Kebler was not there. His clerk said he was off on one of his jaunts. It was late then. Macklin rested his horse while he ate, and then he set out for the Dewhurst place. He was a patient man, and he was following an idea. If he couldn't run it to the ground, he would try another. Houghton had told him to go ahead if it took a year. Macklin was prepared to take the year if necessary.

Ann overtook Lee where the short cut started down to Island Ford. She came in with a rush, smiling when she saw the startled look on Lee's face.

Iris had ridden in to Chaunce's place just as Ann was leaving. Iris had been a sight, her eyes red and dust in streaks where tears had run. Ann had found satisfaction in that, but Iris had controlled herself very well, and Ann recognized a straightforward will that might be dangerous. Whatever it was that had upset Iris was a mystery—until Ann met Sandy Macklin.

Lee was on this side of the river. A quarrel, of course! Everybody in the land knew that he and Iris had been meeting somewhere on Gothic Creek . . . together on a hillside . . . like a pair of animals. The place, more than the act, shocked Ann Houghton.

Lee watched her uneasily. "What are you doing over here?" he asked.

Ann thought perhaps she liked him better when he was ungracious. Before, she had considered him too even-tempered, too much under Roderick's dominance, with a streak of cruelty that would have made him impossible to handle when he grew older. She was sure now that the cruelty, at least, had been imagined.

"I ride a lot of places, Lee." Ann was careful not to ask why he was here. She knew he would think about the omission and give her the bitter edge of his glance, wondering how much she knew about him and Iris.

The glance came. She rode beside him, keeping her expression impersonal. Inevitably, he must compare her and Iris, and at the moment Ann's position gave her an advantage. She said casually, "Do you mind if I ride along to the other side?"

"Why should I?" Lee tried immediately to lighten his statement. "I'm glad you came along." He stopped to let her go ahead down the steep trail.

Dust from sliding hoofs came up in clouds. Ann rode with only half her mind on the descent. In some ways Lee was not enough like his father, although she would not have wanted him at all if he had Roderick's quick veering temper, which brought trouble without any apparent gains for the risk involved.

Her vision was far-reaching. She wanted a man who would be, twenty years from now, a power in the state, not merely a comfortably fixed cattleman unknown beyond the boundaries of the Sapinero country. She had plans for herself and her children too. There was no impatience in Ann Houghton. Her mind ran straight ahead down a clear track. She would give as much as she needed to give, wait as long as she had to wait, and work as hard as was necessary to accomplish her aims.

There was pride in knowing that she could look twenty years ahead, when most women of her age did not care to anticipate the future beyond two weeks, from the present moment.

Lee was the man she needed. She could guide him so skillfully that he would not realize it for a long time; and when he did—he was not stupid—he could look behind him and see that her guidance had been good. That he had carried on with Iris meant nothing. He would be easier to handle because of doing so. Someday he would own Diamond and that was a prime consideration. It would be foolish to start with a man who had nothing, when the struggle ahead would be long enough, without the drag of poverty.

She had a tiny moment of panic. He was too cool. She smiled, sending a slow, deliberate glance at the hill they had just come down. "You take things up pretty fast, don't you? I said only that I've always *wanted* to go swimming over there."

"It's a good idea now and then to do something you *want* to do."

Ann revised her judgment of him a trifle; he wouldn't be quite as easy to handle as she had thought. She gave him an oblique look, still smiling. Her horse finished drinking and began to stall. She started across the ford.

They crossed at the upper lance point of the island where the washed sand was deep and warm among the willows. "Someday, I will go swimming here," Ann said. She watched the expression on Lee's face and was satisfied. He was not nearly as cool as he had made out.

On the meadows of the south bank, when it was time for her to turn toward home, she swung down to tinker with a cinch that did not need adjusting. Lee stepped out of the saddle and brushed her hands aside. He looked at the cinch only an instant before he turned to Ann with a steady, appraising look.

"Well?" she said.

He kissed her then, pulling her to him so hard her breath ran short, and the excitement she had been afraid of all the time fumed up in her like the swell of dizziness. Instincts that were no part of her careful planning made her respond fiercely; and then, after a time, the plans, the future, and the goal twenty years away, were nothing but a misty, untroubling dream.

It was Lee who stepped away, drawing a deep breath. "Good Lord," he murmured. "I've wondered—"

"Yes?"

"Nothing," Lee said, but she saw that he was shaken. Mechanically he tightened her cinch. The horse looked around in startled protest.

"So it's nothing?" Ann said gently, smiling.

"No. I didn't mean that. I—"

One instant more, poised toward him as she was, and he would kiss her again and the fire would surge up higher; and that was what Ann wanted too, but an inner caution rose up through her longing, warning her that this was enough for now. She moved quickly to pick up the reins, but even after that she hesitated before going up into the saddle so quickly Lee had little chance to help her.

Now she was above him, removed from something that could drag her ambitions down to a common level of living. But she did not feel safe even then. The clarity of thinking which seldom failed her told her that the danger was in herself. The woman in her rallied smoothly to hide the thought. She smiled at Lee and rode away.

Her horse was grunting, reluctant to keep going because of the too-tight cinch.

She saw Lee ride away slowly. He looked back and she waved at him. After a time she loosened the cinch.

Ann kept rebuilding her plans, but there was a weakness in them now that bothered her. She veered from a mood of thoughtful introspection to self-induced anger. Nothing was quite as sure now as it had been. She had discovered a potent weapon, but it was double-edged.

CHAPTER THIRTEEN

BLASS ROOD holed up in his cabin like a sullen animal. Little jets of uneasiness were prickling him. Sandy Macklin, cold-eyed and stone sober, was up to something. Twice he'd been here and the second time he waited all day to see Cantonwine, still on some business of his own in Buena Vista.

Everything had gone wrong. Roderick was

untouched and Sam Harvey, not even involved yet, was a man to reckon with; and the events surrounding Maxwell's death had proved something Bliss always suspected: Lee Vail was about as tough as his old man.

All the pussyfooting, all the jockeying around. . . . Bliss goddamned the preacher's high-flown plans, although he had none of his own. Worst of all the slow poison of greed was in him. Roderick's hold on Union Park was a fragile thing, merely his own existence and that of Lee and Harvey. Greed warred with fear.

By slow degrees Bliss had committed himself to going ahead until he had a great share of Union Park. It seemed to be his own idea now. But caution held a heavy hand on him. He couldn't forget how Lee had stood against odds. He cursed the fact that his own thinking had run out and that he was dependent on Cantonwine, for Bliss had dark doubts about the man and the night Tony Alarid was killed.

Preacher Cantonwine rode in late that afternoon. Jeremy's wife and the other women came out of the main house to greet him and receive some trifling purchases he had made for them in Buena Vista. With his short arms sticking out from his body Bliss stood in his doorway and watched, glowering. There were people around who thought Cantonwine was a little tin Jesus.

When he had bowed and scraped and made enough pious talk before the women, Cantonwine took his stallion to the corral. Bliss followed. "You took your time, Cantonwine. What have you been doing?"

211

"Is there some kind of rush?"

Bliss studied the forelegs of the stallion. There were scars enough, some old, a few fresh ones. Cantonwine was a hard rider, and sometimes people had seen him surging up through rocks where there was no trail.

"Sandy Macklin has been trailing all over the land. It's got out that he's looking for a big, strong horse with legs that got scarred up the night Alarid was killed." Bliss watched the preacher's deep-set eyes. He could not tell anything.

"Has he had any luck?"

"I don't know." Bliss was suspicious of the man's casual attitude, and yet he took encouragement from it. There had been a puzzling change in Cantonwine. He had taken to wearing a pistol under his waistband. Some kind of assurance had been growing in him. It flashed from his eyes now and then in a wild, uncertain way that made Bliss wonder, but still it was there. The man seemed to be rising above his cravenness.

Bliss said, "I don't know what Macklin's found out."

Cantonwine was taking care of his stallion. "It would be helpful if you could find out something besides rumor, Bliss."

"It ain't rumor! He's been here twice. The last time he waited to see you."

"Did he? Let's go to the cabin."

Bliss wished they had stayed outside. The cabin windows were dirty and there was gloom inside. It seemed to gather most heavily around Cantonwine.

The preacher said, "I have much better plans than before."

"Yeah? Well, the first thing I want to know is—did you kill Alarid?"

"Does the idea make you squeamish?"

"I want to know." Bliss thought of the dark, of that long, deep-slashed face waiting in the willows, staring into the night. Yes, he wanted to know.

"We did," Cantonwine said.

All the implications of the statement threaded slowly through Rood's mind. "You can't get me into it, damn you!"

There was no answer. The gloom seemed to grow more oppressive. Cantonwine was a dark figure, completely still in his chair, but a tenseness seemed to pulse from him. His mouth was partly open, his teeth showed, and his eyes were smoldering. After a time he said, "Who has done the obvious things? Who has talked the loudest against the Vails? You, Brother Rood."

"Don't call me brother!"

"You are, in this," Cantonwine said solemnly.

Bliss could smell his own sour sweat and it was like the foul odor of fear. He could break Cantonwine in two with his hands and he held no high regard for the man's ability to use the pistol he was wearing; but in spite of that he knew Cantonwine was the master and he the servant.

"I have changed my plans," Cantonwine said. "I will break the Vails from within. Then I will handle Roderick myself, and later there will be time to see about the son."

"Alarid was afraid of that sort of thing. I—"

"Be quiet. Listen. I will kill Roderick Vail myself in a fair fight." The same wildness that was in Cantonwine's eyes was in his voice. He spoke as if from madness, saying something that was impossible.

One part of Bliss wanted to laugh but another part of him, more superstition than imagination, made him believe he had heard the truth. His mouth hung open as he stared. "You'd meet Roderick—"

"I!" Cantonwine made the word a ringing pronouncement. "Yes, I!" He drew to his full height. "I have a destiny to fulfill, not only in this narrow place but in a larger sphere, a tremendous future to meet. And you, Bliss, will be my strong right arm in all things!"

Bliss could follow only so far, but there was promise enough in what he grasped.

After a time Cantonwine spoke in a voice that seemed to drop to normal with reluctance. "You've been aware that Mrs. Vail and Sam Harvey are lovers?"

"There's been talk, yes. I—"

"It is so. When I spoke at Maxwell's grave I saw them looking at each other. I can read deep into the souls of people, for I have trained myself—" Cantonwine broke off his wordy flight. "Tomorrow I will leave here. After I have gone tell your father that I went to Diamond to speak to Maureen Vail of her terrible sin."

"My God!" Gramps Rood would spread the story all around in no time, Bliss knew. "You're not really going—"

"I am! I'm going to Diamond to plead with Mrs. Vail to repent, to let me help drive the devil from her. Do as I say, Bliss, and then come to Kebler. I will have more work for you to do. There are men you must go talk to. I will tell you how to gather them to us."

Pete Kebler and Joe Emmet were going into the sawmill business as partners. There was no written agreement and one most important aspect of the plans had been glossed over casually by Kebler. In the back room of the saloon the two men were studying a list of new equipment they would need.

"It's a pile of money," Emmet said doubtfully.

That was better, Kebler thought; Emmet was getting away from his reluctance to have anything to do with the Vails. For two days Kebler had seen the man's spirit rising. He didn't need Iris Meeker, Kebler thought. Machinery and work were enough for Emmet and someday he would realize it.

"I can get the money," Kebler said. The venture was sound enough. "We've got the timber here. We'll build that road on your route to Buena Vista. The way they're booming over there, we'll have a market for the next twenty years. We won't even have to haul. They'll be glad to take delivery right here."

Emmet nodded absently, still poring over the list of

equipment. His failures before had been lack of management. He had always been far more absorbed in the making of his product than in selling it. Kebler was already getting great satisfaction from the plan: it would give Emmet a chance; it would boost the country; and they would both make money. Once the operation was in full swing, Kebler was confident that Emmet would be all right, but there was still a delicately balanced matter of personalities.

They were talking of Emmet's proposed trip to look over a saw rig, when someone entered the saloon. Kebler leaned back in his chair and saw Preacher Cantonwine walking toward the bar.

"Just a drink of water, if you please, Brother Kebler."

"There's a pump outside."

"I thought you wouldn't mind if I rested a moment in here where it's cool. I have a most difficult mission to perform."

Kebler went behind the bar and poured a glass of water. He saw Cantonwine crane to see who was in the back room. Anxious for the preacher to be gone, Kebler waited, reconstructing a pattern of unpleasant thoughts about the man.

Cantonwine smacked his lips over the water. He wiped his mouth and Kebler watched the pulpy way his lips slid along his dusty sleeve. "Brother Kebler, I am about to undertake a mission which I dislike so much I would almost rather leave the ministry than do it, but it is my duty and I must meet it."

He waited for a comment. Kebler watched him with cold dislike.

"The Lord has directed me to speak to Mrs. Vail of her sin with Samuel Harvey. I am on my way there now."

Disbelief, at first, and then a shock of rage ripped through Kebler. His face turned white. "My advice to you is to stay to hell away from Mrs. Vail!"

"Oh?" Cantonwine studied Kebler's expression and he made a filthy thought of what he saw. "You're unusually vehement." He let the thought slide on greasily.

"My advice—"

"Your advice is not the Lord's advice."

Kebler's rage turned to disgust. "You foul sonofabitch. I hope you get killed. I hope Roderick—"

"There is a possibility that I will. But I must do as I am directed. I will overlook your name-calling because I know—" Cantonwine's glittering eyes carried some deep amusement over his unfinished statement.

Kebler did not know when he had let a man get the best of him by unsettling him so deliberately. The strong control of a lifetime leveled Kebler's anger after a few moments. Something had turned over in Cantonwine; he must have fed upon his own fanaticism until it had worked like a powerful stimulant, overcoming his natural cowardliness. It struck Kebler that all his mouthings about religion had never been sincere, but now he was doubly dangerous because the black cunning that had risen in him could still take refuge behind religion.

Cantonwine raised his voice. "Mell Crawford tells me that you and Brother Emmet are going into the sawmill business together."

Kebler was warned then to pitch the man out but he tried to let words take the place of action. "That's none of your business, Cantonwine."

"Where will you cut, I wonder? When I tried to help Brother Emmet, Roderick Vail cursed both of us. Has he changed his mind toward Brother Emmet? Does he feel that because of what his son has done to Emmet—"

Kebler moved swiftly, going around the bar. Cantonwine turned sidewise. He put his hand upon a pistol under his belt, staring with parted lips at Kebler. The saloonman stopped.

He'd use that pistol, Kebler thought. *So help me, the man is suddenly a stranger.*

"I'm wondering if you and Emmet have asked Roderick Vail about his timber," Cantonwine said. He was stronger, more confident than he had been a moment before.

It worked that way, Kebler thought. He had seen it so when an immature man discovered the power of a pistol. But Cantonwine was not a wild youngster. He had brought himself deliberately to this point.

"Have you completed all arrangements with Roderick?" Cantonwine asked. "I'm surprised that Brother Emmet could swallow his pride—"

"Get out!" Kebler said.

Cantonwine looked past Kebler. He smiled and then he left. Emmet was standing in the doorway to the back room, and his face said that all his doubts and the blackness had returned.

"Well," Kebler said, "did you let that get under your hide? You could see how deliberate it was, the same thing he pulled at the dance to make you hate Roderick."

"I saw that, all right," Emmet said slowly. "Have you asked Roderick about the lease? You sort of slid around that question before."

"There hasn't been time to see him yet. Don't worry, I'll get the lease. You don't think I figured to throw money away, do you?"

"No, but—" Old wounds were open again. Joe Emmet was in the same cast-down mood as when Kebler had seen him at the mill right after Iris rode away. "Maybe the whole idea ain't worth Roderick's insults."

"You're thinking of Lee, not Roderick."

"I guess so."

"Make up your mind," Kebler said. "If you haven't got the guts to go ahead, I want to know now."

"I've got the guts," Emmet said. "It's just that a man gets beat down sometimes so he don't give a damn. I'll go on home and give the idea some more thought."

Kebler let him go. You could do so much for a man and then the rest was up to him. Emmet might leave the country now, drift on into other failures. Worse yet, he might fall in with Bliss Rood and become an active enemy of the Vails. Pete Kebler was sure now of who was directing Bliss.

He watched Cantonwine ride away. For the first time, the carbine rocking at the man's left knee did not seem out of place. The big stallion went down the street with a surging stride. There was no doubt that Cantonwine was going to do as he had said. In all matters except the one he was carrying to Maureen Vail, she could handle herself, Kebler was sure. It brought a grinding rage in him to think that she might be defenseless where Cantonwine was going to strike.

I could have killed him, Kebler thought. *I could have got my shotgun from behind the bar . . .* His thoughts left him shaken and astonished. Never in his life had he wanted to kill a man, or even considered the idea.

He started to take a drink. The whiskey touched his lips. He spat and then he hurled the glass across the room.

CHAPTER FOURTEEN

ANN HOUGHTON rode into the twin cabins camp shortly after Roderick and Lee had eaten dinner. Roderick strode outside to help her down. He was gallant and easy in her presence, complimenting her upon her looks, smiling, saying that he was honored by the visit. Lee observed that she was pleased by the attention. Long ago Roderick must have been like that with Maureen. It was a bleak thought that lay in the midst of other difficulties Lee had been mulling over.

He said, "You must be hungry, Ann. What can I fix you?"

"No more than a cup of coffee." The woman gave Lee a long, direct look, then glanced at Roderick.

"All right, all right," Roderick said. "I know a hint when I'm hit across the nose with it." He was grinning when he led Ann's horse toward the corral at the creek.

The moment he was gone Ann's face settled into an intent expression. She walked inside. "Lee, that Cantonwine has made trouble. He's been at your house and talked to your mother about Sam Harvey."

"He did?" Lee's face was quiet, but a rocketing charge of anger whirled in his brain.

"It's all over the country. Gramps Rood was spreading the story even before Cantonwine went to your house, from what I heard."

"You mean the man said in advance he was going to talk to Maureen?"

Ann nodded.

A meddling preacher, Lee thought. He wasted no more anger on the man. It was Maureen he was thinking of now; she needed all the help Lee could bring to bear upon her problem. He said, "I'll go home right away."

"Where's Harvey?"

"The camp on Ballou Creek. Why?"

"I think it's his place to do something about Cantonwine."

Lee shook his head. It was Roderick's business. Since Cantonwine was a preacher, Roderick might do no more than run him out of the country, or at worst give him a beating. Neither act would help Maureen. In fact, any act at all against Cantonwine would serve to increase the talk. There was a foulness in what Cantonwine had done that was beyond Lee's understanding. He started toward the door.

Ann stepped in front of him. "Don't tell your father right now, Lee. Take him home and let your mother talk to him first. Maybe she can cool him down. Anything the Vails do directly against Cantonwine will make an unholy scandal, do you understand?"

"Let's understand one other thing, too." Lee's face was grim. "Maureen is in love with Harvey but that's all there is to it."

"I believe that, Lee, but others won't. They'll talk, and if you or Roderick—"

"You don't think they'd talk if Harvey did something?"

"Of course they will, but it won't be a Vail—" Ann hesitated. "You've killed one man, Lee. I know it wasn't your fault, but you can't afford to do it again."

Lee had no intention of killing another man, but he asked, "Why not?"

"It would ruin both our lives."

She was assuming now that which Lee had hesitated to ask. He had no time to wonder how this had come about, but he accepted the fact at the moment, for it seemed to settle one of his worries.

"Don't let Roderick kill him, either," Ann said.

"I can't control Roderick."

"I think you can. You must!" Ann kissed him, withdrawing her lips quickly. He heard her going toward the corral, and a little later her voice running lightly as she talked to Roderick.

Lee stood in the middle of the room staring out on the trees where men had been hanged. Some things he had grown big enough to handle; the others—like this—he must handle. He stood there trying to draw his plans. Sometime later he heard Ann ride away. Roderick came back to the cabin, still vastly pleased about something.

"What's the matter, Lee? Good Lord! You two didn't fight again? She was pleasant enough a minute—"

"Why has Maureen hated you for years?"

Roderick stared. The red spots started in his cheeks. "What brought that up?"

"Answer me."

"Why, you pup! You—"

"Answer me, Roderick!"

Roderick tried to carry through behind his anger, but his effort broke against the quietness of his son, and Lee saw an inferiority behind the screening outburst.

"She hasn't always hated me," Roderick said. "After she was hurt—"

"She cursed you the day she was hurt. I know now that she's hated you at least since you killed those two men. I've had a little of her side. What's yours?"

"The two of you talked me over, did you. That's a fine thing. That's like—"

"You're no martyr, Roderick. What's been the trouble between you and Maureen?"

"What did *she* say?"

"She didn't tell me." Desperately Lee wanted to find something on his father's side.

"I guess she just never loved me," Roderick said.

"Do you love her?"

"Yes," Roderick answered gently, with a musing expression, as if he were bewildered.

Lee guessed that love could be an abstract, independent force existing apart from little courtesies and considerate acts; in Roderick's case, it must be so. It was all he could find on his father's side.

Lee tried to put his next words gently. "Have you ever admitted to yourself that Maureen is in love with Harvey?"

Roderick nodded. His face was tortured.

"And you let him stay here? In fact, you sent for him in the first place."

"I needed him. I didn't know Maureen loved him until a year or two after he came. He's wanted to leave a dozen times but I talked him into staying. I need him!"

"What for?"

"I've got enemies," Roderick said.

Lee recalled that Maureen had said that Roderick had always depended on Sam Harvey a great deal. The thought confused Lee. It suggested that Roderick had no strength of his own.

"You can trust Sam," Roderick said. "You can trust him in all things, Lee. No matter how he felt toward Maureen—"

"Your trust put an awful weight on him! Your kind of trust must have made a hell out of his life."

"I suppose so. Well, he can go now if he wants to. I can depend on you, Lee. Once I doubted that you had any guts but now I know better. It's better if Sam leaves."

"With Maureen?"

Roderick's face turned white. "She won't! She wouldn't do that to me, Lee!"

Lee found a hollowness in the words. He wondered whether Roderick would suffer more from wounded vanity if Maureen left him than he would from actual loss. Maureen had said that he never needed her. Lee made no judgment either way, distrusting his own ability to think clearly.

There still was one unsettled matter that he had not mentioned. He forgot Ann's advice and stated the facts bluntly. "Cantonwine has been at Diamond, talking to Maureen about Sam. The story is now all over the country."

Expecting the change in Roderick, Lee was still startled. Roderick's evil temper rippled across his face in an instant, contorting his features, twisting his expression into a hellish cast. His cold eyes blazed murder. "Cantonwine! I'll kill him!" He began to rage and curse.

"That will only make it worse."

"I'll kill him, I tell you!"

"He doesn't carry a pistol."

"He did the other day!"

"He's a preacher. You'll turn the whole country against us again. You'll make it so Maureen can't hold up her head. You're not going to do it, Roderick. You can slap him around, run him out of the country, but you can't kill him."

"You're telling me what to do, you whelp?"

"I am. You're not going to kill Cantonwine."

The force of Lee's will was greater than his father's. He saw the bending in Roderick, the reconsideration.

"He's made a fool out of me!" Roderick said.

There it was again: the personal feeling overriding all, the crippling fear of what people were thinking. A man unsure, a man feeling inferior before the world.

"Cantonwine is a meddler," Lee said. "For all we know, he may have thought he was right. In spite of that he has to have *a* lesson, but you can't shoot him."

"Maybe you're right." Roderick clenched one hand, rubbing it with the other. "I'll beat some sense into him. I'll show him how the boar ate the cabbage." He started out. "Let's go."

"I'm not going with you. I'm going home."

Roderick swung around. "You're not going with me?"

"No."

"He might be at the Rood place. I don't trust those Roods."

Lee saw caution in his father, as if Roderick were

weighing the odds. It had been like that before, initial boldness and then a hint of withdrawal before going ahead. It was, Lee guessed, natural that a man who had lived a violent life, who had killed other men, must reach the point where he could trust nothing, where he lived in fear that his string might run out.

"Nobody will mix into it, as long as you're going to do no more than cuff him around," Lee said.

"You won't go with me?"

"No. Wait for him in town. If he had the guts to tell everybody what he was going to do, he'll not be afraid to meet you."

Roderick rode away while Lee was saddling. He swung out southeast, in a direct line toward Kebler.

Two miles from Diamond, Lee met Pete Kebler, who stopped his gray and waited in the trail. "I was hoping you were Roderick," Kebler said. "Is he still up in the park?"

"He headed for town just before I left. I suppose you've heard the story that seems to be going around."

"If it concerns Cantonwine, I have." Kebler's tone had a savage edge. He turned his horse and started back toward Diamond with Lee.

"How'd my mother take it, Pete?"

"I never got out of the saddle when I passed. I was there just long enough to ask where Roderick was."

"You don't gossip or give much advice, do you, Pete?"

"Are you looking for either?"

"I could stand advice."

"I wish I had it then. I don't. This isn't like telling you when it's time to leave town, Lee."

They rode a long way in silence before Kebler said, "I was going to ask Roderick about a timber lease along the south edge of the park."

"For yourself?"

Kebler gave Lee a sharp look. "For Joe Emmet and me. We're figuring on a partnership."

"You can't tinker with people's lives, Pete. It don't work. Emmet won't thank you for—"

"I'm not tinkering," Kebler said. "Emmet's smart enough to see through me. I'm just betting that doing what he's always liked to do means more to him than"—Kebler gave Lee a level look—"Iris Meeker."

"It's a tricky bet."

"I'm trying to give him the chance. He makes up his own mind. I don't consider that tinkering."

Lee was thoughtful. He seemed to be trying to apply the principle to some problem of his own. "You think Emmet would take the lease?"

"I was fairly sure once that he would." There was a rising blade of anger in Kebler's voice. "What do you think of Cantonwine, Lee?"

"A big-mouthed meddler."

"That's all?"

Lee sensed a deeply disturbed current behind Kebler's smooth face. "What else should I think?"

A small spurt of viciousness came out of Kebler. It was unlike him. "He's dangerous as hell, Lee! Men like him have torn up whole societies because there was something dirty and twisted in their thinking. You can't say they're crazy, not exactly, but—" Kebler saw Lee's curious, unbelieving expression. It shamed Kebler; it made a gossip of him and brought sharp realization that he had violated his own code of not making judgment of men before others. He could be wrong about the preacher. The man had put his hand on a pistol and made Kebler back away; and maybe Kebler was carrying more resentment than he knew.

Still, he was reluctant to drop his effort to warn Lee. Then he remembered that Roderick had gone to deal with Cantonwine. Roderick was a match for four men like the preacher. Kebler said no more.

When they crossed the meadows toward the house Kebler started a detour to go directly to the road. "I'll see you, Lee."

Lee called after him. "You and Emmet can have the lease. Give me a day or two."

Kebler waved casually, as if the matter were not of great importance. His gesture covered a great leap of pleasure, not entirely because his objective was in sight, but because Lee Vail had taken stature as a man. Too practical to be sentimental, Kebler still rejoiced when he saw a human being rising strong and sure in the uncertain struggle.

Given the opportunity, Lee would have weighed Cantonwine accurately, Kebler was sure. In spite of Roderick's continual delusions of danger to himself, he probably was taking Cantonwine lightly. Roderick might kill him and never realize how dangerous an enemy he had disposed of. Kebler rode on unhurriedly, heavy with his thinking. Unless Cantonwine was completely unbalanced, which Kebler did not allow, there must be a practical consideration behind his actions. There had to be.

Pete Kebler kept chewing steadily on this premise. Just before he reached the steep drop to the Sapinero he made his conclusions. He paused to look back on the great meadows of Diamond and the rich basin far beyond that was Union Park.

Lee stopped at home with the conviction that there was no way to make an unpleasant subject less painful by trying to creep up to it. He would be blunt. And then he found himself taking more time than usual to unsaddle and care for his horse. He fiddled. At last he forced himself to go into the house.

Maureen Vail had seen him coming, of course. She was cooking. A short-order house, a place to sleep, Lee thought bitterly. Maybe it was too late now to make a home of a place that must have been a prison to Maureen.

He saw no shocking change in his mother's face. She must have taken Cantonwine in her stride; and then it occurred to Lee that the man might have boasted of what he intended to do and then not come here at all.

"How was the park?" Maureen asked.

"Fine," Lee said automatically. "The grass is better than I can remember."

"That's nothing unusual, is it?" Mrs. Vail smiled. "Where's Roderick?"

"Riding around."

"When are you going back?"

"Not for a long time."

The tone of Lee's voice caught all of Mrs. Vail's awareness. She gave him a long look and then he knew that she, too, had been stalling. Tension grew between them, coming from the knowledge that each knew what lay in the other's mind, with both hesitating to speak out.

"Do you want a cup of coffee now, Lee?" Mrs. Vail still tried for casualness, but her voice had tightened. Lee saw the hurt, the numbness.

"What did he say, Maureen?"

"He said he'd come to save me." Mrs. Vail pushed a pan to the side of the cooking surface of the stove. She sat down, staring at a fork in her hand.

"Why didn't you put a rifle on him?"

The woman shook her head slowly. "What he said was true, up to a point." She spoke with detachment, as if she were reviewing her life. "How did you find out, Lee?"

"Ann told me. Before he came here Cantonwine seems to have made a public declaration of his intentions."

Mrs. Vail took the fact as if nothing had the power to hurt her. "I suppose people have been talking for years, anyway."

"It's time to make some changes then."

"That sounds like your father. Do you think you can beat everybody into being still, or scare the timid with a pistol, or—"

"I didn't mean that at all. I mean it's time for you to make a change. Go away with Sam, Maureen. Get a divorce." Lee saw a longing in his mother's expression that hurt him; and then it brought a feeling of pity for Roderick, and anger against himself for being blind so long.

Maureen shook her head.

"Why not? You've wasted your life here!"

"Wasted my life? No, Lee." Mrs. Vail smiled gently. She looked at her son and was happy, and Lee did not understand the sudden change. She asked, "Why didn't you go raging after Cantonwine?"

"It wouldn't have helped you. Go away with Sam, and to hell with the talk."

"No, Lee. The time for that was long ago. Then you were born and I couldn't leave. You remember when I hurt myself? I was actually running away then. I didn't take it as an omen when the horse threw me, although it seemed to be one. Then when Sam came here, I revived the idea of going away with him, but I've managed to put it all out of my head now."

"Have you? It's so strong in your mind that you can't stand to have Sam around any longer. You've made him promise to leave."

"He will and that will be the end of it."

"You're still young. You're a beautiful woman, Maureen. Why won't you—"

"No, Lee."

Lee closed his mouth on his unfinished protest. He stared at his mother. "Isn't Sam all right? Is he too much like Roderick, do you think?"

"Sam is all right. I'm married. I've been married for a long, long time. No matter how much I love Sam Harvey, I'm a married woman."

Lee got up and paced around the room. He was young enough to oversimplify but not too young to understand his mother's deep sincerity. But he still was in rebellion. Circumstances had caught Maureen; there ought to be some way to cut her loose as cleanly as one might slash a strangling rope. And then he remembered that Kebler had refused to give him advice.

If anyone could understand human problems, it was Pete; but he had refused to give advice. Lee felt balked but he would not allow defeat. And yet he knew he was defeated.

"Where did you say Roderick was, Lee?"

"He went to town. I made him promise not to kill Cantonwine."

"Cantonwine wore a pistol when he came here. He was rude enough not to take it off when he came inside."

"Then let him get what he asks for."

"He might kill Roderick."

"Cantonwine?"

"Yes, Cantonwine, or any other man with a will to destroy," Mrs. Vail said. She shook her head. "But Roderick won't let it develop that far, unless you or

Sam are there. Sit down, Lee." She watched his expression carefully. "Roderick has never killed a man in all his life."

Lee sat down.

"He was a carpenter in Granada when I first met him," Mrs. Vail went on. "He was a handsome man, a wonderful builder. He loved the work, and I know that if he had stayed with it he would be a different man today. But one afternoon there the marshal was killed by three men. They ran for their horses behind a building where Roderick was working.

"They knocked him down in their hurry. He had a level in his hands at the time. Roderick broke one of the men's legs before he even got off the ground, and then he got up and hammered the other two into submission. He was standing over them, cursing, when the crowd got there. That same day they made Roderick marshal. He had always been handy with a pistol, just as he was with anything that requires dexterity. He was a good shot. I remember that he had won shooting prizes.

"But overnight he changed. A pistol was no longer a tool for an hour of pleasant target practice. He became arrogant. He built a reputation without shooting a single man. He did have fist fights, a great many of them. They wanted him then in Hays City. That was where I first saw Sam. He was Roderick's deputy. Our first week there he and Roderick had a fight with four cowboys in the Trail's End. Two of the cowboys were killed."

Mrs. Vail's face was almost expressionless. She was sitting straight in her chair, with her hands folded on the table, and her eyes never moved from Lee as she spoke. "The other two were wounded, one of them crippled for life. Roderick provoked the fight without good reason, but it was Sam who had to do most of the dirty work to save them both."

"You're hinting that Roderick was afraid to use his pistol, that he—"

"Let me finish. Roderick became more unsettled all the time. He was quarrelsome. He was continually knocking someone around with his fists. Sam Harvey stayed with him, not entirely because of me. Sam is his friend and friendship between men sometimes goes beyond my understanding. Roderick had built up a reputation, a false power that he knew he could not maintain. He quit suddenly.

"He went back to work as a carpenter, but something had changed in him. He couldn't find any joy in his work. I think his brief taste of glory had ruined him. It wasn't that he wanted to be a killer, not that exactly." Mrs. Vail frowned, searching carefully for words. "I think when he came to the point of killing, the natural goodness in him rebelled at the idea, but afterward he regarded it as failure rather than a virtue.

"Anyway, he had the sense to quit, but that only made things worse because that, in his mind, was another failure. We came out here. I hoped things would be different, and for a while they were. Then Roderick began to use his record to intimidate men.

He never had a single pistol fight because everyone turned away from him. Then he hanged those men in Union Park."

"Cannon Ridgway was in on that too," Lee said.

"Ridgway didn't want to do it. Roderick forced the issue on him. Cannon never had any use for Roderick afterward."

A coldness that was sickening was growing in Lee as he stared at his mother. "Roderick never had a single pistol fight out here?"

Maureen Vail shook her head.

The room was very quiet. Lee wanted to shout a protest that would roll away everything he was thinking. *Three men had come by night to hang Roderick. Two of them had died on the ground and Lee had seen them lying there.*

"He had a pistol in his hand when I saw him!" Lee cried.

"They took him from the house without one. You saw the pistol he picked up when it fell from the hands of one of the men. He did, I think, fire it at the third man who was running away. I think he did that, yes."

Oh, Christ! The crash of a rifle was all Lee could hear from that night. "You had to do it."

"I guess so. Mrs. Ridgway said the same thing. She was the only person besides you I ever told. Sam Harvey has always suspected it."

Lee knew now the reason for Maureen's sleepless nights, her wild rides. The one time she started to run away fate left her helpless with an injured back. Lee knew also why Maureen had cursed Roderick and thrown a rifle at him after she drove Kebler's delegation from the yard; and he knew why Johnny Maxwell was buried where he was.

Maureen Vail had laid the blame for those three graves on Roderick. Still, Lee had his doubts about the total picture Maureen had drawn. From boyhood he had held Roderick as the symbol of a fighting man; no few minutes of talk could kill completely his belief.

"In some way you must have misunderstood him," Lee said. "I know he was ready to fight Kebler and the bunch of them. He was—"

"*You* would have fought them, Lee. Perhaps near the end he would have brought himself to it, but it was you he looked to that day. He's been waiting a long time to find out what's in you. Now he knows you are not like him, and he's happy. He'll try to make you the extension of the man he could not be. He no longer needs Sam."

I can depend on you, Lee. . . . It's better if Sam leaves. And then Roderick had hesitated about going alone to face Cantonwine. The raging temper, the great show of boldness, and then the shrinking away that Lee had always regarded as natural caution. . . . But this time Roderick had gone ahead alone, thinking that it was only a fist fight, against a coward.

"You say Cantonwine was wearing a pistol?"

Mrs. Vail nodded.

A meddling preacher? He had worn a pistol when he came to Diamond before with Kebler and

Houghton and the others; and now Lee recalled the hate in him, the cruelty and cowardice. Preacher Cantonwine began to uncoil before his sharpening consideration. He remembered the man's slyness at the dance, his deliberate baiting of Roderick about Joe Emmet.

Most clearly of all, he recalled Cantonwine's terrible intentness when he studied Roderick's reaction to going outside to meet an unknown man who never existed. Cantonwine had run a test on both Roderick and Lee.

Lee rose quickly.

"No," Mrs. Vail said. "Let him face just once the consequences of his own acts!" She stood up, her eyes blazing. "He's spent a lifetime of making trouble that other people had to settle. He's made a murderer of every person he should have loved, and his regret afterward, if there was any, was never evident.

"If you run to help him now, that will be just what he wants. He'll use you like he always used Sam, to do the dirty things he started and couldn't finish! He's not going to do it to you, Lee!"

Lee said quietly, "Will you go away with Sam?"

"No."

"Then how can you ask *me* to run out on Roderick?"

"You won't be running out, Lee. If Roderick discovers that Cantonwine intends to use a pistol, he'll also find some way to back out of the situation, but it might teach him that he can't use you as he has used Sam."

Lee said, "He might not find out soon enough about Cantonwine." He went outside quickly.

It was incredible that Roderick was what Mrs. Vail said he was. Lee hesitated on the porch. He himself knew small details that pointed to the conclusions Maureen had made, but still he did not want to believe them. He did not doubt his mother's honesty, but yet her own unhappy life must have colored her attitude toward Roderick.

Lee found himself staring at the shed he and his father had re-roofed. The ridge line was hard and straight, there were no sags in the shingled roof, and the rafter ends matched cleanly, running in beautiful alignment.

There was a time when I thought I'd never want to be anything else. I got away from it, that's all.

Lee ran to the corral. He took a buckskin that was a groundeater.

CHAPTER FIFTEEN

SANDY MACKLIN finally got his look at Cantonwine's stallion in Crawford's livery stable. In the semi-gloom the big, lump-jawed blue roan stood stock-still, watching Macklin from the sides of its eyes as he eased into an empty stall next to it. Macklin knelt, peering across a slat at the horse's legs. The light was too dim to tell anything.

He closed his eyes and waited and then he opened them and tried again. He still could not tell much. The scars, if they were there, would be healed by now. Each day of delay had made things tougher; but Macklin had to know. For a while he stood scowling, with one hand on the back of his corded neck, and then he went around a stanchion so quickly the stallion had no chance to kick him as he started in beside it.

It stepped aside readily enough, but something warned Macklin. He leaped back just as the horse threw its weight sidewise in an effort to crush him against the side of the stall. The slats were two-inch planks, and Mell Crawford had put in extra posts especially to contain Cantonwine's horse when the stable was crowded.

The planks and posts shuddered as the stallion crashed against them. *You sonofabitch,* Macklin thought. He went back into the vacant stall and stretched around a stanchion in an effort to untie the short rope on the stallion's halter. His right wrist slid along the cool, smooth top pole of the manger until he touched the knot.

The stallion dipped its head and tried to crush his arm. Its teeth snapped as Macklin jerked back. *Why, you double-dyed sonofabitch,* he thought, still without anger.

After a time he reached through the slats and clamped his thumb and forefinger on hair near the blue roan's shoulder, hauling back in time to keep his arm from being broken when the stallion surged against the stall once more. Macklin put the hair in his shirt pocket and tried to button the flap. The button had been gone for a month. He finally put the hair in his tobacco tin.

He went to the grain room and got an empty bucket, looking up and down the street for a few moments afterward. Mell Crawford was busy in the blacksmith's shop. Bliss Rood and Cantonwine were in the church, the last Macklin had seen of them. In the church. . . . The thought gave Macklin a moment of uneasiness; he might be so far wrong it was pitiful.

He dumped a few handfuls of loose hay into the bucket and went back to the vacant stall beside the stallion. Striking a match on the side of the bucket, he lit the hay and held the bucket around the end stanchion as close to the blue roan's head as he could.

Hell broke loose. The stallion screamed and tried to kick the stall apart. It lunged from side to side, hauling back on its halter rope. The manila proved stronger than Macklin had anticipated. Consequently, the manger was coming apart before the rope finally broke. The blue roan bolted to the front doors, but Macklin had slid them open only far enough to let himself inside. The horse wheeled and ran out the back way into the small corral.

Macklin put the bucket down quickly. Rubbing his blistered palms on his shirt, he searched carefully until he was sure no spark had escaped to cause a fire. Then, using his hat as a hot pad, he took the bucket outside, dumped the feathery residue from the burned hay, and returned the bucket to the grain room.

A hell of a way to treat a horse, he thought; and then he went into the corral to have a look at the stallion's legs in good daylight.

Immediately the blue roan came at him, teeth bared, rearing. Macklin narrowly made it over the top of the corral logs. With tight interest he watched the rippling power of the big horse as it swung back and forth on the other side of the barrier, moving with him as Macklin walked slowly around the corral. All four legs had been raked plenty, but no man could say when and how.

Macklin went back to his own horse. Mrs. Crawford, almost obscured by the tall bushes of her raspberry patch, called to him as he rode along her fence on his way to the street. "Sandy Macklin! I thought it was you over there at the corral. Did you hear about—"

"The preacher's horse broke out of its stall."

"He always does." Mrs. Crawford's plump face peered from under her sunbonnet with a lush interest that had nothing to do with horses. "Did you hear what the preacher said to Maureen Vail?"

Macklin shook his head. Only politeness held him.

"You knew he went to see her?"

"I guess so."

"Well, it seems that she and Sam Harvey have been carrying on all these years, right under Roderick's nose. Crawford says it isn't so, but I've been thinking about—"

"Why didn't you ask Mrs. Vail about it when she was staying here with you, nursing Johnny Maxwell?"

"Why—" The woman glared at Macklin. "You sound like Crawford. The whole lot of you men think a hussy is just fine. A decent woman stays home and works her fingers to the bone, and—"

"Yes, ma'am." Macklin tipped his hat and rode away.

He observed that the door of the church was open. Cantonwine had been staying, off and on, in the lean-to living quarters at the back end of the building. Macklin glanced at the saloon. A few bottles of beer, dripping with the coldness of the water that ran through Kebler's storeroom, would not be bad right now. Macklin licked his lips and rode on.

About two miles from the buggy crossing he met Cliff McLeod and would have passed him without a nod, but McLeod said, "Hold on a minute, Sandy." McLeod had been drinking his own whiskey. His eyes were glittery with the bite of it. "Could have given you a horse the other day, I guess. Must have been sore about something."

"You generally are," Macklin said, and watched McLeod beat his temper down. *Why, the man really had something on his mind, or else he would have cursed and gone on.* It was not whiskey that was loosening him up, either, for whiskey only made McLeod peasant cautious.

"Things could change around here," McLeod said. "Some of us who ain't had nothing all our lives might find a way to do a little better. Did you ever think of that?"

Macklin said, "I don't know what you're talking about."

"Come into town with me. You'll find out. Cab Dewhurst, Billy Rella—quite a bunch of us—might see a way to do all right."

"Bliss Rood, too?" Macklin was more puzzled than interested.

"Him, too. Come on into town, Sandy."

"I been there once today." Macklin rode away.

McLeod called after him hotly, "You're a damned fool, Macklin! You'll see."

Macklin forgot the incident long before he reached the twisting gut of rock that led down to the river where he and Ann Houghton had come up from the Sapinero. Macklin went down on foot, searching the bushes and the jagged lips of rock for horse hair. He went all the way to the river where his dead horse lay festering beside the big pool.

The sight of the horse increased his sense of failure, but he turned and went up the channel again, still stubborn and careful as he made another search. Once more he found nothing. Time. A man never thought of things until it was too late. Morning winds and evening winds had raced through this narrow passage many times since Alarid was killed.

Discouraged but with a terrible patience working in him, Macklin went back to the Teepees. Cal Houghton came tramping out of the house. He had been working on his books and was still wearing steel-rimmed glasses which gave him the appearance of a pudgenosed schoolmaster. "Well?" he asked. When Macklin kept staring at him curiously, Houghton remembered the glasses. He jerked them off and jammed them into his pocket.

"Can't say. I had a look at Cantonwine's stallion. It could make that jump, I know, but—" Macklin rubbed the back of his neck with a blistered hand, wondering for an instant why the movement hurt. "The scars were there. Too old to make anything of now."

Houghton twisted irritably. "We should have used our heads right after we found Tony."

Macklin nodded glumly. Cantonwine's stallion was the last horse on his list. Both Macklin and Houghton had ridden with the preacher two days after Alarid's death; but it was like Chaunce Meeker had said: Who was wondering about the skinned legs of anybody's horse then? "I looked for hair in that hole going down to the river, Cal." Macklin shook his head. "Always four jumps behind."

"What do you think about Cantonwine, Sandy?"

Macklin's eyes set like the still muzzles of two pistols. "Nobody seems to know where he went after the dance."

"Did you talk to him?"

"No. Why would he—"

"Why ain't it," Houghton said. "We don't give a damn about why. What do you want to try next?"

"I figure to ask Bliss Rood some questions."

"Uh-huh. Him and the preacher have got awful thick, sure enough. You try Bliss. I'll take Cantonwine."

"Tonight?"

"Tomorrow will do."

"They're both in town," Macklin said. He looked at his burned hands, flexing them slowly.

"We don't want to jump wild," Houghton said. "We want to be sure."

"You don't have to tell me." Macklin could not forget the sorry mistake he had made about Lee Vail. He did not intend to be that wrong again.

"Tomorrow then." Houghton went inside.

Ann came into the mess shack while Macklin was eating alone. She stood across the table from him, with one foot up on a bench. "How do you like the new horse, Sandy?"

"Pretty good," Macklin said warily. He saw at once some purpose that a smile and clean young beauty could not hide.

Ann looked at the cook and kept looking at him until the man took the hint and walked out. She sat down then, sidewise on a bench, looking across her shoulder at Macklin. "I heard you and my father talking about Cantonwine."

"Did you?"

"Sam Harvey and Roderick Vail can take care of him. It would be much better if Harvey did it alone. Was there much talk in town?"

"I guess," Macklin said. "I wasn't interested."

"I am. Cantonwine will be taken care of. I don't want my father mixed up in it. The facts would become confused."

"Tell Cal then, not me."

"You know better than to say that, Sandy. I don't want the Vails involved and I don't want the Houghtons in either. It would make too much nasty talk. I have enough to contend with as it is. You think perhaps Cantonwine killed Alarid?"

"I didn't say so."

"Don't stall," Ann said crisply. "I wasn't born yesterday. You can find a way to keep my father from running head-long into Cantonwine. I don't care how you mislead him—"

"Even if we think Cantonwine killed Alarid?"

"Yes. Even then."

Macklin saw the same singleness of purpose that had forced him into the upper canyon of the Sapinero. He did not know how to combat it.

"Alarid is dead," Ann said. "He was no real friend of yours, no matter what you think. You owe your loyalty to Diamond, not to a man you can't help. Keep my father from going any farther on this thing. Let it dwindle away. I don't mean to quit suddenly. You can still pretend to make an effort to find who it was that killed Tony.

"I have a future to think about, Sandy. I can't stand to have it entangled with any more scandal than can be avoided. Cantonwine will get his. I'm depending on Harvey for that. You stay out of it because anything you do will reflect back on all of us here."

"I see." Macklin put his fork down slowly. He stared into his plate, too disgusted to look at Ann.

"Of course you see," Ann said gently. "I know how hard you've worked and what a disappointment it must be to give it up, but that's what we must do."

Macklin heard her rise. She leaned across the table and touched his shoulder. "Poor Sandy. Don't take it so hard." He still did not look up. "You need a new saddle to go with that horse I gave you. I noticed your old rig is pretty badly used up."

Buy me with a horse and saddle, Macklin thought bitterly. *The hell she will!* He raised his head and his boiling reaction was in the look he gave her.

She was expecting it. "You've been here since I was little, Sandy. I wish you could stay here always. You want to, don't you?"

She meant it, Macklin thought; in her way she was sincere. But he did not overlook the waiting spear behind the shield of words. He'd always figured to run out his years at Teepees. A man got into a comfortable groove that fit him like the configurations of his saddle after years of use.

Ann could change things for him. Cal might not realize the fact, or admit it if he did, but Macklin knew. Ann's ways were hers. She never met her father head on, but she handled him just the same. Her unholy determination got her what she wanted; and there would be no softness in her if Macklin crossed her.

He stared at his plate again. The weariness of all his riding came down on him at once. Old. You can't make a new start against younger men. The sudden change would be a brutal wrench. But he could go along with Ann and find his way to the sunset pleasantly smoothed. Probably she would never again demand anything of him as bitter as this. Then, too, she'd no doubt be married before too long.

The stubbornness of being right fought with expediency.

With a faint smile on her lips Ann left him.

CHAPTER SIXTEEN

AT THE FOOT of Shurfino Mountain the lonely talus of centuries lay like ice from the breakup of a great river. Here Cantonwine paced the granite while Bliss Rood sat, a sweating lump in the bright sunshine.

"He's probably in town now," Bliss said.

"Let Roderick Vail wait. The waiting will prey upon him. Look out there, Bliss. Look upon it." Cantonwine extended his arm. He could picture himself poised there, a prophet, a man of power and vision. "And all that is but nothing to those with the strength of spirit to act strongly."

The green lands of the Vails, the park that was like a gold mine. The canny side of Bliss told him that it was much more than nothing; but another part of him that had fallen under the spell of Cantonwine began to reach out farther. He looked at the Teepees holdings also, and that was as far, for the moment, as his mind could grasp.

Cantonwine walked back and forth. The urge to

remove his boots was powerful. "How many of our group will be there?"

"McLeod, Billy Rella, Cab Dewhurst, maybe the two drifters I talked to in Arnold Basin."

"They are not to interfere," Cantonwine said. "They are to be witnesses to the fact that all I have told you will be true. Afterward, we will gather them closer to us, but you will be my strong right hand. The day of the dispossessed is coming. What of Emmet? What did he say?"

"He ain't made up his mind yet."

"He will depend on it. My success will bring him to me. He will be another of our band." Studying Rood's expression, Cantonwine was sure that he had broken through the brutish shell and tapped the mysterious springs of belief that make followers of men.

Cantonwine removed his boots. He walked barefooted on the rocks. Bliss watched him curiously for a moment, and then he seemed to find nothing unusual in the act. It was, Cantonwine thought, the final proof that Bliss would follow all the way. His objections had become questions. After the first bold stroke he would be a worshiper.

The time I have wasted talking to the stupid faces of men and women in pews before me, to people who believed that meekness would bring them a reward.

"What if both Harvey and Lee show up?" Bliss asked.

"Harvey cannot do so. He is publicly set against Roderick because I revealed the truth about him and

Roderick's wife. Roderick's great vanity cannot stand the shame of allowing the accused man to do his work, any more than he could let his son face me. No, we will not have to worry about Harvey. If he has not left the country by now, he will do so after I have killed Roderick."

"Why will he?"

"For one thing—can Lee Vail allow his mother's lover to remain here? I think not. But if he does I will speak against their lust, arousing the decent people of the land. Roderick's death will be on them, not me, and it will start the disintegration of the Vails. Only Lee will be left to stand between us and our goal. It is not only land and riches, Bliss, but power that will grow and growl"

Bliss tried to hold to what he could understand, but the preacher's hypnotic voice carried him beyond the immediate to something that was cloudy, mysterious, but nevertheless pleasant. All the roiling discontentment in him had been funneled into a longing to stand big before the world. There was a blazing in his being, a feeling of strength and success already close at hand. The whisper of a last doubt came from him. "Are you sure you can kill Roderick?"

"I can and I will!"

The doubt was gone. Bliss looked up with awe at the gaunt, intense man posed on the rocks.

"None of our band must interfere," Cantonwine said. "I want no unfair advantage, and I must be protected from unfairness too."

"I'll take care of that!" All at once Bliss felt an unreasoning hatred of anyone who might harm Cantonwine, for the man was leading him toward the realization of a dream, the first dream Bliss had ever risen to.

Cantonwine looked across the sun-drenched land. Empires had been built from meaner starts than this. One stroke would make him feared as Roderick had been feared. He would have then the followers he needed, and his power would grow and there was no ending of it in his mind.

There was a tremendous lie in Roderick's life. Hints of it had come in the answers to letters Cantonwine had written from Buena Vista to the places where Roderick had been a marshal. More sure was the hollowness Cantonwine had seen himself when he made a clever test of Roderick's courage at the dance.

Cantonwine's own cowardice, which he had never denied to himself, had been swept under by his emotional upsurge. He was walking on sure ground. His only genuine fear had come when he swam his horse down the river the night he killed Alarid. There was no proof of what he had done that night; there never could be.

"We will go now," he said. "I am ready."

Bliss picked up Cantonwine's boots and knelt to help him put them on.

When the rider stopped at the side door of the saloon, Pete Kebler was busy behind the bar. He could not see outside, so he watched the tightening of expressions on the faces of men who could see through the doorway. Wild young Cab Dewhurst had his look and then he glanced at Billy Rella, a hard-bitten homesteader from the Upper Gothic.

The Gallatin brothers were next to Rella at the bar, lean, bearded men who had been living all summer in an old cabin in Arnold Park, high in the Fossils. Nobody doubted they had good reason for hiding out, and nobody bothered them. But now they were in town. And McLeod was here again, alone at the far end of the bar, beyond Chauncey Meeker and Mell Crawford.

One of the Gallatins murmured, "Cantonwine?"

Looking outside, Rella shook his head.

The scent of trouble carried far, Kebler knew; but this time it had penetrated to strange places. He knew that Dewhurst and Rella and Bliss Rood had been talking to Emmet at the sawmill. There was no telling how Emmet was lined up now.

Sam Harvey came through the side door. His restless eyes covered the room. He spent a sharp moment sizing up the Gallatins. He settled on McLeod with an expression that was like a warning. McLeod stared back, his own expression keen with malice.

"Roderick here, Pete?" Harvey asked.

Kebler pointed to the closed door of his living quarters. He watched Harvey go to it. He was dressed in his best clothes. When the door closed behind him Kebler had a look outside. Harvey's warbag was lashed behind the saddle.

The same Gallatin asked, "Who's the salty old roan?"

"Sam Harvey," Cab Dewhurst said.

"He ain't so old." Rella dragged the last word out with peculiar significance that brought a smile to some of the men at the bar.

Kebler felt his temper sliding up. He looked at the smirk on McLeod's face and had half a mind to throw the man out again, just to see—he told himself—how much unity there was among the irresponsibles.

Harvey walked into Kebler's kitchen and poured himself a cup of coffee. Roderick was sitting at the table, his arms folded, his boots hooked back in the rungs of the chair. He watched Harvey quietly.

When it concerns me, there's never been any fear in him, Harvey thought. *Well, I guess that's the way friendship ought to be.*

Roderick said, "What's the idea of the clothes?"

"I'm leaving. You know damn well I should have a long time ago."

Roderick nodded. "All right."

"*After* the deal with Cantonwine." Harvey saw the relief in Roderick's expression.

"That won't amount to much."

"Shouldn't," Harvey said. He thought of the times he had seen Roderick beat men senseless with his fists and he wondered why the source of such violence always turned to water when the chips were down in a straight-out killing fight. Harvey wasted little time on the thought, for long ago he had accepted Roderick for what he was, understanding without trying to analyze.

"Who told you?" Roderick asked.

"Houghton's girl." Harvey took a drink of coffee. "Lee going to marry her?"

"I'll see to it." Roderick nodded. "Where'll you head, Sam?"

"Montana, I guess." Harvey wondered just how Roderick thought he was going to order Lee's life around.

"Did you go by the house?" Roderick asked.

Harvey shook his head. The two men met each other's thoughts without evasion.

"That was best," Roderick said.

His matter-of-fact attitude broke the calmness in Harvey and left a bitterness because Roderick's trust had been so complacent. "You could have been a damned fool! I hope you know that, Roderick. Three times I've asked her to go away with me."

"I supposed you had." Roderick's craggy face was pale. "But I knew you wouldn't do it without coming to me and telling me; and then, if Maureen wanted to go, I couldn't have stopped her. So I tried not to worry about it, except that I knew I'd failed her."

All Harvey's torment was distilled in his dark eyes. He thought, *It's not my integrity that's trapped me but Roderick's simple trust. Before me, he's never tried to deny his weaknesses and he's always known that I would be there when he got in too deep.* Out of a helplessness came savageness, and Harvey tried to find a mockery in Roderick, the laughter of a man who uses another and regards him as a fool.

Harvey's scrutiny of Roderick was bleak and terrible, for behind it was the rage of a man searching to find if the high faith he had lived up to had been based on deceit. But the falseness Roderick threw against the world, the self-deception he must have used against himself, was not with him now. He stood the probing without flinching, using no defense, merely stating in a look one simple fact: Harvey was the only friend he'd ever had.

The tension went out of Harvey. He leaned back in his chair. His suspicions were gone, but the bitterness still shoveled deep inside him. He got up like a tired man.

"So long, Roderick. I guess there's no need to wait on this Cantonwine thing."

"It's nothing. So long, Sam."

There was a moment when the bond that had been a life-long force between them, built on need and faith, cried out for more than this casual parting.

Harvey hesitated and then he went out, closing the door quietly, putting behind him forever that which he had known and that which he could never have.

He stopped at the bar for a drink, once more making a swift inspection of the men in the room. Long practice in reading the general temper of a group served to warn him there was something more in the wind than a fist fight. Kebler set out a bottle and glass. He said nothing, but there was a tiny hitch in his expression as he looked at Harvey's clothes and then squarely into his eyes for an instant.

Harvey took the drink. "I'll see you sometime, Pete," he said, and started toward the side door. Just before he went out he turned his head quickly. All the men along the bar were watching him. A tingling feeling of unease was still with Harvey when he mounted.

He rode slowly up the street. All the tiny reflexes from a day when threat was probable around any corner that he turned, inside any doorway that he entered, were working in his system now. He had come here to say so long to Roderick, to stand behind him one last time; and so he might as well see out the hand. It would be Lee's job thereafter. Maybe Lee could handle things in a different way, in a better way.

Harvey turned his horse toward the livery stable behind the Crawford house, and it was then he saw Joe Emmet riding in at the head of the street. Another one to wait like the bunch in the saloon?

Crawford's handyman was hammering away in the blacksmith's shop, making loud sounds on a quiet, waiting day.

Lee Vail came into town on the long-striding buckskin that was a brother to Roderick's favorite mount. The quietness of the place made him wonder if he had worried needlessly; and it reminded him of the afternoon when he and Roderick had ridden to the church grove and started the grinding of events which had led to this day.

He went through the side door of the saloon. The drinkers at the bar threw their hard interest at him immediately. There seemed to be another pattern here like the shifting under-layers of preliminary moves the night Johnny Maxwell had come bursting in, covered with filth and out of his head.

The feeling caught in Lee and made him wary and cold with apprehension. At the far end of the bar Chauncey Meeker raised his head and gave Lee a troubled look, either a warning or an appeal.

Pete Kebler pointed toward the back rooms. "Roderick's in there."

Before Lee closed the door behind him he heard someone say, "That's the boy," and someone else asked, "How many does it take?"

Roderick was sitting in the kitchen, with his feet jammed under the table and against the wall. There was a half-filled coffee cup clear out of his reach. He looked up at Lee and grinned. "You, too!"

"Who else do you mean?"

"Sam. He just left. For good."

"How'd he find out?"

"Ann."

I think it's Harvey's place to do something about Cantonwine, she had said. There was a strong desire in Ann to have her way. The thought threw Lee completely off track for a moment.

"Did you see the bunch at the bar?" Lee asked. "Two strangers, McLeod, Rella—"

"Coyotes," Roderick said. "They drifted in to see

the fun." He stared at Lee. "Still, they could get ideas. I'll depend on you there, Lee."

"You know Cantonwine's been wearing a pistol?"

"He won't come at me with it."

"Won't he? Maureen said he didn't take it off when he came inside to talk to her." Lee watched the blotches run on Roderick's cheeks. He listened to his father curse Cantonwine until the anger ran out and left tight speculation.

"Suppose he comes at you with a pistol?" Lee asked.

"Damn the man! He's surrounded me with enemies. He'll have Bliss Rood with him, sure as hell. We'd both better step out when the time comes."

"I'll be here," Lee said. "Pete and Chaunce Meeker are here, but Cantonwine is your problem."

"He won't have a pistol. I know he won't. I pushed him around in the grove. I slapped his face at the dance that night. He's yellow, Lee. He'll want to talk. He won't be looking for a pistol fight."

Lee's voice bore down ruthlessly. "I think he will." He walked out to the door that opened into the saloon. He opened it and stood there waiting to catch Kebler's attention. Joe Emmet was at the bar now, and Lee heard him say, "I don't know where you got the idea Harvey left town. I saw him taking his horse into the livery stable when I came down the street."

A moment later Kebler noticed Lee, who said, "Will you bring us a bottle, Pete." Kebler nodded. Lee closed the door and walked back into the kitchen.

Roderick was on his feet: "Well," he said, smiling, "Sam didn't leave, after all. Go get him, Lee."

"Why?"

"I want to talk to him."

"You already have."

"What's the matter with you, Lee?"

"This is one time you're getting along without Sam. You don't need him. You don't need me either."

"You traitorous damned whelp! I thought—"

Kebler came in with a bottle and glasses. He put them on the table and gave no indication that he had heard anything.

Lee said, "Pete, Cantonwine has been rigging trouble three ways from the ace. What do you think happened to Alarid?"

"I don't know," Kebler said. "Houghton and Sandy Macklin would damned well like to find out."

"Yeah," Lee said. "So would I. That deal almost ruined the Vails. It looks like another try coming up."

"Seems to be," Kebler agreed.

"Breaking Harvey away, leveling down for Roderick, drawing those no-accounts into town. . . . What's he want, Pete, Union Park and everything that goes with it?"

Kebler frowned. "It's reasonable, but it wouldn't stop there. Cantonwine scares me, Lee. I told you men like him have wrecked whole societies—"

"He doesn't scare me a damned bit!" Roderick said. "You two are talking trash."

Both Lee and Kebler ignored him.

"Would it work?" Lee asked.

Kebler nodded. "Take a cold-blooded look at it. Your hold on the park is pretty thin. Ninety per cent of it has always been Roderick. What worries me most is he hasn't got the ghost of a chance to get Roderick in a fair fight, and I don't think the gang in the saloon is ready to jump—not yet, so what's he got in mind? He's got something up his sleeve or he wouldn't be making his play."

Lee was silent. All at once the situation was worse than he had thought. For all his shrewdness, Kebler still believed that Roderick was a deadly pistolman, and yet Kebler was taking a grim view.

"Will he fight?" Lee asked.

"I started to throw him out a few days ago," Kebler said. "He made me change my mind."

"Is he crazy?" Lee asked.

Kebler shook his head. "I've been crazier at times than he is. I laid out a townsite here for ten thousand people and was sure we'd have them, too. Cantonwine has his plans, too, but the difference is—he might make them work." He glanced at Roderick. "If he lived long enough."

"He drew a pistol on you?" Roderick asked.

"He would have. I—" Kebler saw something in Roderick's look that startled him— "I backed up."

Lee's face was grave. He watched Kebler studying Roderick and he knew the saloonman was seeing something and hardly able to believe it. For once Kebler could not make the smooth planes of his face hide his thoughts, and so he tried to do it with talk. "I guess there's enough of us here to see that no one interferes. I've talked to Chaunce. Mell Crawford will go so far with us. Harvey's still here. Emmet— I don't know about Emmet yet, but I'm betting on him."

Kebler's tongue was smooth, but what he was seeing in Roderick was all over his face; for Roderick Vail, at this moment, was a man shocked numb by fear.

"All right," Lee said. "Thanks, Pete."

Kebler went out.

"Go get Sam," Roderick said.

"No."

"They're boxing us in, I tell you!"

"We'll be all right." Through a window Lee saw Houghton and Ann riding in on the southeast road. This was becoming a Roman holiday, he thought. Roderick pushed the bottle of whiskey aside and sat down on the edge of the table, staring at the floor.

"How about that timber lease for Emmet?" Lee asked.

Roderick heard the question but it made no impression on him for a moment. "Oh, that," he said vaguely.

"I'm giving it to him," Lee said. "Him and Pete."

Roderick nodded. He was staring at the floor again.

"I'll tell them now," Lee said. "And then I'm going to find Harvey and talk to him. I'll be back."

Roderick's head jerked up. "Tell Sam to hurry."

"I'm not sending him back here." Lee saw his father slump once more. It was not cowardice; it could not be, Lee thought. But there was no doubting that Roderick had come apart, and Lee knew that he had forced it.

In the saloon, Lee walked straight to Emmet. The man eyed him somberly. "Anytime you're ready, Joe, put your set in Union Park."

The bitterness and anger that Emmet had held to use against this moment showed in his eyes. There was a long moment when he seemed on the verge of hurling it at Lee, but at length he said, "What are you trying to buy?"

Lee shook his head. "If you take it that way, you're wrong. I'm not trying to buy anything from anyone in this room." He looked down the bar, man by man, until his glance touched Cliff McLeod.

"How are you, boys?" Lee did not expect an answer and none came. Meeker and Mell Crawford and two other neutrals who had joined them at the bar and near McLeod knew the greeting was not for them. Lee walked out. Let them chew on his civility now, work their minds around it. Some would think it was a warning; they would have to wonder in their various ways. But he knew he had seen a careful respect in all of them.

That much was good, but it was not very much at all. He went to find Sam Harvey.

Sitting just inside the doorway of Crawford's livery stable on an upturned bucket, from where he had been watching the street, Harvey looked up at Lee and said, "Yes, I started to leave. I changed my mind. Habit, I guess."

"It's been a bad habit, Sam. He was always ready to try again because he knew you'd be with him. He's in Pete's kitchen now, whimpering for you."

Harvey's face stiffened. "No, Lee, it isn't that. I don't know what it is. He's got all kinds of guts for some things, but—"

"I talked to Kebler right before him, and we showed him he stood to lose the park and everything else, but he still can't bring himself to face Cantonwine."

"It's a pistol fight then?"

"Yes!"

"I know what he feels like," Harvey said. He started to rise.

"No, you don't," Lee said. "You've carried him far enough, and I'm not taking over the job."

Harvey settled back on the bucket. Still as brown rock, his face looked up at Lee. "You know what'll happen to him?"

"Maybe not."

"Your father, Lee. You can't do that."

"He made your life hell, Sam, and he made hell for Maureen. She killed two men because of him, and maybe it was because you had always been there to haul him out of every jam he got into!"

Harvey got up slowly. .

"I hold you responsible for not taking Maureen away from him a long time ago," Lee said.

Harvey shook his head. "Start again, and see if you want to say the same thing."

Lee let his breath out in a long sigh. "You're right,

I'm running wild. But I'm right about Roderick. He gets no help from us, except that we'll see nobody cuts in from the side when it starts."

"He can't do it, Lee!"

"He'll have to. If I step in, I've taken on your job for the rest of my life."

Harvey's words fell gravely. "He's a crack shot. He's fast on the draw. Whatever stopped him beyond that I don't know; but suppose he ever went through the barrier. You'd have something on your hands then, Lee, much worse than a man who is afraid to kill. Every time I had to take on one of his fights, I thought about that. Maybe I used the idea to help justify what I did. I don't know. It's hard to say now."

"Was he honest with you, Sam? Did he ever admit that he—"

"Yes," Harvey said. "He called it lack of guts." He shook his head. "It isn't that, Lee."

Lee pushed his hat back and wiped his forehead with his sleeve. It was stifling hot. He pulled his sticky shirt away from his body. Every way he tried to approach his problems, they grew worse. He thought of something then and clung to it, hopefully trying to build it up: maybe Cantonwine wouldn't show up. What real proof was there that he had penetrated Roderick's myth? Even Kebler had been fooled until a short time ago.

Why sure, it was possible that Cantonwine was high-tailing it across the Fossils at the moment.

"There's our man," Harvey said quietly.

Cantonwine and Bliss Rood were dismounting on the shady side of the church. Cantonwine paced slowly around to the front, looking down the street. Tall and spectral in his rusty black clothes, he stood a few moments on the church steps before he went inside.

"Where's he wear his pistol?" Harvey murmured.

"Waistband, last I saw."

"Don't think it can't be used from there."

Hammering in the blacksmith's shop ceased. The sounds seemed to hang on with measured beat even after Lee saw Crawford's helper running toward the saloon. Chaunce Meeker trotted up the street on a long-legged dun. He rode to the church and went inside.

His lips tight, Harvey watched Meeker all the way, and then he gave his head a slight shake. "Too late for talk." He turned to Lee, waiting.

"I'll go back to the saloon," Lee said. "If Roderick has changed his mind—" He and Harvey looked steadily at each other, both knowing where the truth lay.

At last Harvey said, "I guess it's my job, like Ann said. It won't bother me too much, Lee. I'm leaving. You have to stay here."

Lee shook his head. "One Vail or the other." This was his last pretense before Harvey that Roderick could be considered as a factor in the settlement. "You'll keep an eye on Bliss?"

"Him and all the rest, if need be."

"All right."

"Look at your pistol now," Harvey said. "Then forget it."

"I wish I could forget the whole miserable business," Lee said bitterly. He checked his pistol. He went toward the saloon.

Ann intercepted him at Mrs. Crawford's front gate. She made no pretense of concealing her anger. "You said you weren't coming here."

"I changed my mind."

"You promised to let Harvey handle this!"

"I don't remember that I did," Lee said. She might be right, but he could not remember. He glanced toward the church.

"You promised to take Roderick home, to let your mother talk to him—and now you're both here."

Anger gave the woman's lips a thinness Lee had never observed before. Later maybe he could explain; now there was no time. "I'll see you later, Ann." He walked around her.

"Where's Sandy Macklin?" she demanded.

"I haven't seen him." When Lee glanced back, Ann was almost running toward the livery stable where Harvey stood.

Talk in the saloon ended suddenly when Lee walked in. He found Roderick standing at a window in the kitchen, looking south toward the Broken Diamond.

"He's here," Lee said.

"Kebler told me." Roderick did not turn around. "Where's Sam?"

"He's gone. It's your play, Roderick."

"All right." Roderick turned slowly. His face shocked Lee. His lips had loosened, his eyes were staring as if they had already seen and accepted death. "Sure," he said, "it's my play." He seemed to gather confidence from his own voice. He started across the room and he brought his features under control, step by step, until at the door to the barroom he was the man Lee had thought him to be long ago.

Roderick reached toward the doorknob. His hand hesitated. It fell back and he stood there staring into the panels. He turned and his face was worse than before because all the terror of a lifetime was smeared across it.

His steps were uncertain as he returned to the kitchen and sat down. "A preacher," he muttered. "I can't kill a preacher, Lee, no matter what he's said. You go talk to him and see—"

Someone rapped on the door. Chaunce Meeker came in, a curiously outraged expression on his long face. "I can't get anywhere with Cantonwine," he said. "He's set to go through with it. Bliss Rood drew a pistol on me. He—"

"What are you trying to say?" Lee asked.

"I'm saying the whole thing is idiotic! What kind of a reputation are we going to have over here if a preacher gets killed? Sure, he shot his mouth off, but I don't see that he has to be killed because of that. I thought if I could take word back to him that Roderick is willing to let him go—I've got the board together and we've already fired him as our minister—then maybe he'd be willing to call it quits."

"No!" Roderick said. "We're not backing away."

"But—" Meeker turned to Lee, who watched him quickly for an instant and then shook his head.

"I still say it's senseless. I—" Looking from Lee to Roderick, Meeker saw something he did not understand. "Then it's no?"

"Damned right!" Roderick said. "He started it."

Meeker went out.

Sick at heart, Lee studied his father. Before death itself Roderick could not drop his false pride. Only with Sam Harvey had he ever been honest. Even now he could not meet Lee on a forthright basis.

If I go ahead with this, Lee thought, *I'll be doing it over and over as long as he lives.*

Kebler called through the doorway. "He's coming down the street, Lee."

Lee! Kebler knew the truth. Roderick's face said, *I can depend on you, Lee.* Facts compressed against Lee like the cold jaws of a trap, and he wanted to rage against circumstance and injustice. But he knew that the job was his. Roderick could not do it and Lee could not escape it.

At the door Lee turned to look at his father. Roderick's arrogance was returning. He was safe. Another Sam Harvey was bound to him, this time by a kinship that could not be denied.

"Remember what I've taught you," Roderick said. "You're more than a match for him. I'll be behind you, boy."

Lee could look no longer. He stared at the door and he saw the dreary pattern of his life stretched out before him. Acceptance was not of this moment; he must have accepted it, he thought, when he rode from Diamond after talking to Maureen. Everything in between then and now had been futile effort.

He walked out. Kebler was waiting, carrying a shotgun. The saloon was already empty.

Sandy Macklin came into town by way of the tall cottonwoods on the creek, leaving Teepees a half hour before he and Houghton were to have ridden away together. He left his horse in the trees and went to the lean-to living quarters at the back end of the church. No one was there.

He dropped back into the trees and crossed above the end of the street, working down to Crawford's livery stable, arriving soon after Lee returned to the saloon. Harvey, at the front of the building, heard him enter the back way. At once Harvey spun out of sight behind one of the heavy sliding doors.

"Me! Macklin!" the Teepees rider said. He went down the line of stalls. Cantonwine's horse was not here. Harvey did not put his pistol away until he had a good look at Macklin's face.

"Have you seen Cantonwine?" Macklin asked.

Harvey nodded toward the church.

"I'll be damned," Macklin muttered, looking at two horses that had not been beside the church when he was there. "Maybe I'm too late." The thought made him savage. He watched Bliss Rood ride away from the church and disappear behind the trees on the east side of the street. Before long he heard the sounds of the hoofs and then Bliss came into view, his horse trotting directly toward the livery.

"Where's Roderick?" Macklin asked Harvey.

"In Kebler's."

It was a long pistol shot to the street from here, to where the two might meet, Macklin guessed. Bliss was coming to neutralize Harvey, and that made time brutally short. Macklin drew his pistol. "Don't move a hair, Sam."

Bliss came up while Harvey was staring bitterly at Macklin. "This one won't bother us any," Macklin said. "What do we do with him?" He could not risk a glance at Rood.

There was a sullen moment of doubt when Macklin thought it was no good, and then Bliss said, "So you listened to McLeod, huh?"

"He talked to me." Macklin watched Harvey until he heard Bliss reach the ground. The Teepees rider swung then and put the pistol on Bliss. "And now," Macklin said, "I want to talk to you."

A piggish hatred settled on Rood's features, the expression of a man who has been tricked. He glanced toward the church, as if his failure had been noted there.

"Who killed Tony Alarid?" Macklin asked.

The hint of something Macklin had searched long to find lived just an instant in Rood's eyes, and then

Bliss shook his head. From the corner of his eye Macklin saw a drift of smoke from the pipe of the blacksmith's shop. He marched Rood to the doorway and there the man hesitated. Macklin grabbed his pistol. Bliss wheeled, driving his right elbow in an arc, but Macklin had stepped clear. He struck Bliss between the eyes with the pistol, harder than he meant to.

The blow should have dropped him like a poleaxed hog. It served to drive Bliss into the doorway. He spread his arms and held himself upright, dazed. Macklin kicked him in the groin. Bliss started to double over, and Macklin struck him again with the pistol, driving him through the doorway.

Bliss staggered against the horn of the anvil and fell sidewise into a rack of angle iron. He rolled to the floor and lay there, too hurt to rise. Macklin watched him narrowly for a moment. He holstered his own pistol and pitched the other one outside.

Smoke was still drizzling from the forge. Leaning against the anvil block was a wagon-box brace that the smith had been welding when he saw Cantonwine and Bliss ride into town. Macklin put the brace back into the fire and began to pump the bellows. Bliss groaned, drawing back his legs. His eyes were alive and wicked.

A quick glance at the street told Macklin it was still empty. He sweated as he wrestled the anvil block, lowering it until both block and anvil lay across Rood's legs, and then he pumped the bellows again.

The brace had been welding-hot not long before. It began to take on a dull cherry color.

Bliss raised himself enough to look at the weight on his legs. Blood was running down his forehead. "What are you going to do?" he mumbled.

"Who killed Alarid?"

"I don't know." Bliss fell back, rolling his wrist across his head.

Macklin tried to lift the brace from the fire with tongs, but the iron twisted in his grip. He grabbed the blacksmith's leather apron from a nail on the sooty wall and wrapped his hands in that. The brace came from the fire dripping red-hot cinders, jetting little white, hissing rockets of flame.

"Who killed Alarid?" he asked, and stepped across Bliss, holding the fiery metal toward his belly.

"I don't know!" Rood's voice was hoarse and quavering.

"Who did it?"

Bliss put out his hands as if to grab the brace.

"Grab it," Macklin said. "I'll yank it away and your palms will come with it. It's going into your belly, Bliss, in there where it's wet and warm."

"Jesus, no!"

"Who killed Alarid?" Macklin lowered the metal until the acrid odor of burning wool filled the room.

"He did it! Cantonwine!"

"You're sure?"

"He told me so! He swam his horse down the river afterward and went up a narrow cut."

Macklin threw the brace into the forge. He leaped outside, almost colliding with Mrs. Crawford. She gave him a look of unabashed horror, but she was not too repelled to peer inside the shop.

Harvey looked at Macklin and nodded. Cantonwine was stalking down the street. A group of men had come from the saloon and were stringing out on the west side of the street, close to the ditch.

Roderick Vail was not in sight.

Macklin wiped his sweaty hands on his trousers. He pulled his hat down tight and began to walk.

In measured strides Cantonwine came pacing to fulfil his destiny. It was a long way from the church to the saloon, but he chose to walk it and he savored every step, for all around him was a great song that rose to frenzy, and he was the center of creation, a cold, hard instrument that could not fail.

Doubts and fears were all behind him; he had fed upon his ego until he had risen above the dragging little anxieties that hamper all mankind. He could not be tired, he could not be afraid. Soon this would be over, the first sharp stroke that would open the way to a limitless field of operation.

He had kicked his boots off inside the church. His toes were long and spatulate, brown from exposure to the sun. Deliberately he set his feet against the dust, against the earth that he was master of. His immediate goal was a miserable building down the street. A craven man would come forth from it to be hurled from life as quickly as if he had never existed.

Cantonwine saw the heads of waiting men turned his way, and then they turned to look at the saloon. He was striding on like an avenger. Roderick must be cowering inside, trying to gird his vanity and pride around him to make it serve as courage.

Three men came from the saloon, Lee in front, behind him Kebler, and last, Roderick. Kebler swung away, facing the line of men near the ditch. Soon Lee would do the same, leaving Roderick alone to come ahead, or stand and wait. It pleased Cantonwine to think he would do the last.

Instead, Roderick moved aside to join Kebler. Lee Vail came up the street. Annoyance touched Cantonwine's strong flowing feeling of superiority. They were trying to upset him. Lee would stop in a moment, stand aside. But he did not do so; he kept coming, and then Cantonwine realized at last it was Lee he must face.

With the realization his annoyance passed; he was geared too finely to his purpose to swerve aside. because of minor changes in the program. Why, it was even better to kill Lee Vail than his father.

On Cantonwine's right a voice called his name. That was another minor irritation. Someone was trying to disrupt his purpose, but it would not work. Bliss Rood was on the right somewhere, and Bliss could cover irritations there.

"Hold it, you sonofabitch." The voice was too sure and deadly to be ignored.

Cantonwine spared a glance. Sandy Macklin was

275

standing across the ditch, a dusty, nondescript man who counted nothing in the lay of affairs.

Cantonwine upbraided himself for bothering to look at the man. "I will have time to speak to you later, Brother Macklin." Cantonwine walked on.

"Don't take another step."

Once more Cantonwine stopped. The annoyance had to be considered. Bliss, damn him, should not have allowed this to happen. "What is it, Macklin? Be quick."

"You killed Alarid. Bliss just told me. Sam Harvey heard him say so, and so did Mrs. Crawford. You killed Tony."

"I'm afraid you've heard a terrible lie." Cantonwine glanced down the street. Lee was motionless. Bliss, the lumpish brute! Cantonwine felt the curse of betrayal, but one failure must not ruin his plans. The fanaticism that had driven his will this far overswept his feeling of shock. All things were still simple and clear.

This unexpected intrusion had to be taken in stride. He must kill Macklin and then go on the few more paces that were necessary and do the same to Lee Vail.

Sandy Macklin waited, a lean man past middle age, a weathered brown man with a streak of soot on his forehead.

A simple, meddling fellow, Cantonwine thought, mere grit in the certain gearing of the plan. Cantonwine drew his pistol with astonishing speed. He was quite sure of himself when he fired.

He reeled back from a blow. He felt no pain, but there suddenly was no strength in his body. It was incredible that this could happen to him. His pistol would not obey him. He felt it tipping, falling from his hand. The great song around him ended with a crash and then a terrible stillness was everywhere.

He no longer owned the world. He was a miserable man on the long street of an unknown town. He wanted to turn and walk to the blessed peace of the church, at his back, to see again faces looking up at him as he preached. No shred of dream or dignity was left to him in the brief time he stared at a quiet brown face.

This was but a flicking instant before Macklin fired two more times. Afraid, alone, and knowing it, Cantonwine went down into the warm dust.

Down the street the complete disorganization that follows violence held men stunned for a moment. Kebler recovered first. Cradling his shotgun, he looked at Rella, at Dewhurst, at the Gallatins. "Let's say this winds it up." He saw something run out of the expressions of those he meant his words for. They were only spectators now; whatever Cantonwine had held out to them was gone.

Roderick's voice was loud, "Anybody here who wants to say it wasn't fair?" He was himself again. He looked at Houghton. "I say he got what he deserved, don't you, Cal?"

Starting up the street, Houghton glanced back at Roderick, but he did not bother to answer the question.

In a few moments there were only two men left near Lee, Kebler and Emmet. The full weight of Kebler's character lay in the look he gave Lee. "You'll find a way to handle him, Lee. I'll bet on it."

Emmet said, "We decided to take the lease. I was the one that was holding things up. Just to keep things straight, I want you to know I told Pete *before* you came out here on the street."

Lee nodded. He put out his hand. Emmet studied him a long moment, growing red in the face, but he did not take the hand. "No," Emmet said, "I can't say that I like you well enough right now to shake your hand." He walked up the street.

Kebler said, "You took the girl away from him, Lee. He's man enough to stand that, but what sticks in his craw is the wondering whether or not you intend to marry her." Kebler strode away toward the group gathered around Cantonwine.

Lee stood where he was. He saw Harvey passing the corner of the fence where Ann and Mrs. Crawford and two other women were. Macklin started toward the stable. A man ran from the crowd and walked with him, gesturing excitedly. Macklin walked on, waving his arm for the man to leave him alone.

Ann left the women. Lee heard her call, "Sandy! I want to talk to you."

Macklin turned and started toward the saloon, and Ann angled over to intercept him. She was almost running when she caught up with him. The two were then not far from Lee. He heard Ann say, "You deliberately disobeyed me, Sandy!"

"Yes."

"I'm afraid you'll regret it."

"I know I would," Macklin said, "if I intended to go back to Teepees any longer than it takes to pick up my plunder." Macklin walked on.

"Wait a minute, Sandy." Ann's manner changed quickly. "Maybe you did what you thought was best. It did keep Lee from having another blot on his name."

"I wasn't thinking of that."

"Don't quit. Go on back to the ranch and forget what I said."

Macklin shook his head. "It wouldn't be worth it. You never forget anything. So long, Ann." Macklin turned away once more.

Lee saw Ann's lips thin with determination. Her expression robbed her of beauty and left a hard will exposed; but by the time she again stopped Macklin, almost in front of Lee, she was smiling.

"Please, Sandy?"

Macklin shook his head.

"What will you tell my father?"

"The truth, if he asks. Cal's no fool, and you've never twisted him around your finger. He'll know what I'm talking about."

"You're not going to find another easy job, Sandy. You're too old. You'd better forget what I said and stay where you are.

Lee said, "Sandy has the foreman's job at Diamond for the rest of his life, if he wants it."

"Please don't interfere, Lee," Ann said.

"I'm not. You heard the man say he'd quit. If he wants the job at Diamond, he's got it."

"You can't make that offer," Ann said. "Your father—"

"I think Lee can make it," Macklin said. "I think I'll take it too." He went on toward the saloon with his shoulders high and straight.

"Why did you interfere, Lee?"

Lee said nothing. Up the street, Roderick's voice was loud among the men milling around Cantonwine. Harvey walked past Lee and Ann, reading their faces with a quick glance. He nodded and went on, following Macklin into the saloon.

Ann sighed. "I'm upset, Lee. I lost my temper. I'm sorry."

Once more she was the woman who had made Lee's blood surge that day on the mesa above the Sapinero. But he was not the same man he had been that day. He knew now that her unspoken promises were freighted with too many considerations of her own.

He said, "I'm sorry too, Ann." His level look, his tone, caused a run of panic on her face.

Harvey and Macklin were the only two people in the saloon. They had a drink. They watched McLeod get his horse and ride out of town. Harvey said, "You made a fast draw, Sandy, all things considered. Did I see that once in Hays a long time ago?"

"Maybe. I was younger then."

"We all were."

They were silent, caught by the thought of flowing years. Macklin kept looking out through the doorway to where Ann seemed to be pleading with Lee Vail. "You leaving, Sam?"

Harvey nodded.

"Lee offered me your job."

"Take it. You'll find Lee running Diamond from now on, I think."

"Yeah, but—" Macklin kept watching Lee and Ann. His loyalties were simple and the break he had made was hurting. He had been too long with Cal Houghton to say what was in his mind.

"If he marries her," Harvey said, "You can quit, can't you?"

"How'd you find out about her?"

"She just the same as ordered me to take care of Cantonwine." Harvey paused. "If she was a man, she'd be governor of this state in time." He spun his glass and watched it tip and fall into the scupper of the bar. "I was leaving once. Now I guess I'll start again. I'll take the anvil off Bliss as I go by."

"Did you pick up his pistol?"

"No, I didn't. Do you think—" Harvey's face was still; and then he smiled at the thought of this last touch of a responsibility that he had placed in other hands. "I looked in on him and he was laying there like he figured to stay a while, but maybe I should have picked up that pistol, Sandy,"

"He'll sneak away," Macklin said. "Still, let's go see about him."

They walked out together.

Bliss Rood struggled a long time with the great weight on his legs. He got one foot free. The curving side of the anvil base now rested entirely on one ankle, and for a time he lacked the strength to make an awkward lift from a sitting position.

He heard the shots. Then there was a silence, and afterward men set up an excited babble.

When he pried himself loose at last he knew that the affair outside was over. He staggered to the door and had a look. There was a group in the street. Harvey was going toward it. Macklin and Ann Houghton were talking near the ditch, down toward the saloon; and Lee Vail was standing there by himself.

Bliss could not determine what had happened until he saw Roderick's tall figure moving in the group of men that surrounded something in the street. He knew then. Cantonwine was dead. Even then, so strong had been Rood's belief in the man and his plans, that for a time he refused to accept the truth.

He heard someone say, "What was he doing barefoot? Did some of you fellows pull his boots off afterward?"

Cantonwine was dead, Cantonwine was dead. His death was not what gave Bliss the terrible feeling of loss. It was, rather, that everything Cantonwine had promised was gone. Bliss had been nothing and he had owned nothing all his life. He had been discontented but never violently unhappy because of what he lacked, and then Cantonwine had drawn a future for him.

Better things. A greater life. *Those who have suffered much shall be lifted up. I will have power and men will know me. And you, Bliss, will be my strong right arm in all things.*

The future was gone, fallen in the dust with Cantonwine, the glowing dream, the greater life. The loss now magnified its wonder.

Sorrow for himself took hold of Bliss. He saw McLeod leaving town. He saw the others he had talked to, idle spectators now. He had lured them on with careful words Cantonwine had given him. *Our band.* They were nothing now, but if Cantonwine had not died under the smash of Roderick's lead, those men would have rallied to the dream; and Bliss would have been a leader.

His discontent was fearful now, for he had seen a vision and then it had been torn away from him, and he knew that he alone could not bring it back. He felt like weeping for himself, but the animal in him gave way to rage.

His pistol was still lying where Macklin had thrown it. Bliss picked it up and put it under his shirt. A limping figure, with blood seeping from a deep cut on his forehead, he started walking. His mind was fixed on the man who had wrecked everything.

• • •

Ann was standing close to Lee. There were tears in her eyes, and she was saying, "You can't be that cold. I know better, Lee. Don't you remember—"

"Get over across the ditch, Ann."

For another instant Lee watched Bliss Rood walking toward the scene up the street. The man's dragging steps, slow but direct, reminded Lee of the way Johnny Maxwell had come at him in the saloon.

"Lee!"

"Get out of the way, Ann." Lee went up the street at a fast walk. He heard someone coming behind him, but he had no time to look. Watching Bliss narrowly, he observed that his holster was empty.

Someone said, "There's Rood. I wonder where he's been all this time."

Lee kept walking even after he decided he was mistaken. Bliss, like anyone else, had a right to join the men up the street. And his holster was empty. Lee glanced behind him. Harvey and Macklin were coming.

He heard a man yell, "Duck!" And then the men around Cantonwine were all ajostle in an instant, diving to the sides, crashing into each other. Someone knocked the shotgun out of Kebler's hands, and Kebler dropped to the ground to recover it. Roderick was all alone, facing Bliss, who was dragging a pistol from under his shirt.

Roderick had time to draw, but he turned his head for a quick glance down the street, and in that instant Bliss killed him.

Lee cleared his pistol. He took careful aim and knocked one of Rood's legs from under him as the man turned to run. Bliss went down on his knees. He put his pistol across his forearm, steadying it on Lee.

Lee pulled the trigger again and again. He was still aiming when he saw Bliss sink slowly forward into the deep grass of the ditch bank. Harvey and Macklin ran past him while he stood there numbly, staring at the second man he had been forced to kill.

Kebler got up, looking around him like a man bemused, and then he dropped his shotgun and ran to kneel beside Roderick. Lee saw him rise at once. Kebler pointed to his heart as Harvey and Macklin reached him.

The dust was in Roderick's tawny hair, smeared across his face. His features were brittle sharp. Lee looked down at him a moment and turned away as Harvey took off his coat. Lee looked toward Union Park. This was not Roderick here on the ground; Roderick was riding somewhere in the park, at peace, Roderick was building something with his hands, at peace.

"He had time to draw," Macklin muttered. "Didn't you think so, Harvey?"

"No," Harvey said. "He didn't have a chance." His glance at Lee said: *Let the myth go on, no good will come from disputing it.*

And men would not let it die anyway, Lee thought.

Later, he stood beside Harvey and watched a wagon

start toward Diamond. Macklin was driving it, towing his horse at the tail gate.

"You'll stay a while now?" Lee asked.

Harvey nodded.

Maureen was free. The two of them could go somewhere and pick up their lives where they should have started long ago. Lee looked toward the park. "I won't go home with you right now, Sam. Chaunce and Emmet and I are going to take Bliss up to his brother. Then I'm going over to the Meeker place to see Iris. Tell Maureen that. She'll understand."

Lee watched the wagon for a moment. "Take him high in the park, will you, Sam?"

Harvey nodded.

They turned away from each other with their eyes filled with tears.

Center Point Publishing
600 Brooks Road ● PO Box 1
Thorndike ME 04986-0001 USA

(207) 568-3717

US & Canada:
1 800 929-9108
www.centerpointlargeprint.com